An American Novel

Antoine Bello

Translated by Bérangère Callens

Portraits by Noli Novak

For B., the one and only

Week 1

Death And Taxes

By Vlad Eisinger

The Wall Street Tribune, Tuesday, June 26, 2012

When Citibank threatened to foreclose on her house, Cynthia Tucker, 77, pored over her finances one more time. Liquidating her 401(k) or pawning her engagement ring would cover only part of her mortgage. With a heavy heart, she resolved to auction the $75,000 life insurance policy she had contracted prior to her wedding. After one month of intense negotiations, Mrs. Tucker signed the assignment form and pocketed about $23,000. The buyer, a local architect, was now responsible for paying the premiums. On Mrs. Tucker's death, he would collect the $75,000 indemnity.

The trade of life insurance policies, also known as life settlement, has been growing rapidly over the past 25 years. Yet it accounts for but a tiny fraction of the overall life insurance market. Only $5 to $6bn worth of contracts change hands every year, compared to an aggregate value of $19,000bn for all policies currently in force in the U.S.

The very notion of life settlement is subject to controversy. Insurance companies invoke repeated instances of fraud in order to prompt states to regulate more stringently, if not ban altogether, the resale of policies. Conversely, consumer rights organizations rely on a 1911 judgment by the Supreme Court that affirms the right of policyholders to transfer their contract without limitation.

This article is the first in a series devoted to a little-known market, the development of which could significantly affect the way Americans prepare for retirement, the prices of millions of new policies issued every year, and the solvency of some insurance companies.

To carry out this investigation, the most comprehensive ever conducted on the subject by a national newspaper, we have met dozens of players in the life settlement industry — asset managers, lawmakers, individuals who sold their policies — between September 2011 and May 2012. Our experts also created their own computer model to evaluate policies by combining the most recent life expectancy tables with statistics published annually by the American Council of Life Insurers (ACLI). After reviewing more than

24,000 transactions conducted after 2005, they've concluded that either life settlement buyers overestimate their potential gains, or insurance carriers underestimate the threat posed by the negotiability of policies.

We will also see that, in their quest for ever-increasing returns, insurance companies, policyholders and life settlement buyers sometimes resort to deceptive or illegal practices.

No state is more closely associated with life settlement than Florida. The absence of income and estate taxes makes the Sunshine State a highly attractive destination for affluent seniors. In 2010, 65-year-olds and over accounted for 17.3% of the population, the highest percentage in the country. According to a report by the Government Accountability Office, Florida is home to 503 life settlement brokers. Not surprisingly, the Life Insurance Settlement Association (LISA) is headquartered in Orlando.

For the purposes of this series, we will draw many of our examples from a 580-people community located in Florida, on the Gulf of Mexico, halfway between Pensacola and Panama City. Completed in 2005, Destin Terrace is a 234-unit residential program and near-perfect miniature replica of the American insurance ecosystem.

Originally a small fishing village, Destin has enjoyed phenomenal economic growth over the past decades. It is often listed as one of the most gorgeous cities in the U.S., thanks to its white-sand beaches and blissful weather. According to the Florida Department of Environmental Protection, over 80% of the Emerald Coast's 4.5 million visitors each year stop off in Destin.

Source : Google Maps

In 2009, the median annual income of a Destin household was $57,554, vs $44,736 and $49,777 for the whole state of Florida and the United States respectively.

Destin Terrace, whose entrance is right across the beach, comprises three types of units: 115 1-, 2-, or 3-bedroom condos, 99 single-family homes built on lots of 0.15 acres, and 20 mansions, each set on over an acre of land. Amenities include a pool, two tennis courts, a gym, a pond, a playground and a clubhouse. Association fees run at $650 quarterly.

The housing crisis that struck Florida in 2007 hasn't spared the 97% of homeowners of Destin Terrace. The mansions, each of which was offered at $1.2m at the completion of the program, reached a low of $650,000 in 2009. They now sell for around $800,000. The prices of houses and condos have followed similar patterns.

What makes Destin Terrace especially interesting is that several of its inhabitants have a connection with the life settlement industry, be it as insurance agent, auditor, investor, or even lawmaker. Their testimonies will help us understand the forces currently at play in the life insurance sector.

Life insurance — which could more accurately be named death insurance — is one of Americans' favorite investments. Our fellow countrymen hold 150.7m individual policies, as well as 112.1m so-called group policies purchased by their employers (per ACLI, 2011). The face value (i.e. the indemnity payable at death) of all policies currently in force is a little over $19,000bn, roughly equal to the entire market capitalization of Wall Street.

According to Jeremy Fallon, spokesperson for the Life Insurance Brokers Association, "it's not a question of whether you need life insurance; it's a question of how much you need to buy." Sure enough, most of the financial advisors we met consider life insurance the cornerstone of any financial and estate-planning strategy. None of them would advise their clients to forgo it altogether.

As Tim Rollo, president of money-management firm TR & Sons, puts it: "It doesn't matter whether you're rich or poor. You want to leave a minimum of four to five years' worth of income to your family, preferably even more, especially if you're the breadwinner."

The average death benefit of policies underwritten in 2011 was $162,000.

Another reason for the success of life insurance lies in the tax benefits it provides. Death indemnities paid out by carriers are not taxable, prompting many seniors to buy large policies with the sole goal of reducing their estate liabilities.

"Let's say you take out a $10m policy. Even if you pay $10m in premiums between now and the day you die, you'll still come out on top. That's because if you wanted to leave the same $10m to your heirs, they'd have to cut a $3.5m check to the IRS," Mr. Rollo says. The top federal estate tax rate currently stands at 35% and is scheduled to rise to 55% as of January 1, 2013.

The life settlement market gained its footing in the 1980s, when many AIDS patients sold their policies in order to fund their final months or years. Most of them managed to obtain a good price — typically between 50% and 70% of the face value — as buyers were lured by the prospect of quick returns.

Bruce Webb, 48, is a flight attendant at Southwest Airlines and a Destin Terrace resident since 2009. He learned he was HIV-positive in 1986. Soon afterward, he noticed an ad in the men's room of the Pink Paradise, a Miami Beach nightclub. "The text was very short: HIV = $$$, followed by a phone number. The person at the other end of the line asked me a few questions about my viral charge and lymphocyte count. One week later, I had five offers on my desk."

Bruce Webb

Mr. Webb eventually sold his policy to Sunset Partners, a specialized firm based in Panama City, Fla. "After all the fees and expenses, I netted a bit under $160,000, more than enough to carry me through the two years I thought I had left. Then I had the good fortune of being selected for a clinical trial of AZT. Twenty-five years later, I'm still here!"

Mr. Webb's case is far from unique. The introduction of antiretroviral therapy in 1987 and the continuous progress in tritherapy have led to a substantial decrease in mortality for people infected with HIV. According to a 2008 study performed on 14 cohorts of patients from 10 different countries, a 35-year-old patient now has a life expectancy of 32 years, compared with about 47 years for the entire population.

Investment firms that hadn't prepared for this phenomenon quickly ran out of cash. In their models, indemnities collected upon the death of the first patients were supposed to fund the payment of premiums for the rest of the portfolio. For lack of sufficient reserves, those funds had to choose between letting the policies expire (or 'lapse' in insurance jargon) or continuing to pay the premiums, sometimes for more than 20 years. Dignity Partners, a San Francisco firm, filed for bankruptcy in 1996. Sunset Partners, the fund that had purchased Mr. Webb's policy, followed suit in 2002.

Bruce Webb says he sympathizes with the investors who lost their savings, some of whom live in Destin Terrace. Yet he doesn't harbor any guilt. "I offered to sell my policy; they agreed to buy it. I received five bids. I picked the highest, as anyone would have. This money enabled me to quit my job and to receive proper care. I invested the remainder and, three years ago, I fulfilled an old dream by buying a condo."

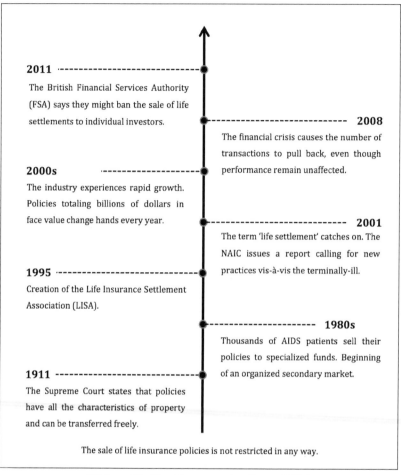

2011 ----------------------------
The British Financial Services Authority
(FSA) says they might ban the sale of life
settlements to individual investors.

            ---------------------------- **2008**
The financial crisis causes the number of
transactions to pull back, even though
performance remain unaffected.

2000s --------------------
The industry experiences rapid growth.
Policies totaling billions of dollars in
face value change hands every year.

            ---------------------------- **2001**
The term 'life settlement' catches on. The
NAIC issues a report calling for new
practices vis-à-vis the terminally-ill.

1995 ----------------------------
Creation of the Life Insurance Settlement
Association (LISA).

            --------------------- **1980s**
Thousands of AIDS patients sell their
policies to specialized funds. Beginning
of an organized secondary market.

1911 ----------------------------
The Supreme Court states that policies
have all the characteristics of property
and can be transferred freely.

The sale of life insurance policies is not restricted in any way.

History of the life settlement market. Source: LISA

At the request of the government, insurance carriers retooled their products. In 2001, the National Association of Insurance Commissioners (NAIC) published the Viatical Settlements Model Act, in effect providing a blueprint for states to reform the laws applicable to terminally-ill patients. More than 150 carriers now offer their clients with a life expectancy of less than two years the opportunity to collect part of their death benefits in advance.

Michael Hart, 43, lives in one of Destin Terrace's mansions, within a stone's throw from Mr. Webb's condo. As a Republican state senator and member of the Banking & Insurance Committee, he helps craft the laws governing the insurance industry. "Our rules on accelerated death benefits for the terminally-ill are a model of cooperation among legislators, insurers and consumer rights associations. Considering how critical the situation was, not reaching an agreement was simply not an option," Mr. Hart says.

The advent of tritherapy nearly killed the life settlement industry. It took several years and the emergence of a new type of players to purge past excesses.

Jean-Michel Jacques recently moved to Destin Terrace with his family. He is the president of Osiris Capital, a fund set up in 2007 to take advantage of the mishaps of life settlement's historical actors. Osiris, which has raised about $60m from European investors, purchases policies at rock-bottom prices from funds struggling to pay their premiums.

In 2009, Mr. Jacques made what he considers the best deal of his career by laying hands on 2,700 policies previously owned by Sunset Partners. "Just think about it. We acquired for 10 or 15 cents [10% to 15% of the face value] policies for which they had paid 60 cents 20 years ago. At that price, you simply can't lose. Those people may have survived AIDS, but they will eventually die like everybody else."

Mr. Jacques targets an annual return of between 15% and 20% until the extinction of the fund. According to his estimates, there are about 30,000 AIDS policies in circulation in the U.S. Osiris owns close to 5,000 of them. "We're ready to buy more, provided, of course, they're reasonably priced," he says.

Today's market has little in common with that of the 1980s. Nowadays, most sellers are seniors seeking to finance healthcare procedures, or to support their children or grandchildren, or who simply can no longer afford their premiums. Says Lawrence Johnson, professor at the Ross School of Business at the University of Michigan: "For many seniors, selling their policy is like killing two birds with one stone. Not only do they eliminate an expense, but they also free up capital they thought was blocked until their death."

Due to a lack of nationally consolidated data, the size of the life settlement market isn't known with any degree of precision. The Government Accountability Office estimates it at $9bn in 2007, $12.9bn in 2008, and $7bn in 2009.

Trade association LISA's numbers, based on transactions reported by its members, run 10% or 15% higher. Depending on the year, sellers pocket between 17% and 20% of the face value, net of fees and brokers' commissions.

Notwithstanding temporary fluctuations, the future of life settlement looks bright. Eighty-two percent of all asset managers surveyed by the American Society of Investment Managers (ASIM) this year said they were open to the idea of including it in their portfolios, up from 36% five years ago.

Ken Gardner Jr., ASIM's president, ascribes this surge in interest to the recent financial crisis. "For the sake of caution, we usually recommend that our clients diversify their investments. Yet in 2008, all major asset classes — be it stocks, bonds, commodities or real estate — tumbled at once. Life settlement was one of the few assets to hold its ground. For one reason: people kept on dying."

In an uncertain environment, there is something reassuring about life settlement. Lawrence Johnson quotes Ben Franklin: "In this world, nothing can be said to be certain, except death and taxes." Mr. Johnson adds: "Life settlement buyers sleep like babies. They don't care about unemployment numbers or the latest report on manufacturing activity in China. The performance of their assets is totally uncorrelated with the usual economic indicators."

Presented in this light, life settlement looks like the Holy Grail of money management, an asset simultaneously profitable and risk-free.

"Smart investors can now build portfolios that will steadily appreciate, shielded from the volatility of markets," wrote Tony Babbitt, president of Sunset Partners, in a message to his underwriters dated February 4, 2002.

Three months later, Sunset Partners filed for bankruptcy.

Write to Vlad Eisinger: vlad.eisinger@wst.com
Next week: *Insurance Companies' Dirty Little Secrets*

*****

From: Dan Siver <danielgsiver@gmail.com>
Date: Tuesday, June 26, 2012 10:03 A.M.
To: Vlad Eisinger <vlad.eisinger@wst.com>
Subject: Coincidence…

Vlad,

Imagine my surprise upon discovering your prose in the *Wall Street Tribune*! I have to thank my neighbor, Mrs. Cunningham, without whom I would have forever remained ignorant of this outstanding piece of journalism. She told me you interviewed her. What a shame you didn't come knocking on my door. It would have been a treat to see you again after so many years.

My God, you must be pondering right about now, how could a man as brilliant as Dan, the finest Céline exegete this side of the Atlantic, end up in a hole like Destin? A legitimate question that calls for a thorough answer.

I moved to Florida last summer, after the death of my parents, who had retired here. Dad passed away, two years ago. Mom followed a little later, leaving the house to my sister and me. A fine gift indeed! They had bought it for $450K pre-construction at the peak of the market. The realtor told us we could get $280K for it at most. I was about to politely turn down my inheritance, when I realized the 30-year mortgage payment was lower than my rent on the Upper East Side. I had just broken up with my girlfriend (or, to be more honest, she had just broken up with me), and decided I needed a change of scenery. I haven't looked back. My quality of life has gone up and my taxes have gone down. Best of all, no more distractions! I write eight hours a day, I buy groceries at the local Publix, and I walk on the beach mornings and evenings.

You're probably wondering why I waited to turn 40 to become a property owner. That, my friend, is success — I have none. My first novel enjoyed a bit of a buzz; the next ones, none at all. Anyway, I get by. I write pieces here and there, a few reviews for *Harper's*, and I work freelance for a PR firm where I proofread nauseating reports written by consultants with mini-skirts and not-so-mini bosoms.

How about you? I used to read your articles in the *New York Times* when you first started. And then one day, you disappeared from the credits. I

9

have to admit I wasn't curious enough to track you down. The *Wall Street Tribune*, how very impressive! Do you still write (real books I mean)?

Dan

PS: Vivian Darkbloom says "Hi."

*****

From: Vlad Eisinger <vlad.eisinger@wst.com>
Date: Tuesday, June 26, 2012 10:50 A.M.
To: Dan Siver <danielgsiver@gmail.com>
Subject: ... I think not!

Sacrebleu! I wish I had known! I'm looking at the 2011 Destin Terrace directory and could kick myself. I had noted the presence of a Lydia Siver, but, ignoramus me, I hadn't recognized your mother's first name. Too bad, your couch would have been a thousand times better than my impersonal digs at the Hilton.

My condolences on your parents' passing. I only met them once, on the first day of school at Columbia in 1994. Your father was sweating like a showerhead. He had just gruelingly climbed three flights of stairs with the portable AC unit slicing into his arms. He nearly choked when he discovered our hovel, the size of a medicine cabinet. "You could live in a mansion in Cincinnati for that price," he exclaimed. You winked at me, and right away I knew you had no desire to set foot in the Midwest again.

I, too, followed your career at first. I read *Wrong Move* — very neat — and another one whose title I can't seem to remember. I was hoping to run into you the other day at our 15-year class reunion. Matt Padilla told me you'd moved down to Florida. To tell you the truth, I pictured you in Miami Beach rather than Destin, but to each his own, I guess.

As for me, life is swell. Still a Brooklynite at heart, I have a pad in one of those new residential complexes for yuppies called Asterid Center. I've been living with a fantastic girl, a publisher, for the past year. I switched employers in 1999. Nothing beats the prestige of the *New York Times,* but the *Tribune*'s editor-in-chief made me an offer I couldn't refuse: a title of senior reporter, a thirty percent raise, and the expense account of an

African dictator. More importantly, he made the case that the business world would provide me with greater topics of investigation. He was right. I've published several noteworthy series — one on companies that backdate their stock options, one on nosocomial infections in public hospitals, and the most recent on Detroit carmakers' pension funds, which almost earned me a Pulitzer. Let me know what you think of my articles. Personally, I'm rather pleased with them.

I know what you're thinking. Rest assured, I haven't given up my dream of writing the great American novel. For now, I'm gathering material — I have 12 journals filled with notes. All I need is time to dive into them.

Hope to hear from you soon,

Vlad

PS: I had totally forgotten about that anagram game! How does it work again? You can't respond until you've figured out the writer hidden behind it, right? That one's easy: Vivian Darkbloom = Vladimir Nabokov. For your information, Nabokov also published under the pseudonyms Adam von Librikov in *Transparent Things* and Baron Klim Avidov in *Ada*. By the way, have you heard from Sir Jangled?

*****

Dan's journal

Tuesday, June 26
I had forgotten how conceited Vlad could be. Not much to be proud of, though. Six years of comparative literature at Columbia to end up plowing through General Motors' books — talk about a nosedive...

And always the braggart! Mister Big Shot lives in a residence for yuppies (understand, "No hicks need apply."); he has an open reservation at Jean-Georges; and he missed the Pulitzer by a hair. Not to mention his TA's pedantry: "For your information, Nabokov blah blah blah." What a prig!

I wish him good luck with that girlfriend-publisher of his. The moment she realizes he's not the next Hemingway, she'll dump him like an old sock — and I know what I'm talking about.

(But who am I to bad-mouth anyone? Vlad might very well be the next

Hemingway. He's pleased with his articles — that's an auspicious start.)

(…)

Mrs. Cunningham caught me as I was taking out the trash tonight. She was vaguely fiddling with her begonias in her bathrobe, waiting for me to step outside.

"So, you read the article? Did you see how much Bruce got for his policy? Makes you think, doesn't it?"

"Put my mind at ease, Mrs. Cunningham," I teased her. "You don't have AIDS, do you?"

"Not AIDS, no, but uterine cancer, yes!"

I was dumbfounded. She seems in tip-top shape and rises with the lark.

"Does your daughter know?" I asked.

"Not yet. I think I'll talk to Chuck about it first. He's the one who sold me my car insurance. I bet he'll know what to do."

I told her it seemed like a good idea. Incidentally, if she keeps Patterson busy, maybe he'll get off my back for a while.

(…)

I came across quite a little gathering in front of the Phelps' residence, as I was coming home from my evening stroll. Sharon Hess (the nurse) hailed me with her prison-warden's voice.

"How about you Dan: what do you think of that *Wall Street Tribune* article?"

I was vainly looking for something intelligent to say, when Melvin Phelps came to my rescue.

"Only good can come of it as far as we're concerned. After that idyllic description of Destin, real estate agents' phones will be ringing off the hook."

Jennifer Hansen emphatically nodded in agreement. If I were in her shoes, I, too, would want to believe the market's picking up. The price of her house was virtually cut in half the day the bubble burst. Even if the mansions and condos fared a little better, I'm sure I'm not the only one to owe the bank more than my house is worth.

Phelps is taking this story very much to heart, as if he were personally responsible for the price per square foot in West Florida. You can tell he's been on a quest for new challenges since he settled down in Destin for good and was elected president of the Homeowners Association. I heard he had a big job at Bank of America, in Charlotte, before he retired.

Ed Linkas, who was coming home from work (no nine-to-five in auditing, I guess), stopped his Nissan convertible by the huddle and lowered his window. Vlad's article didn't teach him anything he didn't already know, and for good reason — he's an actuary. That didn't stop him from finding it well put together, informative, and remarkably documented. In the course of the conversation, he mentioned that he owns four life insurance policies, totaling up to $3m in coverage. As we were all staring at him in astonishment, he explained that he invests only in tax-free products "because, over the long run, the savings are gigantic."

With a hint of hostility in her voice, Sharon asked him who his beneficiaries were, since he has no wife or children to speak of. Unflustered, Ed answered that he had designated his brother and his niece, until the day he could start his own family. He seems to know exactly what he's doing. I bet dealing with numbers all day long must come in handy when managing one's finances.

Phelps wanted to know who, among us, owns life insurance. He obligingly went first, sharing that he's personally insured to the tune of $10m, split among his wife, their two daughters, his alma mater, and various charities.

The Hesses don't have any (strange, considering he's a doctor); the Hansens just took out a $500,000 policy; and Mary-Bee, the French woman, couldn't remember if her husband has $1 or $2m in coverage.

The fact that I've never owned life insurance didn't come as a shock to anyone.

Wednesday, June 27
Worked on my book all day, mainly doing research on the Web.

Wikipedia doesn't cease to amaze me. Jimmy Wales has made Diderot and d'Alembert's dream come true. There's a special place for him in Heaven.

Corrected dozens of spelling mistakes as I read. I can't help it — typos and punctuation errors just seem to jump off the page. I guess it's one of the benefits of having lived with an editing professional for 10 years — I'm not selling a single book but the manuscripts I turn in are impeccable.

I was moving a comma on Hermann Broch's English page when the idea for an innocent little hoax crossed my mind. According to Wikipedia, the author of *Sleepwalkers* and *The Death of Virgil* counted famous Austrian writers among his friends, such as Rilke, Musil, and Canetti. For a moment, I pondered the possibility of adding to that list the name of Leo Perutz, also a German novelist and contemporary of Broch. Who would ever know?

To further delve into the question, I read an article describing Wikipedia's editing process. I discovered that all modifications to the website are documented and readily accessible to anyone. Broch's page, created by a certain RodC in 2004, is thus the product of about 150 iterations. We owe RodC — whose profile doesn't say whether he's American, German, or Fijian — some twelve other biographies of twentieth-century writers, among them Pavese, Radiguet, and Hölderlin. He seems to have been somewhat inactive since 2010. I doubt he would get wind of my little spoof.

Two other users have significantly enriched Broch's page: Simonides, AWOL since 2004, and Prof02, whose access to Wikipedia was blocked in 2010, when he was found guilty of numerous violations (self-promotion, personal attacks, etc.). Neither one has amended Broch's page since 2006.

In short, my chances of getting caught look fairly slim, especially since the scores of corrections I've made in the past vouch for my expertise on the subject of European literature.

Even so, I wasn't taking my imposture lightly. Corrupting the corpus of Wikipedia means infringing upon the fundamental pact hundreds of millions of users implicitly adhere to. Could I keep trusting an encyclopedia whose editors might be pranksters the likes of me? Groucho Marx once said he wouldn't like to be part of a club that would accept him as a member…

Yet the more I thought about it, the more determined I became. The problem was indeed ill-defined. It wasn't a matter of finding out whether Broch had been friends with Perutz, but why he wouldn't have been. Everything brought the two men together — their language, their age (they were born four years apart), their taste for mathematics, even their favorite subjects (history, destiny…). They must have rubbed shoulders in Vienna between the two wars. Was it conceivable that Mailer had never met Styron? Or that Derrida never ran into Bourdieu? Come on now, let's be serious.

Of course, one cannot rule out that they had been introduced, but felt a strong dislike for one another. Yet that, too, deserved to be reported; a man's enmities are often more telling than his friendships.

Here is how I envision things: assuming I followed through with my plan, a grad student, better informed than I with regard to Broch's life, would end up stumbling across my note and make a point of reestablishing the truth. "No, Broch did not enjoy Perutz's company. He envied the success of *Little Apple*, and deemed *The Swedish Cavalier* an insignificant whim."

In either case, I would have served the truth by sending Perutz's exegetes on a fruitful trail.

Ended up making the change. Let's see how long it lasts.

Thursday, June 18

Ran across Chuck Patterson as he was parking his metal-gray panzer in front of his palace — one of the downsides of living in a cul-de-sac, I have to walk through the entire community to gain access to the beach. With his silver mane, steel-blue eyes, and attaché case, he looked like a Nazi returning home from work.

Chuck can't accept the fact that he will never sell me a policy. I don't need life insurance (even less now that I've read Vlad's article), I don't own a car, and I bought my homeowner's insurance on the Internet. But you have to admire the fellow's savoir faire. He casually sprinkles the conversation with allusions to the vagaries of everyday life, especially to the necessity of preparing for them. "Poor Sharon fell asleep at the wheel. Her car's ready for the junkyard. There's another one who tried to cut corners by opting for a high deductible…"

He's also an expert at drawing the attention of his interlocutors to dangers they hadn't previously considered, e.g. asbestos in their basements, kidnapping, identity theft, nuclear war, etc. In Chuck's world, 15 separate policies are a minimum requirement for a good night's sleep.

True to form, he asked me out of left field whether I had medical insurance. Before I had time to come up with a fib, he shoved a glossy brochure in my hands and made me promise to review it.

To change the subject, I inquired if Mrs. Cunningham had paid him a visit.

"We struck a deal," he answered. "I should be able to get a good price for her policy."

"Did you know she had cancer?"

"What? No, I sure didn't. Such a shame."

Friday, June 29

Perutz is still there. Another possibility I had failed to consider is that nobody gives a hoot.

Despite my best efforts, I found myself thumbing through Chuck's brochure — although I wonder if I can still call it a 'brochure,' it's so fancy. I've seen art catalogues that weighed less.

I don't know whether it's the news of Mrs. Cunningham's cancer or the prospect of my dentist's appointment, but not having medical insurance is really starting to bother me.

The last time I requested a bid, I thought the broker had accidentally thrown in an extra zero. I was so stunned by the price ($6,300 for barely decent coverage), I had calculated that I would need to sell an additional 14,000 books each year to offset the expense! (I earn 60 cents per paperback copy, 7% of the retail price of $9.99 less 15% for my agent. After taxes, all I'm left with is a paltry 45 cents.)

Fourteen thousand books! One every half-hour, Sundays included! Instead, I had decided not to become ill.

At first glance, the Emerald Basic Health plan looks like what I need. It doesn't include dental or eye care, but it does cover doctors' visits, prescription medicine, and hospitalization fees up to $1m per year. I'm going to ask Chuck for a quote and suggest — you scratch my back and I'll scratch yours — that he buy 100 copies of *Double Play* as Christmas gifts for his clients.

Saturday, June 30

Watched Mrs. Cunningham this morning, as she was bustling about in her garden.

Nothing in her demeanor would lead anyone to believe that she has but a few months to live. I'm ashamed about the way I reacted when she told me her terrible news. Let's hope she didn't mistake my shock for insensitivity or, worse yet, indifference.

Earlier, to appease my conscience, I gave her a copy of *The Usurper*. She put it away on her bookshelf, between two volumes of Jackie Collins, then offered me a cup of tea, which I had no choice but to accept.

Oddly enough, she didn't want to talk about her health so much as her finances. Her policy, taken out by her late husband, Otto, is for $500,000.

She hopes to walk away with at least $300,000 — quite a hefty sum for someone who recycles her plastic bottles for pennies.

"I'm going to show that simpleton Bruce Webb how it's done," she told me with a knowing look. "He netted forty percent of the face value. I'm older, sicker, and most of all I'm not going to get bamboozled with a bunch of fees."

After she cashes in her check, she'll head to Las Vegas to realize her dream. She'll sit at a roulette table with a huge pile of chips, look the dealer straight in the eyes, and bet $10,000 on black while sipping a daiquiri.

"I can hold my own at gambling, you know? Otto and I used to treat ourselves to a Vegas getaway once a year, in April, for our anniversary. One-armed bandits in the morning, blackjack in the afternoon, and, if we had done well, we went to a show in the evening. Sinatra, Tony Bennett, Siegfried and Roy — we saw them all!"

I asked her if they had a favorite hotel in Vegas. She burst out laughing.

"You must be joking! Otto knew how to work the system. The week before our trip, he would call all the hotels on the Strip to catch up on the latest deals — dinner with champagne on the house, the honeymoon suite, free cocktails… And once we were there, if we heard of a better offer, we'd pack our bags and leave!"

Sunday, July 1

(…)

What surprised me most when I read Vlad's article was learning what Jean-Michel Jacques does for a living. He's one of the first people I met when I moved to Destin Terrace. A frumpy and mischievous goblin, he expresses himself in a colorful English with a thick French accent (I've since learned that he's a compatriot of Hercule Poirot). He was delighted to hear that I had studied French literature, and generously complimented my accent.

We sometimes work out together, he perched on a stationary bike and I huffing away on the treadmill. When my heart rate permits, we discuss the European Union in the language of Molière. Jean-Michel is a fervent supporter of the annexation of Wallonia by France. Having no opinion on the matter, I take great delight in stirring up his hatred of Flemish extremists.

I knew he worked in finance, but he's the last person I would have suspected of managing an investment firm — what I think is called a hedge fund. Although he could probably afford one of the mansions, he lives in a condo with his Vietnamese wife and their two young sons. I must shed light on that mystery.

Monday, July 2
Just left the dentist's office.

I had called the nearest practice, unaware that Dr. Steve Lammons is no other than that grumpy 50-something-year-old man who walks his dachshund in the evening when I return from the beach. I foolishly felt compelled to mention it.

Bad idea — Lammons waited for my gums to go numb to unload.

"Did you read that article in the *Wall Street Tribune*?"

I nodded, unable to speak.

He then launched into a nonsensical homophobic diatribe, all the while examining my molars with a probe. I eventually realized that he was talking about Bruce Webb, our neighbor, who sold his policy in the '80s.

"The gall of that guy! And wouldn't you know, he's a flight attendant, probably a gold member of the mile-high club, if you know what I mean… When I mention that in conversation, everyone applauds him — he took a sabbatical year, he chilled out at home, and with the leftover money, he was able to buy himself a condo on the beach! Between you and me, if that's what it means to be sick, I'll gladly take a virus or two!"

I screamed in pain. In his excitement, Lammons had hit a nerve. He didn't look especially contrite.

"But that money, Dan, do you have any idea where it came from? It was mine! I invested in Sunset Partners in 1994. You know about them, don't you? Of course you do, they're the firm who bought that fairy's policy, plus those of hundreds of his little playmates. The word was they had one or two more years to live, three tops. How do you explain that 25 years later, they're still here?"

If I hadn't had a mouth full of cotton, I would have made a case for medical progress. But Lammons really didn't seem that eager to hear my opinion.

"All the savings I had accumulated went down the drain. Over half a million total. That's a big problem for us dentists: how to invest our money without being taken for a ride by crooks? My colleagues were buying studios in Jacksonville or shares of biotech companies. That didn't appeal to me. The stock market drives me bonkers. As for renters, frankly I think they're a big pain in the butt for not a whole lot in return.

"And then one day my golf partner cancels. The club finds me a replacement on the spot, a chap named Babbitt. We get in the cart, he asks me what I do for a living, and then, out of the blue, he starts talking about his investments earning 18% a year. According to him, it wasn't even rocket science. He kept on saying that all he did was to buy, and to let Nature take care of the rest. On the third hole, I asked him if he could make room for me in one of his funds. On the sixth, I committed to $300,000. On the eighth, he told me he happened to have a subscription form in his car. I filled out the paperwork at the clubhouse. We didn't even play the back nine.

"Six months later, I still haven't seen the first dime. I'm beginning to smell a rat. Babbitt, cool as a cucumber, tells me not to get my panties in a wad. Those fruities aren't dropping like they used to, but they're bound to kick the bucket sooner or later. In the meantime, I've got to hand over more cash to cover the premiums."

I was so enthralled by Lammons's story that I didn't notice he had swapped his probe for a drill. I flinched at the distinctive buzzing sound and sank a bit deeper into the chair, in order to delay the fatal moment of contact. Hardly a novice, Lammons forced the bit between my teeth while continuing his tale of misfortune.

"It was the same hassle every year. The Sunset accountant, and later the bankruptcy trustee, would send me a list of the policies in which I had invested. I had to choose between paying the premiums or allowing the policy to lapse. I coughed up for 15 years like a jackass. Every once in a while, some fag bit the dust, but the death benefit rarely covered that year's premiums. I'd go to Rhonda Taylor for advice, since she's kind of in the business. Rhonda Taylor, see who I'm talking about? Fortyish, divorced, she lives in a condo behind the pool with her daughter. Believe it or not, that ding-dong goofed every single time. If she recommended I drop a policy, you could be sure the guy cashed in his chips the following winter! That damned woman, I swear — she's not the brightest crayon in the box!

"Bottom line: I'm 56 years old and still filling cavities, while all my college buddies spend their days on the greens. That just makes me sick."

To let off steam, Lammons bore his drill into my gum, making me scream in agony.

"Oops, sorry about that. All right, you're going to have to come back to see me again. It's not very pretty in there."

I gagged when I saw the bill: $380 for X-rays I hadn't requested, one cavity, and a cleaning. Evidently, Lammons is quite eager to join his friends at Pebble Beach.

I asked the receptionist if they offered a payment plan. She called Lammons who shook his head, as if bitterly regretting having misjudged me.

"Four monthly payments of $100, first one due right away, non-negotiable."

I handed five $20 bills to the receptionist, promising myself to get back at that moronic boss of hers one day.

(…)

Oh shit — a Wikipedia editor is asking me to name my sources.

Week 2

Insurance Companies' Dirty Little Secrets

By Vlad Eisinger

The Wall Street Tribune, Tuesday, July 3, 2012

The rise of life settlement, the sale of an existing life insurance policy to a third party, is rooted in the way life insurance is priced as a product.

Anyone who has ever taken out a policy is familiar with the procedure, which has hardly changed over the past 25 years.

The candidate first fills out a comprehensive medical form. After the usual info — such as height, weight, treatment and family history — several questions focus on tobacco use.

Indeed, depending on their age and the type of insurance, smokers pay between 30% and 100% more for their coverage than non-smokers. The Center for Disease Control (CDC) estimates that tobacco consumption is responsible for 443,000 deaths annually in the U.S. Also according to the CDC, the life expectancy of habitual smokers is 14 years shorter than that of non-smokers, a gap that keeps widening.

After undergoing a medical examination, which, above a certain amount of coverage, includes blood tests and an EKG, the candidate is placed in one of the following categories: super-preferred, preferred, standard, or tobacco. That category, age, and gender are the three main factors used to calculate the annual premium.

To determine the life expectancy of their clients, insurance carriers rely on mortality tables published and regularly updated by the Society of Actuaries (SOA). For instance, a 35-year-old man has a 0.16% probability of dying in the coming year; a 36-year-old 0.17%; and so forth. A woman celebrating her 100th birthday has a 31% chance of dying within the next 12 months.

Two lesser-known factors play a substantial role in the pricing process.

The first one is the proportion of total premiums absorbed by the underwriter's overhead. In 2011, life insurance companies spent $7bn on office equipment and supplies, $3bn on rent, another $3bn on advertising, and approximately $1bn on travel, according to the most recent annual report of the American Council of Life Insurers (ACLI). This is a lot of money — and it flows directly from policyholders' pockets.

However high they might seem, those numbers pale in comparison to the $60bn spent last year by ACLI members on home- and field-office expenses, a category which includes management compensation.

Prudential Financial is the second-largest life insurer in the country. In 2011, the four members of its executive committee earned a total of $17.8m. Over the same period, Prudential's stock price fell 14%.

Smaller carriers are not to be outdone. In 2011, Matthew Fin, founder and president of Emerald Life, a Pensacola, Fla.-based insurer whose agents include three residents of Destin Terrace, personally received $4.7m in salary, restricted stock and stock options. Mr. Fin also received $643,050 worth of fringe benefits that year, mostly in the form of home security measures and corporate jet use.

Assets under management at Emerald Life on December 31, 2011, were smaller than at Prudential Financial by a factor of 229.

But by far the biggest drain on insurers' finances is their sales force. Carriers paid over $52bn in salaries and commissions to their agents last year, showering top performers with tickets to sporting events, first-class trips to Paris or Venice with the companion of their choice and invitations to lavish seminars in the Caribbean.

According to Linda Andreesen, spokesperson for the American Business Travel Association (ABTA), expenditures of $25,000 per participant are not unheard of at elite-circle sales conventions. "Private performances by Celine Dion or Billy Joel don't come cheap," she says, adding that only pharmaceutical companies spend more on their staff.

Agents work almost exclusively on commission. On a new life insurance policy, they earn between 100% and 120% of the first year's premium at signing. They sometimes receive additional payments over a period of up to 10 years. They also reap smaller commissions — usually between 10% and 15% — on recurring business, such as homeowner, auto and disability policies.

However, Richard Wicks, head of studies at the American Association of Insurance and Financial Advisors, rejects the notion that agents' compensation is excessive. "There are a lot of misconceptions on the subject. The truth is that half of our members earn less than $47,000 a year. Only 10% take home more than $115,000."

With commissions not capped in any way, however, star agents can pocket several million dollars a year.

While nowhere near such numbers, Charles "Chuck" Patterson, insurance agent for Emerald, earns a very comfortable living. He lives in one of Destin Terrace's mansions, for which he paid $1,175,000 in cash in February 2007. Okaloosa County property records show that he's also the co-owner, along with his brother-in-law, of six houses and one apartment building in the nearby town of Niceville.

"My clients have worked hard to get where they are. I help them protect their families against the vagaries of everyday life," says Mr. Patterson, who's belonged to the prestigious President's Club of Emerald's best agents since 2008, and is "proud of [his] financial success."

In an industry where market share is notoriously difficult to capture, companies sometimes offer hundreds of thousands of dollars to top agents to lure them to jump ship. Chuck Patterson scoffs at that notion: "I'm loyal to Emerald. Champions stick with champions."

Chuck Patterson

Those expenses add up. At the end of the day, payments to policyholders account for a mere 51% of the revenue of market leader MetLife. Emerald, Mr. Patterson's employer, has an even worse record, redistributing only 46% of the premiums it collects. By comparison, roulette players recover 94.7% of their wagers on average.

Payout ratios haven't always been so low. In the 17th century, Lorenzo Tonti, a Napolitan banker, launched a new investment scheme with the blessing of King Louis XIV. Participants would deposit various sums of money in a joint account and agree to share the annual interest income proportionately. Every death within the pool automatically improved the yields of surviving investors. The last man standing collected the jackpot.

The tontine, named after its creator, was gradually banned in the nineteenth century, when it became apparent that unscrupulous investors had other participants killed in order to secure a bigger slice of the cake.

The other factor influencing the price of a policy is what insurance companies call the lapsing rate. Jeffrey McGregor, 38, is vice-president and chief actuary of Emerald, and has been a Destin Terrace resident since 2008. "Some of our clients stop paying their premiums. The policy is then deemed to have lapsed," he says.

There are several reasons why someone might let their policy lapse: they no longer need it, they can no longer afford it, or they simply forget to pay the premium.

According to the ACLI, 6.1% of all individual policies lapsed in 2011. One fifth of those policyholders, having contributed more than the required minimum during the preceding years, were entitled to a refund from their carriers. The remaining 80% receive nothing. All of them forfeited their benefits permanently.

Six percent of lapsed contracts annually doesn't look like a very high percentage. However, this statistic must be viewed in the context of the typical policy's duration of 20, 30, or even 50 years. Ultimately, death benefits are paid on only 10% of the contracts.

Rick Weintraub, president of the Insurance Consumers' Association, bemoans the general public's ignorance about this issue. "People don't believe me when I tell them that 90% of all policies will go unpaid. But it's true, and it's been going on for a hundred years!"

Insurance companies maintain a rather equivocal position toward lapsing. According to the ACLI's annual report, they "vigorously seek to minimize the lapsing of policies. For example, agent training focuses on realistic identification of clients' life insurance needs and careful analysis of the application of family income for protection."

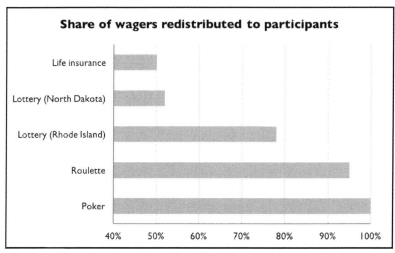

Share of wagers redistributed to participants

- Life insurance
- Lottery (North Dakota)
- Lottery (Rhode Island)
- Roulette
- Poker

40% 50% 60% 70% 80% 90% 100%

Source: Wall Street Tribune

Nevertheless, Jeffrey McGregor admits that lapsing is the friend of the insurance man, who is suddenly released from his contractual obligations. "Financially speaking, it's somewhat of a boon for us. Those clients have paid for years, yet will never collect the indemnity." Mr. McGregor is quick to add that high levels of lapsing enable insurers to offer very competitive rates. "If all our clients kept their policies until maturity, we would have to double or even triple our prices," he says.

Chuck Patterson agrees wholeheartedly. He says one of his neighbors at Destin Terrace recently took out a policy to protect his wife and two children in the event that he should die within the next 20 years. "He's 35, in tip-top shape, and a non-smoker. He was able to buy $500,000 of coverage for $22 a month. That's the kind of price you get thanks to high lapsing rates."

Although those very rates have made the insurers' fortunes, they could well become their Achilles' heel. Life settlement funds do indeed intend to keep the policies they acquire until maturity.

Rhonda Taylor has lived in one of Destin Terrace's condos since 2006. She works for Integrity Servicing, a company that manages thousands of life insurance policies on behalf of several life settlement funds.

"When I call an insurer with notification of a change in ownership, I hear a momentary silence, while the agent digests the bad news," says Mrs.

Taylor. "The company thought it had insured Jack Smith, from Wichita, Ka. and now it's dealing with a hedge fund out of Miami or New York. It means the policy won't lapse, and, ultimately, they'll have to pony up."

Jeffrey McGregor won't deny that insurance companies are concerned with the rise of life settlement. He calls for both stricter and more permanent rules. "No industry needs stability more than ours. What would happen if, over the course of a few months, hedge funds were to acquire half the policies in circulation? Insurers would be wiped out, plain and simple. Nobody wants that."

With secondary transactions upward of $6bn per year, compared to the $19,000bn in aggregate in-force contracts, insurers' doomsday scenario still appears far-fetched.

According to Mr. McGregor's wife, Susan, who is vice-president of the life settlement fund Osiris Capital, insurance companies are less vulnerable than they seem. "Some fund managers think they can buy just any policy and hold it until maturity. They're so convinced they're smarter than insurance companies' executives that they gloss over the price. Well, they're in for a nasty surprise if you ask me. Insurers weren't born yesterday."

Investors vie for the most lucrative policies: those of the inoperable liver cancer patient or the degenerative disease sufferer, whose progressions can be predicted with a high degree of probability. "Most of such investors end up overpaying, without realizing the risks they incur. If the death occurs within the first few years as expected, they realize a return of 8% to 10%; but as soon as the going gets tough, they lose their shirts," says Mrs. McGregor.

Buyers sometimes face a different sort of competition from the insurers themselves, who secretly repurchase the policies with an almost certainly short duration. Jeffrey McGregor sees nothing wrong with that practice: "We'd rather pay $300,000 now to retire a policy instead of $1m in a few years. It's common sense."

When calculating life expectancies, other, more sophisticated investors take into account criteria that go beyond age and gender. For instance, actuarial tables have consistently shown for more than a decade that, on average, left-handed people outlive their right-handed counterparts by a year. To cite another example, a zip code is in itself a mine of information. "People in Beverly Hills are known to receive better medical treatment than Bronx residents. It'd be foolish to deny it," says Mrs. McGregor, who mentions other telling factors such as wealth and education levels.

The law prohibits insurers from using race as a factor in their underwriting decisions. Yet, according to a recent article in the Journal of the American Medical Association, African-Americans live on average 5 years less than Caucasians, 9 years less than Hispanics, and 13 years less than Asian-Americans. Such significant differences are bound to pique investors' interest.

Timothy Harris, president of Targeted Life Settlement, created a mini-scandal last year by revealing that his Denver-based fund used racial profiling to select the policies on which to bid.

"It's time we acknowledged that Emily Yu will live longer than Latoya Johnson," he said in a trade event's panel discussion on the results of the 2010 census. The conference hosts quickly issued a press release condemning the remark. Mr. Harris was later expelled from the Life Insurance Settlement Association (LISA) and forced by his investors to liquidate his fund.

Mr. Harris didn't return our repeated requests for an interview.

Jean-Michel Jacques, Mrs. McGregor's boss, gladly leaves such criteria to his rivals. His fund, Osiris Capital, specialized very early in the acquisition of policies previously held by AIDS patients. "We gathered all AIDS studies ever published in the U.S., Europe and Japan. Then we cross-checked and, whenever possible, cross-indexed all the data to eliminate duplication. We considered such factors as when a patient had been contaminated, the treatments undergone, and a slew of other information I'd rather keep confidential."

When he heard about Osiris's initiative, Roberto Sandoval, director of the AIDS research center at John Hopkins University, offered to purchase a copy of Mr. Jacques' software.

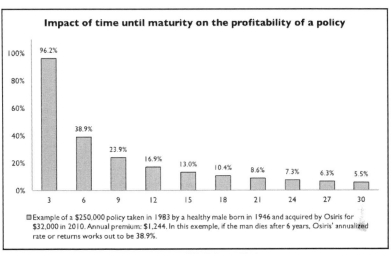

Source: *Osiris, Wall Street Tribune*

"He turned down all our offers, even the ones with a lot of zeros," says Mr. Sandoval. "He was concerned that his model might fall in the hands of his competitors. In the end, he shared with us the data with the greatest scientific interest, in exchange for our word that the information would never leave the lab. He's someone who really understands how research works."

Mr. Jacques buys only portfolios with an expected rate of return of 15% or more, but that doesn't mean he underestimates the advances of medicine. "In our worst-case scenario, AIDS patients live as long as the rest of the population. Even then, we still make money," he says.

What of a cancer vaccine or some miraculous discovery that could suddenly prolong people's life to 120 or 150 years?

"Life settlement funds would go belly up," says Mr. Jacques. "But it's a risk I'm willing to take. And, should it happen, I hope my investors will be wise enough to focus on the years they've come out ahead, rather than the millions they've lost."

Write to Vlad Eisinger: vlad.eisinger@wst.com

Next week: *The Cut-Throat Fight Between Insurers and Premium Finance Funds*

Dan's journal

Tuesday, July 3

I walked over to Jean-Michel Jacques' place last night. I had never visited that part of the community. The impersonal common areas and the rows of mailboxes reminded me of how much I had come to loathe my life in New York in the end.

Jean-Michel's wife, Anh, answered the door and welcomed me in. She was very kind and knew exactly who I was. She ushered me to the children's room. Sitting cross-legged on the carpet, Jean-Michel was reading a story in French to his boys, both listening angelically in their bunk beds. He signaled that he wouldn't be long. While he was finishing, I surveyed their abode. Theirs is a modest two-bedroom, where everything has been designed to create the illusion of quality at the lowest cost. The finishes especially — lighting, floor covering, appliances — are a definite downgrade compared to those in my house. The condos are much cheaper, though — no mystery there.

Jean-Michel seemed delighted to see me. He offered coffee, which I refused, anxious not to encroach on his family time. I explained that I needed his insight into certain financial mechanisms that I describe in *Camelia Van Noren*. Would he be willing to give me half an hour of his time, preferably somewhere other than the gym?

He suggested I swing by his office on Friday around noon.

Wednesday, July 4

Another good work session on *Camelia* this morning. Still, I'm constantly hampered by my limited knowledge of economics. May Jean-Michel prove enlightening.

On another note, Perutz is still there, stuck between Elias Canetti and Franz Blei. I refrain from refreshing the page more than twice a day, as much for time's sake as for fear of attracting the attention of the Wikipedia police.

Broch's profile hasn't been subject to any modification since my prank last week. Then again, good old Hermann's been dead for 60 years. No wonder his page isn't buzzing with news.

I just realized I haven't yet read Vlad's second article. Let's hope Mrs. Cunningham didn't throw it away. I have the feeling it's going to be the talk of the town at the pool party.

Thursday, July 5

Well, my social life must have sunk pretty low for a BBQ at the Destin Terrace clubhouse to stand out as the season's highlight.

There were at least 250 of us, crowded around the buffet, where Ed Linkas, spatula in hand, was skillfully flipping burgers. A long walk on the beach had whetted my appetite, and I found myself shamelessly snatching the last hot dog right under the nose of one of the McGregor boys.

Melvin Phelps was walking from group to group, apologizing that the buffet wasn't as sumptuous as last year's. Apparently a few residents have failed to pay their dues, forcing the association to tighten its belt. So he had to forget about hiring a caterer and send Rafaela to Costco to buy sandwich trays and cupcakes. Manuel, Rafaela's husband, was tasked with keeping a close eye on alcoholic beverages, while Phelps's own grandchildren were helping to clear tables.

Melvin introduced his daughter Kimberly to us in passing. She's living with them "temporarily, just until she finds a place she can call home." After a few years toiling in investment banking on Wall Street, she's made the move to insurance at Saint-Joseph, a company whose agents compete with Chuck Patterson. Phelps dumped his heiress in my lap on the pretext that, having both lived in New York, he bet we had "tons of things to talk about." As if I needed another insurance agent on my heels!

What he doesn't know is that I left Manhattan in part to escape women like Kim. I could no longer stand their twangy voices, their ridiculous dietary quirks, their proclamations of independence belied by their obvious desires to find a husband, and their more or less subtle ruses to assess my spending power (one of them breaking new ground in ingenuity by guesstimating my royalties from my books' current rankings on Amazon).

And yet, in a surge of altruism so typical of me, I decided to give the damsel a chance. Lucky for me, she's quick on the uptake — unlike some who call themselves theater experts just because they saw Mamma Mia on Broadway. She also makes no secret that she's counting on daddy to help her launch her career. I discouraged her by claiming that I didn't own a thing worth insuring (I've noticed in the past that the fastest way to get telemarketers off my back is to tell them I'm dead broke).

"Not even your life?" she asked with a smile.

"Especially not my life," I answered.

As expected, Vlad's article was on everybody's lips. Jean-Michel Jacques and Jeffrey McGregor talked at length about adverse selection, a scientific term used to describe the fact that sick individuals are less prone than healthy ones to let their policies lapse. That makes perfect sense; the whole difficulty for the insurers consists in incorporating that behavior into their mathematical models. Susan McGregor was listening quietly. If I'm not mistaken, she and her husband are rivals in a way. She was gazing at Jean-Michel in awe, imbibing his words. Meanwhile, off to the side, Anh was indicating to her two sons by nodding what they were permitted to put on their plates.

Happened on a little tête-à-tête a bit later between Sharon Hess and Donna Phelps, Melvin's wife, who were diligently dissing Jean-Michel. Their list of his shortcomings was endless — his profession (despicable), his accent (ridiculous), his Vietnamese wife (probably communist), his kids (who sweep all the prizes at school), and even his thriftiness, which they blamed for weakening the American economy. Donna complained that Jean-Michel had declined to contribute to the charity she runs. "He makes millions and he can't spare $100 for our veterans? Shame on him! If he thinks he's ever going to fit in with that attitude."

Chuck Patterson, who usually takes advantage of these community parties to hand out business cards left and right, was also raked over the coals. After observing the Phelps tribe's little game with a worried eye, he incurred the wrath of Mrs. Cunningham, who demanded to know how much money he earns every year from the premiums on her home and car policies. He awkwardly dodged the question.

Mark Hansen, who has just purchased life insurance, asked Patterson if he had really received a commission worth one year's premium for his policy. As a man cognizant of economic realities, he didn't seem shocked so much as curious. His wife, Jennifer, didn't prove that open-minded. She rebuked Chuck for not having knocked down his commission and offered them a friends-and-family discount. Chuck retorted, stone faced, that all his clients were his friends. Mark sportingly came to his rescue, claiming that he had actually found the price of the insurance quite reasonable.

"Of course," chimed in Jeff who was walking by. "As a non-smoking 35 year-old, you only have one chance in 700 to die within the year." (Something tells me the McGregors have a set of mortality tables posted in their bathroom.)

Michael Hart made a late appearance, his entry happily coinciding with the blaring first notes of Bruce Springsteen's *Born in the USA*. He was wearing navy blue pleated pants and a Ralph Lauren polo shirt, which, as expected on this national holiday, featured an American flag. He's a handsome man in his early forties, clean-shaven, with a perfect tan and flawless teeth (he must have had them whitened at Lammons' and then written it off as a business expense).

Ed Linkas, who had been relieved at the hamburger station, told me he voted for Hart at the last state elections.

"He won by a landslide. He does have a lot going for him — he's friendly, wealthy but not too wealthy, he speaks decent Spanish, he's a hunter, a reservist, a Red Cross administrator... Republicans go nuts for that kind of profile; they're begging him to run at the next midterms. But he's playing it cool. He says he won't leave Destin until he sees his daughter's softball team win the county championship. Voters are lapping it up!"

I watched the guy with a certain admiration. Although I'm well aware that all his moves are calculated (exchanging witty banter with Jennifer Hansen, nonchalantly patting Brian Hess on the back, squealing with delight upon tasting Mrs. Cunningham's blueberry pie). He oozes confidence. You can't learn that in books.

Ed introduced us. Hart, who had slightly overdone it in the Cologne department, shook my hand warmly, as if our meeting marked the beginning of a beautiful friendship. He pretended to remember my mother, "such a sweet lady" (an odd choice of words from anyone who actually knew Mom), before asking me if I had had a chance to register to vote.

I brought up Vlad's articles, curious to know his stance on the whole life settlement phenomenon. He launched into a pompous diatribe, a hangover from his lawyer days no doubt. He started by defending the right of senior citizens to sell their policies, "so as to adapt the structure of their savings to meet the challenges of old age. At the same time," he carried on, "insurance companies need rules that are clear and transparent" (This is not the first time I pick up on politicians' penchant for pleonasms. Why not "clear, simple, transparent, and comprehensible" while we're at it?). He closed with

33

"the importance of pragmatic legislation, which would take everyone's interests into account."

I didn't ask a second question.

Phelps's grandchildren, who had abandoned their posts, were playing tag around the pool, gobbling down cupcakes and hot dogs, while Rafaela, who was now flying solo, heroically stayed on top of service, replenishing the buffet at regular intervals and shoving empty plates into an enormous trash bag.

I also had a little chat with Bruce Webb, the flight attendant who sold his policy in the '80s. I recognized him from his portrait in the *Wall Street Tribune*, as he was eating his fruit salad off to one side. He told me he's been feeling a bit ostracized since Vlad revealed that he has AIDS. Donna Phelps and Blanche Patterson are giving him the cold shoulder. He even found a nasty message (whose content he refused to divulge) in his mailbox. Despite the aversion Lammons inspires in me, I don't believe that fool (who thank goodness didn't deem it worth his while to honor our shindig with his presence) capable of such a cheap shot.

While we were talking, a 16 or 17-year-old girl with black fingernails and a pierced nose walked over to Bruce and encouraged him to "hang in there." She disappeared as quickly as she had materialized, leaving us in an uncomfortable silence.

What a strange bird, that Webb. He explained to me without the slightest hint of embarrassment why airline companies purposely hire gay men — they don't get pregnant, they have no family life, they don't make unreasonable requests (since they love to fly and see the world), and they don't get hit on as much by passengers. He moved to Destin to be closer to his mother, who resides in a retirement home, while his partner of 10 years, also an airline steward, lives in Texas. They run into each other at chance layovers and talk on the phone every night before going to bed.

Bruce introduced me to his neighbor, Ray Wiggin, a journalist at the *Northwest Florida Daily News,* the local rag, where he's in charge of the obituary section. He talks about his work with remarkable enthusiasm. When he learned that I was a writer, he invited me over to his place, where he's supposedly putting the final touches on a revolutionary invention. I promised him I'd drop by one of these days.

I left the party as it was winding down around nine o'clock, and walked to the beach to watch the fireworks alone. After having witnessed the spectacle of my taxes going up in smoke, I headed back, making a detour by the pool. Manuel and Rafaela were busy putting everything in order. Phelps's grandchildren were nowhere in sight.

(…)

Ran across Chuck Patterson as he was leaving Mrs. Cunningham's. He was throwing a hissy fit.

"She no longer wants me representing her in the sale of her policy. 'You've made enough money off of me,' she told me. And of course, idiot that I am, I hadn't made her sign an agreement! That'll teach me to trust my clients, goddammit! Did you know I trim her hedges gratis twice a year? Well, she can go and trim them herself from now on!"

I tried to slip away but Chuck needed a compassionate ear.

"The truth is I'm being punished for my success. I've been busting my chops for 30 years. Ask Blanche how long it's been since I've taken any time off. You'll see! Always on the clock, that poor old Chuck! Morning, noon, and night, including Saturdays and even Sundays after church!

"Let me tell you something, Dan, being an insurance broker is one of the most underrated jobs around. Seven out of ten agents throw in the towel after only a couple of years because they can't manage to make a niche for themselves. Half of us are paid peanuts.

"Ah, I hope Phelps's precious daughter isn't afraid to get down and dirty! She's going to learn the full meaning of the word 'competition.' Wall Street is candy land in comparison! We'll see if she ends up sponsoring the local kids' softball team like yours truly. Between the jerseys, the balls, and the trophies, that civic deed is costing me a small fortune! Not to mention I treat all the rug rats and their parents to Pizza Hut at the end of every season! And what about the girl scouts! Do you have any idea how many damn boxes of cookies I buy every year? Enough to feed a small army! Ah, daddy dearest had better not pinch pennies if he wants to keep up…

"And so what if I paid cash for my house. Am I supposed to apologize for that? My banker couldn't get over it. 'Are you sure you don't want something bigger?' he protested. 'Usually, when people have one million to their name, they borrow another and buy a two-million-dollar house.' Can you believe that nonsense? Those are the same people who wonder why they have nothing but debts to leave their children.

"Not that any of them were crying for me when the real estate crisis whipped my ass, mind you. All those wusses who bought their house with a measly five percent down payment, they can always pack their knick-knacks and ditch the bank. I, on the other hand, am stuck. Yes sir, the only responsible person around here is forced to wait for prices to recover and pay off the arrears of the rats who are abandoning ship. So you tell me, Dan, who's the true patriot here?

"By the way, have you given any thought to that health insurance?"

Friday, July 6

At first, I thought Jean-Michel had given me the wrong address. Osiris Capital is housed in a drab building on the Publix parking lot, between a chiropractor and an ambulance chaser.

Despite its glitzy name, Osiris Capital employs only three people: Jean-Michel, Susan McGregor, and Lori, a plump 50-year-old who introduced herself as the office manager, which probably means she answers the phone and orders refills for the coffee machine.

Jean-Michel occupies a room hardly bigger than a broom closet, and whose total furnishings must have cost less than $200 at Staples. In comparison, Susan McGregor enjoys the royal treatment — natural light, immaculate carpet, and freshly painted walls.

In case I had failed to notice, Jean-Michel told me he prefers to run his business on a shoestring. Two employees are quite sufficient to handle Osiris's low volume of transactions. He personally assesses each portfolio, but outsources ancillary tasks (administering policies, paying premiums, collecting indemnities, etc.) to a specialized firm in Niceville.

He was in the middle of answering my questions when a beeping sound signaled a new text message. He glanced at his phone and his face lit up.

"Ah, a maturity!"

Noticing my confusion, he translated: "The technical term for a death. We never say the D-word in this industry."

He let out a quick whistle.

"A quarter of a million! Not bad at all! Hold on a second, Dan."

He shouted through the wall: "Lori, can you look for Lucy Bennett's obituary. Bennett, with two N's and two T's."

He told me he makes it a point of honor to read the death notice of every person in his portfolio.

"Before they die, they're just numbers. It has to be that way. I don't want to wish for anyone's death in particular, you know what I mean?"

I nodded.

He carried on: "When they die, it's different. I allow myself to view them as living people."

I refrained from commenting on the irony of his phrase.

"I sometimes go through the trouble of comparing the main events of the obituary with the medical records. It's so telling! You wouldn't believe the number of divorces that occur in the year following a cancer diagnosis... And I'm not even talking about adult children whose fathers died of AIDS and who refuse to appear on the announcement."

I pointed out that his business seems booming.

"Don't jump to conclusions. Today's the sixth and we're only at $300,000 in maturity. We have to pay $1.4m in premiums every month just to keep the policies active. But all in all, I can't complain. We're having an excellent year."

The time seemed right for the question I'd been dying to ask.

"Will you be moving then?"

"Why would we? We love living at Destin Terrace. And anyway, I couldn't afford to move. I've invested all my savings in Osiris."

"Wasn't that a bit unwise?"

He shrugged.

"I didn't have much of a choice. Without either reputation or a track record, no one would have come on board unless I proved I believed in my product."

He described the circumstances of how he started his own business. He was working in London, in a large American bank, where he was in charge of unearthing unconventional investments for asset management clients. He was having a grand old time buying farmlands in Kazakhstan, works of underground Chinese painters, and great Bordeaux wines *en primeur*. And then one day, some intermediary offered him a portfolio of life annuities. By a fortunate coincidence, the subject of Jean-Michel's doctoral thesis was life annuities. He immediately understood the ins and outs of the life settlement business. Many funds, having underestimated the life expectancy of AIDS patients, were selling off entire sections of their portfolios at that time in order to pay the premiums on the remaining policies.

"In short, it was the right time to invest. I talked to my boss who gave me the brush-off. He swore only by sports memorabilia — autographs of basketball celebrities, Maradona's signed jerseys — a market with turnover of between $2bn to $3bn a year by the way. Personally, I don't understand why some people are willing to shell out $1m for a used baseball, let alone consider it an investment!

"Anyway, I was determined not to spend my entire career in banking. My colleagues' lack of ethics revolted me. They talked about the countless ways to skin their clients, systematically extolling products on which they made the highest commissions and peddling stocks they themselves wouldn't have touched with a 10-foot pole. Ultimately, I cashed in my bonus — $1m— and I left.

"Anh was amazing. If she thought I was being rash, she never showed it. We sold our house in Hampstead and moved into an apartment one third the size. The first year, I worked in the kitchen and didn't pay myself a salary. I started to put together a small portfolio, bidding only on policies I expected would yield exceptional returns. Two or three hefty maturities helped me convince a few relations to invest with me. We managed to get our hands on whole portfolios right when the market was collapsing.

"In 2009, we closed our biggest deal to date, buying nearly 3,000 policies from Sunset Partners. I spent every other week in the US and barely saw my boys anymore — it was getting out of hand. So Anh and I decided to move closer to the hub of my business. It was either New York or Florida. We chose Florida — cheaper and sunnier. We rented in Orlando for a year — depressing. Luckily, a headhunter put me in contact with Susan. She was tempted by my offer but she and her husband were reluctant to relocate to Mickey Mouse heaven. I flew up to Destin to convince them, but, in the end, we were the ones to move!"

He hesitated for a second before telling me point blank that he's just been diagnosed with bladder cancer. He's waiting resignedly for additional test results to determine the seriousness of his disease. Meanwhile Anh is panicking because they have no medical insurance (welcome to the club) and not a penny to their name. I was touched by Jean-Michel's confiding in me but I didn't quite know what to say, other than to assure him of my support.

I decided to change the subject.

"Aren't you worried the *Wall Street Tribune* series might give your profession a bad rep?"

My question surprised him.

"No at all, why? It's going to draw new investors and, hopefully,

38

encourage more seniors to monetize their policies. The only people who have a problem with what I do are insurers and, believe me, they didn't need those articles to hate me."

With that, Lori handed in the obituary she had found in the *Northwest Florida Daily News*, Ray Wiggin's paper. I asked if I could trouble her to make a copy for me. Jean-Michel placed his in his briefcase. He'd read it later, he said. Not to his children, I hope.

*****

Northwest Florida Daily News
Saturday, June 30, 2012

Lucy Inola BENNETT passed away peacefully in her home in Fort Walton, Fla. on Thursday, June 28, 2012, at the age of 94. She joins in heaven her beloved husband, Lester, deceased in 2003.

Lucy was born on November 2, 1917, in Kenoma, Mo. Her parents, Vaughn and Verna Hurst, were farmers. In 1939, she married Lester "Moon" Bennett, who worked on the family farm. Their union was blessed with two children (Raymond in 1941, Mary Sue in 1948).

In 1953, Lucy and Lester became the proud owners of a hardware store in Marion, Mo. They steadily expanded the store, then opened two additional outlets in Joplin, Mo. and Twin Groves, Mo. To this day, the name Bennett Hardware is synonymous with quality, seriousness and kindness throughout Jasper County.

Lucy and Lester enjoyed dancing, hiking in the mountains and spending time with their children. They were members of the Lamar Baptist Church, where they wed. Raymond's accidental death in 1989 strengthened already solid family ties. Soon afterward, Lester and Lucy moved to Fort Walton, where they had spent their vacations for two decades.

After Lester's death, Lucy developed an interest in genealogy. In 2009, she gathered a few distant cousins from Buffalo, N.Y. and Tucson, Ariz. in her home. She also enjoyed knitting, cooking, strolling on the beach and playing bingo with her friends.

Lucy was hard-working, loving and devoted to her husband and children. She touched many lives and will be missed by all those who knew her.

Lucy Bennett is survived by her daughter, Mary Sue, by her five grandchildren (Earl, Marvin, Jenna, Priscilla, and Leonard), and by many cousins, nieces, and nephews.

The funeral service will be held on Monday, July 2 at 2:00 p.m., at the Fort Walton Baptist Church. Lucy will be buried next to Lester in a mausoleum located in the adjoining cemetery.

*****

Dan's journal

Friday, July 6 (continued)

What in God's name have I done to constantly find myself in the middle of other people's business? Earlier, as I was about to slip my key into the lock, Ashley, Mrs. Cunningham's daughter, exited her mother's house, slamming the door. The gentleman in me felt compelled to intervene. No sooner had I asked her what was the matter than she burst into tears. I quickly invited her inside to avoid a scene.

It so happens that Mrs. Cunningham has finally broken the news and informed her daughter that she is condemned. Ashley kept her chin up, at first, like a good little soldier. When her mother told her that she intends to sell her life insurance policy, however, she broke down and started sobbing. Mrs. Cunningham lashed out at Ashley for caring more about her inheritance than about her mother. The conversation became heated, all the more since the two women have been down that road before. Mom had told me that, in 2007, Ashley and her husband Jerry bought the house next to mine, pre-construction, putting ten percent down. One week before closing, Jerry lost his job. The couple, who was no longer able to qualify for a loan, turned to Patricia Cunningham, whom the late and dearly missed Otto had left in relative material comfort. Mrs. Cunningham, who lived in a decrepit little house in Fort Walton at the time, visited the house and found it so very lovely that she substituted herself for her daughter and son-in-law on closing day, adding insult to injury by telling them they were in her debt for saving their ten percent!

I told Ashley she should come back in a few days with flowers. In the meantime, I'm going to try to reason with her mother.

People, I swear…

Saturday, July 7

Chuck Patterson is smiling again. He's been parading around the community all morning at the wheel of his new land yacht, one of those white convertible Mercedes I thought were reserved for Miami Beach pimps and drug dealers. He invited me in for a full-fledged demo — individual screens, sound system, on-board computer, the whole spiel.

He bragged about the way he masterfully conducted the negotiation, pitting a handful of dealers against one another.

"You should have seen me, Dan, I took no prisoners! I told them they could save their manufacturers' prices for suckers and that unless they were willing to throw in the sport package and walnut burl dashboard, I'd take my business elsewhere. The Audi guy folded on the spot, claiming that his dealership doesn't offer discounts. No discounts — and they call themselves sales people! Lexus, BMW, and Mercedes were still in the game. I had my way with them, let me tell you! I would send each of their offers to the other two, asking for another little extra. BMW choked first. I was about to sign with the Japs when Mercedes came back with the leather wheel and electric sun shades. A $1,500 bonus! We closed the deal right there and then — well, not before I had also scored free delivery and registration fees, of course."

I asked whether he was worried that such an expensive car might offend his clients or, worse yet, his prospects. He laughed in my face.

"Quite the contrary: they'll think I must be one hell of an insurer to drive this luxury gas-guzzler. Success works like a magnet, Dan. Didn't they teach you that at Columbia? Plus I'm going to deduct the monthly payments from my income."

I suddenly felt a huge surge of sympathy for Mrs. Cunningham.

*****

From: Dan Siver <danielgsiver@gmail.com>
Date: Saturday, July 7, 2012 4:14 P.M.
To: Vlad Eisinger <vlad.eisinger@wst.com>
Subject: Scolding

I hope you don't expect me to praise you for your articles. The last one is dry as a bone. No flesh, no personal touch. Instead of writing that "Chuck Patterson is proud of his financial success," you would have been better off transcribing the speech with which he favored me earlier. It was lyrical, colorful, grotesque, touching — in one word, human. Inserting his portrait between two paragraphs isn't enough to make him come to life. (By the way, who makes these drawings for you? They're really cool.)

Ditto for Jean-Michel Jacques. You should see how eager he looks when his phone notifies him of a maturity (just that term 'maturity,' Vlad — damn, what a great find!). And how about that habit of his to read the obituary of his policyholders after they croak! But all that goes way over your head at the *Wall Street Tribune*. All you know how to do is to print 0's and 1's, and even then, you consult with your lawyers beforehand.

PS: Sadly, Sir Jangled, alias J.D. Salinger, expired two years ago, leaving behind millions of inconsolable readers, yours truly being one of them. How's Ramona Merlin?

*****

From: Vlad Eisinger <vlad.eisinger@wst.com>
Date: Saturday, July 7, 2012 8:57 P.M.
To: Dan Siver <danielgsiver@gmail.com>
Subject: How dare you?

Jesus, Dan, you haven't cooled off a bit, have you? Your email took me back 15 years.

When will you understand that a good orator has no need for cheap grandstanding? Believe me, in this business, justice will be better served by my articles than by your lectures. Your Chuck Patterson is a scoundrel, as you'll figure out soon enough. As for Jean-Michel Jacques, do you know him well enough to characterize his facial expression as *eager*? When did you ever become qualified to interpret people's countenances?

Beware of your nature, Dan. Even your papers at Columbia were too complacent. You could never resist a one-liner. I've learned at the *Tribune* that searching for comic effect or a convenient alliteration should never take precedence over truth.

As for your shameful attacks on my employer, they deserve but a one-sentence answer: we all have to find our own way. I respect the one you chose; I wish you would grant me the same courtesy.

PS: Ramona Merlin, alias Norman Mailer, has joined Salinger in writer heaven, where they've apparently hit it off with Walter Laich.

*****

From: Dan Siver <danielgsiver@gmail.com>
Date: Saturday, July 7, 2012 9:19 P.M.
To: Vlad Eisinger <vlad.eisinger@wst.com>
Subject: The Vlad I used to love

We all have to find our own way — that's what you said 15 years ago after attending *The New York Times'* presentation at the Columbia job fair. You had driven me half mad for two years, ranting about the great American novel, but suddenly you decided to become a journalist. I remember the night you told me about your decision. You invited me to dinner at Lussardi. I felt no less betrayed than if you had stabbed me in the back.

PS: Did you know that Walter Laich, alias Willa Cather, burned a large portion of her notes and correspondence? She was at peace with herself, for she knew she had brought her life's complete work into being, unlike some who have been procrastinating for 20 years. On a different note, what has become of Lisette Bartelson?

*****

From: Vlad Eisinger <vlad.eisinger@wst.com>
Date: Saturday, July 7, 2012 10:57 P.M.
To: Dan Siver <danielgsiver@gmail.com>
Subject: Truce

Listen Dan, we're not going to harp on all that until the end of time. I've never judged you, so how about giving me a break?

One word though on *Clandestine Passengers*, which I finally found in my bookshelf. The style is there, as are the tone and even the construction. But what about substance, Dan? Where is the substance? A housewife who gives conferences on Virginia Woolf around the world, pretending to be a professor and her neighbor — for crying out loud, did you really expect to stir up the crowds with that?

You're not even an English teacher, nor an editor, unlike so many authors. You don't have children; you live in a hole; you never set foot outside. How do you expect to come up with ideas or to meet colorful characters?

A piece of advice: put your books down, look out the window, and embrace the world.

PS: Your anagram gave me a hard time. Brett Easton Ellis — now there's a writer who has something to say. No wonder he sells more books than you do.

*****

Dan's Journal

Sunday, July 8
Chuck Patterson paid me a visit because he wanted to "hand-deliver his quote personally."

I scrutinized the terms and conditions as if my current situation had less to do with my impecuniousness than the fact that I have yet to find the perfect carrier. Sitting to my left, dashing in his pearl-gray Sunday suit, Chuck was inspecting my library, looking perplexed. When I turned to the last page, he moved his chair closer to mine, probably to catch me in case I fainted.

"I tweaked the caps and deductibles to stay below $6,000," he said, in a way that meant I need not thank him. "It's $495 a month. That's something, of course, but have you been to the ER recently? Last week, my youngest busted her nose jumping on the trampoline. I thought she needed stitches, so I rushed her to Fort Walton. Instead of stitches, they stuck a bandage on her nose and sent us on our way. Do you know how much they billed my insurance? $540, Dan, $540! For that price, they didn't even give the box of bandages! Can you believe that?"

"It's too expensive," I said as firmly as I could. "Never mind, I'll just quit competitive trampolining."

Chuck seemed at a loss. For a second, I thought he was going to try to convince me that a life without aerial acrobatics isn't worth living.

"How much can you afford, Dan? $400 a month? $350? I can try to customize a plan just for you. Where do we cut? On prescription medicine? Physiotherapy? The TV in the hospital room?"

"Nowhere, Chuck. It's just too expensive."

"You're not seeing a shrink, are you? We might be able to shave off $20 to $30 a month by removing psychiatry from reimbursable services... Same thing with the vasectomy — you might want kids one day, right?"

I suggested that he send a copy of *Double Play* to 100 of his clients for Christmas. He wasn't overwhelmed with enthusiasm.

"I usually give out Starbucks gift cards — people love them. What's your book about anyway?"

I tried to remember the pitch in the Polonius catalog.

"It's the story of an MI-6 civil servant who's in charge of creating legends. Not fairy tales, legends: those fake identities that secret agents use during their missions. Little by little, he starts identifying—"

"Never heard of it," Chuck cut me off. "Is it sort of like Tom Clancy?"

There are moments in life, fortunately few, when fate seems to revel in having us glimpse the insignificance of our condition. This was one of them.

"More like Robert Ludlum or Dean Koontz," I answered, mentioning the first two best-selling authors' names that sprang to mind.

Chuck's face lit up a bit.

"Ah, Koontz! They have a whole shelf of his stuff at the airport. Have you met him?"

"No, but we have a lot of friends in common. And I've heard he's been

45

following my work."

Chuck looked at me pensively. Dean Koontz — no doubt that guy had an airtight medical insurance plan, the kind that covers dental floss and sophrology sessions.

"How much does your book cost?"

"The hardcover is $19.99."

"Come on Dan, don't take me for a dummy. Nobody buys the hardcover. How much is the paperback?"

"$6.99."

I could follow his train of thought as if I were in his head: $700, that was about the amount of the commission he would earn should I sign up for his medical insurance. Of course, he could recover part of that amount by prepaying $5 less on the Starbucks cards. But what monetary value would his clients assign to the 15-year-old novel of an unknown author?

"Forget it," he mumbled as he took his leave.

There was my answer.

Monday, July 9

Did my good deed this morning by talking to Mrs. Cunningham. I had trouble convincing her that her daughter is genuinely worried about her health. The truth is it's her son-in-law she can't stand: Jerry, "a bone-lazy dimwit" who's been hopping from one lousy job to the next ever since Citigroup gave him the boot.

"I know what I'm talking about; Otto worked at a bank too. Except that he hung onto his position for his whole working life, like a mussel to its rock.

"Jerry will tell you that he didn't do anything wrong, that the global economy was headed for disaster, and that banks left tens of thousands of average Joes like him high and dry. Oh, sure, when it comes to excuses, he has them pouring out of his ears! They didn't fire all the bank tellers, so far as I know! That Mexican at the Publix branch who cashes in Otto's pension check for me — he's still there. Now, of course, as far as professionalism goes, Jerry couldn't possibly measure up — Jose greets me by my name, makes friends with Baxter, and always gives me a handful of candy for my grandchildren. Do you think it would have killed that schmuck to do as much? He didn't even manage to get out properly. After 10 years of service, he got $5,000 in total severance. Talk about a negotiator!"

46

(…)

It's been over a week since the Wikipedia editor notified me. I had planned on taking care of it sooner but, between my research for *Camelia* and my emails to Vlad, that dear Perutz had completely escaped me.

I read the laconic message again — ("Please indicate your sources") — wondering yet again what in the world had gotten into me that day. I have never deliberately broken the law, cheated on a test, or stolen a neighbor's newspaper, not so much out of virtue than out of an instinctive fear of the police.

I familiarized myself, though not without a certain apprehension, with the "banning policy" page of Wikipedia. It outlines the sanctions to which little smart alecks like me expose themselves. They go from the revocation of editorial privileges to either the suspension or cancellation of the incriminated account.

I let out a sigh of relief — I expected worse.

What are my options?

The easiest one would be to turn a deaf ear, or else to delete my account and create a new one. After a few unavailing reminders, the editor would remove my contribution and everything would return to normal.

Yet I can't resign myself to either course, perhaps because I've seen it in black and white, I'm now convinced that Broch associated with Perutz between the two wars.

I ran a search for "Broch Perutz Vienna friends" on Google. Needless to say, I should have started with that. My search yielded only one page — the one I modified last Sunday. I tried a few keyword variations, with no success.

Far from discouraging me, these failures lead me to ponder the reasons why Broch and Perutz were forced to keep their relationship under wraps. Were they afraid people might suspect them of being homosexual? Or worried about offending their respective churches at a time when anti-Semitism was sweeping Vienna? (Broch converted to Catholicism before his wedding, whereas Perutz remained faithful to Judaism.) Did they belong to a secret society that demanded the utmost discretion from its members? Did they share some shameful flaw?

Since my ignorance about the lives of these two men was limiting my conjectures, I browsed through their biographies on the German version of Wikipedia. Beyond the cruelty of the exercise (and to think I used to read

Goethe in the original text...), I learned that Perutz briefly worked as an actuary in Trieste, at the Italian insurer Generali, which counted a certain Franz Kafka among its employees at the time. Between 1908 and 1923, back in Vienna, he served various functions at another insurer named Anker, where he contributed — thus prefiguring Ed Linkas and Jeffrey McGregor — to perfecting existing mortality tables.

More importantly, I noticed uncanny similarities between Broch's and Perutz's respective paths. Both are Jewish by birth, from textile industrialist families. Both studied mathematics, worked in their fathers' businesses for a while, came to literature late in life, and went into exile under the Nazis.

OK, I think I have my theory.

In 1926, Perutz senior, Benedikt, breathes his last in Vienna at the age of 80. On his death bed, he confides a terrible secret to Leo: he has an illegitimate son, born of his liaison with Johanna Schnabel Broch, the wife of a colleague, whom he met in 1886 at a trade fair in Berlin.

In all probability, Johanna hid from her husband, Josef, that the child she was carrying wasn't his. In any case, Josef raised little Hermann as his own offspring, even appointing him manager of the company he had created.

Once his father is buried, Leo (44 years old by then) requests a meeting with Broch, whom he knows by name but has never met, "to discuss a matter of the utmost importance." The rendezvous takes place in September of 1926, at the apartment of Franz Blei, a mutual friend. Broch, initially crushed by the revelation, begins to recover as he considers the implications. He now understands why he feels nothing for his father, whom he's always suspected of favoring his younger brother, Friedrich. Yet it was with an aim to please his sibling, as much as for the sake of social conformity, that Hermann studied weaving in Mulhouse and then took up the reins of the family factory, notwithstanding a vocation for literature.

The discussion lasts late into the night. Broch admires the way his older half-brother has managed to reconcile his taste for writing and his passion for mathematics.

"You're barely 40," retorts Perutz. "It's not too late." That very evening, Hermann Broch makes a series of decisions that will change the course of his life. He resolves to put the factory up for sale, go back to school, and, most importantly, undertake the writing of a novel, even though to date he's published only short texts for periodicals.

Perutz approves these radical changes, though on one condition — the two men are never to see each other again. Leo wants there to be no room for rumors, for he knows they would be the death of Ida, his very religious wife. Hermann, finding the proposed arrangement rather extreme, pleads for a compromise and suggests they keep their relationship a secret. But Perutz proves inflexible. He will thwart his half-brother's overtures for the rest of his life.

Broch quickly implements his plan. He liquidates the family business and enrolls in mathematics and philosophy classes at the University of Vienna. In 1931, he publishes a first novel, *The Sleepwalkers*, which earns him the praises of Joyce and, later, those of Kundera.

As for Perutz, he keeps his distance. He spends time in Russia and France. In 1928, his beloved Ida dies while giving birth to their third child.

Both brothers pass away in the 1950s, one in Austria, the other in the United States. In accordance with Perutz's wishes, they never did see each other again.

I reread my scenario. It seems ironclad. I have a few days to beef it up.

Week 3

The Cut-Throat Fight Between Insurers and Premium-Finance Funds

By Vlad Eisinger

The Wall Street Tribune, Tuesday, July 10, 2012

The right for a policy owner to dispose of his life insurance policy as he sees fit is firmly established. In a 1911 landmark decision (Grigsby v Russell, 222 US 149), the U.S. Supreme Court stated that "life insurance has become one of the most recognized forms of investment and self-motivated saving." "Therefore," wrote Justice Oliver Holmes, "owners should be able to transfer their policies without limitation."

This judgment may seem at odds with another legal notion that dates back to the eighteenth century and is known as the "insurable interest test." Insurable interest is said to exist when an insured person derives a financial or other kind of benefit from the continued existence of the insured object (or, in the case of living persons, their continued survival). In other words, it's legal to insure the life of your spouse or a business partner, but not the life of your neighbor, let alone that of a stranger.

Insurers have long used this provision to hinder the surge of life settlements — the sale of an existing life insurance policy to a third party. They typically refused to pay the cash benefit when a policy had changed hands between the signing of the contract and the death of the original owner.

Investors who had purchased such policies sued the insurance carriers, invoking the Supreme Court's ruling.

Over the years, judges have come to differentiate between people who, having paid their premiums for years, could hardly be suspected of fraud, and those who sold their policies shortly after buying them. The latter case is referred to as Stranger-Originated Life Insurance (STOLI), meaning that the person insured is not the real initiator of the contract.

Laying out that distinction in the law proved no easy task, especially since in the U.S., the insurance sector is regulated by the states. In 2000, the National Conference of Insurance Legislators (NCOIL) adopted the Life Settlement Model Act, a text conceived as a blueprint to help states fashion their own laws.

"The chief merit of NCOIL is that it set a period — the two years following the signature — during which policies are ineligible for sale," says Lawrence Johnson, professor at the Ross School of Business at the University of Michigan. "Although few states followed suit initially, the impetus had been created."

With greater clarity on the legal front, investors began to devise schemes known as "premium finance," "zero-premium life insurance," or "speculator-originated life insurance." Those ploys, which differ only in the details, all aim to circumvent the two-year ineligibility period.

Here is how premium finance works: an investor approaches a senior, preferably a wealthy one, with an offer that looks too good to be true. The senior will take out a life insurance policy of, say, $10m. The investor will lend the senior $1.4m, the equivalent of two years' worth of premiums.

If the senior dies within two years, his heirs collect $10m, with which they retire the loan plus accrued interest.

If, as is usually the case, the senior is still alive in two years, he promises to sell his policy to the investor for a nominal price plus the cancellation of his debt. The investor is now the legal owner of the policy. Provided he keeps paying the premiums, he will collect $10m when the senior dies.

"The beauty of the scheme is that it generously serves both parties. The senior is insured free of charge for two years and the investor has circumvented anti-STOLI laws," explains Lawrence Johnson.

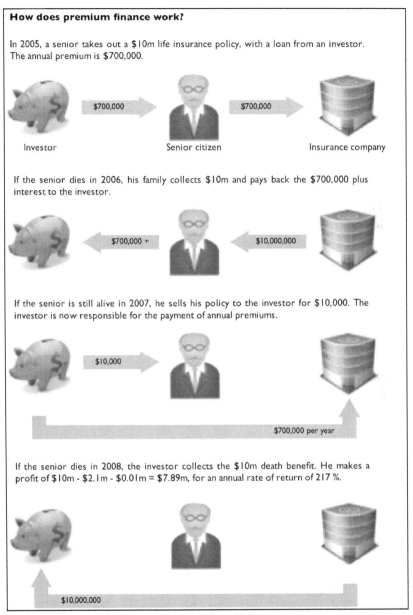

How does premium finance work?

In 2005, a senior takes out a $10m life insurance policy, with a loan from an investor. The annual premium is $700,000.

$700,000

Investor

$700,000

Senior citizen

Insurance company

If the senior dies in 2006, his family collects $10m and pays back the $700,000 plus interest to the investor.

$700,000 +

$10,000,000

If the senior is still alive in 2007, he sells his policy to the investor for $10,000. The investor is now responsible for the payment of annual premiums.

$10,000

$700,000 per year

If the senior dies in 2008, the investor collects the $10m death benefit. He makes a profit of $10m - $2.1m - $0.01m = $7.89m, for an annual rate of return of 217 %.

$10,000,000

Source: Wall Street Tribune

55

Several Wall Street firms sought to exploit what looked like a risk-free proposition. They dispatched salesmen to West Palm Beach or Santa Barbara to visit retirement homes and posh country clubs with the aim of recruiting candidates.

In March 2005, Keith Jennings, head of operations of the Admiral's Club in Boynton Beach, Fla., organized a luncheon presentation at the request of Life Path, a life settlement boutique from San Diego.

Mr. Jennings said he's constantly solicited by organizations seeking access to his patrons. "We only greenlight those who have a real service to offer," he added.

More than 200 members attended the event, feasting on lobster, filet mignon and champagne, courtesy of Life Path, who paid $250 per guest.

Among the several speakers who took turns on the podium, Andrew Marlowe, professor emeritus at Loyola University, argued that seniors possess an unsuspected asset: their age.

"To those of us over 75, he said we had nothing to lose and everything to gain by doing business with Life Path," recalled Reuben Gonzales, a retired CPA who was in the audience. "He later repeated that we'd be stupid not to seize this opportunity. I was shocked."

Life Path's books, which became public when the company went bankrupt in 2011, show that Professor Marlowe was paid $10,000 for his presentation. Contacted by the *Wall Street Tribune*, a spokesperson for Loyola University insisted that views expressed by teachers in public forums are their own and do not reflect those of the university.

Professor Marlowe declined several requests to be interviewed for this article.

During the luncheon, two Life Path executives from California, John d'Angelo and Matt Cosimano, presented what they called "an exclusive offer" to the members of the Admiral's Club.

A survey conducted at nearby country clubs shows that Mr. d'Angelo and Mr. Cosimano offered identical terms at several other venues between January and June of 2005.

Reuben Gonzales says that Life Path offered special incentives to seniors willing to fill out insurance forms on the spot. "For any policy between $2m and $5m, the company treated the whole family to a weekend at Disney World. They covered everything: plane tickets, hotel accommodation, limo rides and even a private tour guide. Over $5m, they'd throw in a $20,000 Mercedes golf cart."

According to Mr. Jennings, about 20 members of the Admiral's Club purchased policies worth between $2m and $15m that day.

Other funds set up vast networks of intermediaries, paying them referral fees for each transaction they help broker.

Sharon Hess has been a Destin Terrace resident since 2009. A professional nurse, she visits Fort Walton, Niceville and Valparaiso retirement homes at least once a week. In 2006, she began to extol the virtues of premium finance to her patients. "It was heartbreaking to see them torn between getting their hair done and spoiling their grandchildren, when I knew they could do both. So I slipped them Fair Share's phone number."

Fair Share LLC, a company from Framington, Mass., paid Mrs. Hess a finder's fee of $500 per policy.

Sharon Hess

According to a study by the Tuck Business School of Dartmouth University, premium finance reached its apex in 2006, with new issues totaling about $6bn in coverage. Life Path and Fair Share were among the most active firms in the market, along with prestigious Wall Street institutions, such as Deutsche Bank and Credit Suisse.

When the policies of the seniors recruited by Life Path started to mature, insurance carriers quickly realized they had a big problem. "They had underwritten those contracts based on standard lapsing rates. Suddenly, they were inundated with indemnity claims: $5m here, $10m there, and they panicked," recalled Lawrence Johnson.

Jeffrey McGregor, a vice-president and the chief actuary at Emerald, a life insurance company headquartered in Pensacola, Fla., finds the term "panic" excessive. Yet he admits to having noted "a substantial inflection in Emerald's lapsing liabilities around that period." "After a bit of digging, we arrived at the conclusion that most of the wealthy seniors who had taken out those policies had never intended to keep them past the ineligibility period."

Insurance companies then pored over all the large policies added to their portfolios over the past five years, systematically canceling any that exhibited irregularities. "They were two sorts," recalled Mr. McGregor, "those where the applicant had lied about his health and those where he had overstated his assets."

Most insurers won't issue a policy above a certain amount, typically $5m. They occasionally make exceptions for high net worth individuals. In order to be approved for coverage of, say, $10 or $15m, some seniors deliberately inflated their assets, sometimes dramatically so. A speaker at the most recent ACLI convention recounted that a retired mailman from Minnesota had bought over $120m in coverage from 26 separate companies, then auctioned his policies for a tidy profit.

In an attempt to discourage a practice that, in Mr. McGregor's terms, "jeopardizes their very existence," insurance carriers took the fraudsters to court.

Emerald, Mr. McGregor's employer, thus sued 86-year-old Emmanuel "Manny" Lammons, a retiree from Delray Beach, Fla., who had taken out a $10m policy in 2005 and sold it to Life Path two years later. In its complaint, filed in Escambia County, Emerald accuses Mr. Lammons of claiming a net wealth of $15m while his real assets, mostly composed of his permanent residence and his 401(k), totaled about one sixth of that amount.

An Alzheimer patient, Mr. Lammons was unable to defend himself. His 53-year-old son, Steve, who has been living in Destin Terrace since 2006, answered the summons on his father's behalf. As a sign of good faith, he vowed to refund all the monies his father had received from Life Path and to return the golf cart, on the condition that Emerald dropped its suit. The insurer rejected the offer, valuing it at only about $60,000 — a far cry from the $10m at stake.

In 2008, following the advice of his lawyer, Walter Oakwood III, Mr. Lammons sued Life Path for having encouraged his father to misrepresent his assets. Life Path filed for bankruptcy soon afterward, leaving Mr. Lammons to deal with Emerald's attorneys. The fund's policies, including the one originally held by Manny Lammons, were distributed among Life Path's investors.

Manny Lammons died last year. His estate has been frozen because of the pending legal procedures.

Steve Lammons says he's appalled at the way Emerald has been harassing his family. "They have no qualms about tarnishing a man's legacy based on one momentary lapse of judgment. It's disgusting."

Frances Gray, another Destin Terrace resident, is Emerald's chief mediator. She denies any persecution against her neighbor. "Cheaters wrong those who play by the rules. We owe it to our clients to protect them against the dishonest actions of a few unscrupulous individuals."

Steve Lammons

Thousands of similar disputes await judgments throughout the country. Although Lawrence Johnson doesn't expect insurers to prevail in every case, he thinks their retaliatory strategy has proven effective. "Boutiques such as Life Path or Fair Share, which couldn't match Prudential or MetLife's legal resources, threw in the towel. Major players like Credit Suisse have refused to fold. They'll probably settle at some point. One thing is certain, they'll think long and hard before trying their luck again."

Insurance companies can also take comfort in the fact that more and more states are siding with them in their fight against premium finance. Forty-one states now regulate the resale of policies. Thirty follow the NCOIL's Model Act. Ten have even extended the ineligibility period to five years.

Insurers are magnanimous in victory. Indeed, many pundits have issues with the way they behaved during the 2000s.

"They'd like us to believe they had no clue some clients lied about their health or net worth," explained Lawrence Johnson. "I don't buy it for a second. Premium finance's mega-policies fueled the insurers' growth, to the delight of their shareholders. I especially recall one Florida company whose production of new policies tripled over the course of a few years. By the time shareholders realized that premium finance accounted for most of that growth, it was already too late. The president of the company had exercised his stock options, pocketing tens of millions of dollars."

Mr. Johnson raises the ante: "The agents who sold those policies must have been aware of what was going on. But one deal alone could land them a commission of half a million. I guess some figures have the power to nip scruples in the bud."

Chuck Patterson, general agent at Emerald, has heard of such practices but says he has never experienced them first-hand. "I know my clients too well to fall into that trap. I wouldn't dream of selling a $10m policy to someone who lives in a trailer," he said.

Several insurance carriers went so far as to turn against their own sales force, accusing its members of collecting unwarranted commissions on contracts they knew to be fraudulent. In return, the American Association of Insurance and Financial Advisors, representing the agents, threatened to disclose a few secrets that could further damage insurers' reputations with the public.

In retrospect, premium finance has created two types of victims:

investors who trusted the likes of Life Path and Fair Share with their money, and senior citizens — or, in the case of Mr. Lammons, their families — mired in a legal battle way beyond their comprehension.

The winners are for the most part limited to the law firms engaged in complex litigation, some of which have been dragged out for years.

As for SLSP and LISA, two associations of life settlement professionals, they are pulling out all the stops with regulators in an effort to dispel any confusion between life settlement and premium finance.

Ryan Landry, SLSP's head of public and regulatory affairs, draws a clear distinction between the two practices. "Premium finance is a disingenuous scheme aimed at circumventing anti-STOLI laws. In contrast, life settlement is the legal sale of a policy legally held by its legal owner. So please don't tar us with the same brush."

Write to Vlad Eisinger: vlad.eisinger@wst.com
Next week: *Creative Destruction At Work*

*****

From: Dan Siver <danielgsiver@gmail.com>
Date: Tuesday, July 10, 2012 11:47 A.M.
To: Vlad Eisinger <vlad.eisinger@wst.com>
Subject: Exercises in style

I'm beginning to understand where you're going with this. You're trying to chronicle our time through the life settlement business, just as Steinbeck and Melville portrayed theirs through the mechanisms of agriculture and whale hunting. Not that they were the first to do it by the way. How about *Lost Illusions*, *Germinal*, or *Bel Ami* (though I would much rather go down in the mine, like Zola, than interview a Lammons).

All right. You know I'm not a big fan of social novels. Still, allow me to remind you that the characters and situations are what make the books you admire so powerful — Lousteau teaching Lucien de Rudembré how to review a book he hasn't read; Dagny Taggart swapping her diamonds for Lilian Rearden's scrap-iron bracelet; Rose of Sharon breast-feeding a starving man. Those are the moments, at the climax of a story, when the characters come alive and the mastery of the novelist shines through.

One last thing: writing articles for the *Wall Street Fucking Tribune* that are read, digested, and excreted within 24 hours doesn't excuse everything. During an investigation, you chance upon a phenomenal scene — I'm talking about those scam artists who force the hands of old men in retirement homes — and you toss it off in three paragraphs. Shame on you! For the fun of it, I rewrote the story to reflect the way I think the events transpired. Let this be an example to you.

PS: Norman Drachydle was a mediocre journalist but a great writer. Could it be you're the opposite?

*****

Greasing the machine
By Daniel Siver

The two men were setting up.

Matt Cosimano plugged in his computer and adjusted the projector. He proceeded methodically, with the quiet ease of the man who has performed those tasks countless times already. He had joined Life Path two years earlier as an account representative and quickly climbed his way up. His six-figure salary was the admiration and sometimes the envy of his family. His father was a roofer who barely brought in $50,000 a year. His mother had proudly raised six children. The eldest sold timeshares. The youngest was a professional butcher, for an industrial meat company during the week and for the New Jersey mafia on weekends.

Cosimano had only two vices: Italian suits and high-class Asian hookers. On Saturdays following the payment of bonuses, he would lock himself up in a room at the Hoboken Holiday Inn with three tattooed Chinese girls.

Close by, John D'Angelo tapped the mike to test the sound system. Fifty-two years old, he liked introducing himself as a Wall Street veteran, even though he hadn't toiled on the southern tip of Manhattan in quite a while. He had started out at Morgan Stanley in the '80s. The remainder of his career was but a long tumble. Each of his employers was less prestigious than the previous one. After Morgan Stanley, he had joined DLJ, then Nomura, then Credit Agricole, and had finally landed at Life Path, where he supervised a team of two people.

D'Angelo didn't delude himself with fantasies of promotion at Life Path, or with other prospects anywhere for that matter. He was too expensive. His Rolodex contained nothing but the names of old geezers, employed at second-rate establishments where they had no more authority than he did. He hoped only to hang on for another year or two, just long enough to pay off the mortgage on his Hackensack house.

The mike was working. D'Angelo scanned the restaurant. He had seen worse. The green and purple carpet — the country club's colors — looked tired, but at least the chandeliers weren't missing any light bulbs. The dark wood paneling, adorned with black and white photographs of legendary golfers (Ben Hogan, Bobby Jones, Sam Snead…), imparted a pseudo-British charm to the room. One could almost forget that the Admiral's Club had been founded in 1997.

The girls arrived shortly afterward. Keith Jennings, the club's event manager, had personally selected them for their "engaging but not provocative demeanor." After sending them to the locker room to change, D'Angelo issued their orders. Each was instructed to sit at a separate table and to enliven the mood, marveling at pictures of grandchildren, and pleasantly responding to the men's compliments.

"Be careful now," he warned them. "Some of the men will be accompanied by their wives. So behave yourselves."

He waited for Jennings to walk out of earshot before adding with a bawdy wink: "That being said, most men will arrive alone. What you do after the luncheon is none of our business."

The girls giggled. D'Angelo whispered a few words in the ear of the prettiest, a blonde majorette-looking baby doll named Priscilla.

The first seniors arrived around noon. Two girls in the lobby placed checkmarks by their names on a list. Jennings had drawn an "x" next to the names of the wealthiest members.

As soon as they found their seats, the gramps seized the menu and, upon reviewing it, whistled in appreciation. Life Path had spared no expense. On this type of occasion, guests could usually choose between lobster and filet mignon. Today, they would have both — and never mind about their cholesterol levels!

The open bar in the back of the room was also drawing a crowd. The bartender had received clear instructions: to serve the members just enough booze to make them euphoric, but not so much that they would be unable to sign contracts.

At half past noon, Jennings signaled the waiters to serve the appetizers. D'Angelo took the stage. He thanked the participants and introduced the guest speaker, Andrew Marlowe, as one of the greatest living experts on life insurance.

Marlowe humbly greeted the assembly. At 56, he taught economics at Loyola University in Maryland, where he held the rank of professor emeritus. After a promising beginning, his career had stalled. According to his wife, the blame lay in a series of unfortunate choices of his research topics. In the 1990s, he had underestimated the market potential for the theory of games. By the time he realized his mistake, he had missed the boat. Then, banking on a boom in the notional market of mortality, he had reoriented his work toward the securitization of life insurance policies.

Sadly, for all sorts of reasons in which the poor fellow played no part, the market hadn't taken off. At the same time, Wall Street was lavishing millions on experts in mortgage securitization. Today, several of Marlowe's colleagues — and not necessarily the brightest ones — were living large and building chalets in Aspen.

Disillusioned and ruined by his divorce, Marlowe was now proffering his title and reputation to investment funds in search of credibility. Anxious to preserve his self-esteem, he claimed to let no one dictate his opinions. One could have argued, however, that for a supposedly incorruptible person, he worked very hard to understand what was expected of him.

His participation that day would earn him $10,000.

He first launched into a quick overview of the history of life insurance, then devoted a full five minutes to the Supreme Court's decision, contending with all the solemnity he could muster that nothing and no one could forbid a policyholder from selling their contract.

He arrived at the meat of his presentation just as the guests were digging into theirs. Insurers, he explained amidst a clinking of forks, had been milking the same cow for too long. They repaid only half the money they collected, rewarded their agents handsomely, and were at the helm of fleets of private jets, which, combined, would have made them the fourth-largest airline company in the country. Worse yet, their business relied on an economic model bordering on fraud — did the honorable members of the Admiral's Club know that only one in ten policies resulted in the payment of the indemnity? He backed his assertions with an array of articles and studies released by the most renowned universities, failing to specify that every single one of them had been funded by the life settlement industry.

He dealt the death blow while the wait staff was serving dessert, a Honduran cacao cheesecake. The members of the Admiral's Club, he asserted, were sitting on a gold mine — their age. The dice, for once, were loaded in their favor; by taking out a life insurance policy and keeping it until they died, they simply couldn't lose. If they didn't wish to wait that long or didn't have the cash to pay the premiums, Life Path offered tailor-made solutions that would allow them to reap a portion of the payout without taking the slightest risk.

Marlowe then left the podium and meandered around the guests, as was his custom whenever he revealed an essential truth to his students.

"To those of you who in the past have let expire a policy that you

65

considered worthless, let me put it bluntly: you were swindled. Insurers have been taking advantage of their clients' ignorance for a century. You now know as much as they do; the time has come to teach them a lesson by reclaiming the portion of their profits that is rightfully yours."

On that note, he took a seat and devoured his cheesecake.

D'Angelo gave the members a few moments to digest Marlowe's exhortation, then presented Life Path's proposition in carefully chosen words so as to not conjure images of the Grim Reaper.

"It's very simple. We're offering you a life insurance policy for a minimum of $2m. You won't have to shell out a single dime. Life Path will lend you the equivalent of two years' worth of premiums, whatever the amount. If, by some misfortune, our good Lord calls you home during that period, your heirs will collect the face value of the policy, minus the repayment of the premiums plus interest. Or, if you're still alive, Life Path will repurchase your policy for a predetermined amount. You have absolutely nothing to lose. The only risk you take is to pocket $50,000 or $60,000. And in any case, you and your family will be covered for free for two years.

"I know what you're asking yourselves: what's the catch? There is none. You're only taking advantage of the insurers' Achilles' heel, that shameful secret on which they've been relying in order to reap their scandalous profit. You're not only about to become wealthier; you're doing the community a service.

"Now on to paperwork. We have prepared all of the necessary documents. Filling out the application forms and medical questionnaire shouldn't take you more than 15 minutes. Matt and I will take care of the rest. In all probability, a doctor from the insurance company will contact you. He'll ask you a few questions and schedule a visit for a blood test. The amount of the premiums will be deposited in your bank account well before the payment due dates.

"Now, listen to me closely. Our yearly recruitment campaign is coming to an end today. Matt and I are flying back to California tonight. We'd love to go home with your file, wouldn't we, Matt?"

Cosimano fervently nodded in agreement. Standing at the foot of the stage, he kept staring at one of the hostesses whom he suspected of being part-Korean.

"We realize all this might seem a bit rushed," D'Angelo continued.

"That's why, to make your decision a little easier, we're sending you and your family on a fantastic weekend getaway to Disney World. Life Path will pay for everything. A limo will take you to Orlando. You'll stay in the Ritz-Carlton's presidential suite, a 2,000-square-foot haven of peace and luxury overlooking the lake. For two days, a VIP guide will escort you around your favorite parks — Magic Kingdom, Epcot, Disney's Hollywood Studios — where you'll be spared hours of waiting in line by entering through the exit doors. That service alone typically costs about $1,500 a day. In addition, you'll receive free tickets to the show of your choice, $200 in vouchers usable at any of the parks' gift shops, and passes for a helicopter ride."

Each new perk was met with approving murmurs.

"I think you'll agree this is a very generous offer. Think of the joy of your grandchildren when you tell them to pack their bags."

D'Angelo pretended to hesitate for a second. All eyes were on him. He turned to Cosimano who gave him the thumbs up.

"Matt informs me that Life Path's president has just signed off on one more prize, reserved for all Admiral's Club members who take out a policy of $5m or more. Ladies and gentlemen, please welcome Priscilla!"

Hidden in the wings, the pretty blonde appeared on stage, driving a spanking shiny golf cart and waving her hand to the theme music from *Wheel of Fortune*. A loud "Oh!" arose from the room, followed by thunderous applause. After a couple of concentric circles, Priscilla stopped the vehicle facing the audience.

D'Angelo took the floor again.

"No, you're not dreaming! For any policy over $5m, Life Path is throwing in a brand new Mercedes-Benz golf cart with hydraulic suspensions — a $20,000 value! Four passengers and their golf bags can fit comfortably, thanks to the space provided in the back. It comes in white, silver, black, or hot pink. Expect six to eight weeks for delivery.

"But I'm sure some of you have questions. Professor Marlowe, Matt, and I will be happy to answer them."

Several hands went up. D'Angelo picked a sly-looking old-timer. Experience had taught him to neutralize objections right off the bat.

"My late father — God bless his soul — used to say that if a deal seems too good to be true, it probably is. So here's my question: is your scheme legal?"

"Totally," answered D'Angelo. "As you can imagine, our lawyers didn't leave anything to chance. Again, we're not doing anything wrong — isn't that right Professor Marlowe?"

D'Angelo had insisted on the word "professor." Marlowe felt everyone's eyes focused on him. This was the part of the gig he hated the most.

"That's right, John," he confirmed, lowering his head.

"What if we already own a policy?" asked a tanned senior, whom D'Angelo recognized as one of the wealthiest men Jennings had identified.

"Professor Marlowe?" said Cosimano.

"There's nothing stopping you from owning more than one policy," the scholar replied reluctantly. "Insurers take all of your contracts into consideration. For up to $5m of combined face value, they don't raise any questions. Beyond that amount, they demand proof that the desired coverage is consistent with your total assets."

"Thank you. One more question, to all three of you: do you own life insurance?"

"Of course," said Cosimano, whose only policy was the one automatically taken out by his employer.

"I own five policies," said D'Angelo. "I bought the fifth one when my daughter was born."

"I took out a $2m policy 15 years ago," said Marlowe. That was technically accurate, though he neglected to add that he had stopped paying the premiums after his divorce.

"One last question?" asked D'Angelo.

An old lady who looked like Barbara Cartland raised her hand.

"Can we go to Sea World instead of Disney?"

Cosimano and D'Angelo looked at each other.

"I think that can be arranged," said Cosimano.

"All right," said D'Angelo. "I want to thank all of you for your patience and your kindness, as well as Professor Marlowe for his invaluable advice. Those of you who are interested can come forward to collect your application forms. Should you need any help, Matt and I are at your service."

The seniors swarmed to the stage, grabbed the forms, and returned to their seats to fill them out. Priscilla was circulating among the tables, handing out pens to those who didn't have one.

The tanned senior signaled to D'Angelo that he wished to speak to him in private.

"I'm going to sign up," he said. "But I was wondering if you see any reason I might want to take out $10m in coverage instead of $5m?"

"I can think of a few," answered D'Angelo. "Is there one in particular you have in mind?"

"How about a new set of Titleist clubs loaded in the back of my golf cart?"

"Done deal."

The senior shook D'Angelo's proffered hand and left on Priscilla's arm.

Other members were negotiating free spa treatments at the Ritz-Carlton or personalized rims. D'Angelo granted almost all of their wishes. He had been given carte blanche up to $1,000 per million above $2m.

Meanwhile, Cosimano was desperately trying to explain to an old man why, under Life Path's guidelines, his assets, which he estimated at $2m, didn't qualify him to purchase $5m in coverage. Manny Lammons wouldn't drop it. He wanted his cart, even if it meant lying on the forms. Cosimano suggested that he add a zero to the value of his retirement plan. Insurers, he said, have better things to do than triple-check their clients' sworn statements.

When the last of the seniors had left, D'Angelo plugged in the numbers. The Admiral's Club's members had taken out 21 policies for a total of $90m in coverage. It was one of their best harvests of the season.

He reached an agreement with Jennings regarding the amount of the bill he would send Life Path — 180 covers at $250 a head, or $45,000. D'Angelo handed the club's event manager an envelope containing $5,000 in cash.

"Come back whenever you want," said Jennings, as he pocketed his kickback.

"Ready?" asked Cosimano, his laptop bag hanging over his shoulder.

D'Angelo sighed, thinking of the sterile rooms awaiting them at the Boca Raton Ramada Inn. Tomorrow they would rise early — the manager of the Magnolias retirement home in West Palm Beach had insisted they set up their equipment before the morning bingo game.

Dan's Journal

Wednesday, July 11
Haven't heard from Vlad. I may have gone a bit too far.
(...)
What a klutz! I fell flat on my face in front of the house while returning from Publix by bicycle. My knees and forearms are covered in scratches. My ankle hurts like hell. I hobbled inside and called Sharon. Luckily she was home. She rushed over at once, felt my ankle, which was swelling by the minute, and came to the conclusion that I had sprained it. It's a lesser evil — after Lammons's bill, I couldn't have afforded a doctor's visit. Sharon bandaged my ankle, cleaned my boo-boos, and went back to her place to pick up a pair of crutches.

I offered her a cup of coffee. She works for several residents in the community — Jean-Michel Jacques, Jeffrey McGregor, Donna Phelps, and a few others I don't know. I was a little surprised to hear her volunteer their names, since I thought nurses were bound by doctor-patient confidentiality, but I didn't say anything. Actually, 1 felt a mild thrill of possessing such information. I bet Vlad knows exactly what I'm talking about.

Speaking of the devil: we talked about the latest *Wall Street Tribune* article. Sharon wishes she hadn't been quoted. It was one of her clients who ratted her out. Vlad called her afterward and she had no alternative but to confess. I asked Sharon what she was afraid of; she hadn't done anything wrong, after all. In fact, she has no doubt she's well within her rights. She says she only intended to apprise her best clients of an incredible opportunity. (She claims she didn't mention it to all of her patients, but I find that hard to believe.) Besides, she said, it's only fair that the Hess household should finally profit from life settlement. In her view, Brian is being exploited, working in his attic for chicken feed. In the end, Sharon's ploy brought in only a few thousand dollars, a far cry from the millions made by some agents. I gathered she was disgusted by the disproportionate sums.

When she found out I had no insurance, she waived her house call fee (I should hope so — she lives only a 100 yards away!). She still charged me $50, exactly what I earn when I sell 110 books. I have to stop thinking in those terms, it's too depressing.

Thursday, July 12

An unexpected consequence of my biking accident is that I totter along morning and night, which makes me an easy prey for my neighbors. God knows I hate small talk, but there's nowhere to hide. Mrs. Cunningham, who was already taxing my patience with her meteorological musings, is now keeping me up-to-date on the status of her uterus; Kim Phelps offered to "give me rides to my appointments" (if she only knew!); Susan McGregor left cookies on my doorstep. Everyone is expressing well wishes as if I were a war cripple.

(...)

Helped Ed Linkas out of a tight corner this morning.

"Please, Dan," he implored me, "would you do me a favor and explain to Chuck that I don't need special disability insurance. I'm an auditor, for Christ's sake, not a fighter pilot."

Without skipping a beat, Patterson delivered a ludicrous monologue, demonstrating that auditing is one of the most dangerous professions in the world, right after alligator trainer and sky-tram repairman. He was completely earnest — it was magnificent.

He seemed relieved not to have been named in Vlad's article. Actually, now that I think of it, I'm surprised Chuck didn't make the rounds of the hospices. He must have a foot in though — his mother lives in a nursing home in Alabama, that he once described to me as "a Sheraton for the price of a Best Western."

(...)

Ran into Jean-Michel Jacques at the beach. He and his boys were flying a kite.

I asked him why Osiris Capital wasn't mentioned in the *Tribune* article.

"Because I've never dabbled in premium finance, simple as that!"

"For ethical reasons?"

"Oh no, because there's way too much competition. My colleagues are lazy, you see; they'd rather put together one $10m deal than fifty at $200,000. Yet although small policies require as much work as bigger ones, they don't draw as much attention. Insurers are prepared to take a case to court for $10m, not for a few hundred grand, especially when lawyers specializing in life settlement bill $600 an hour."

He shared another advantage to his approach.

"Let's say you purchase a policy worth a few million, due to mature in

10 to 15 years. Who knows whether the insurer will still be around to pay the indemnity? No one's safe from bankruptcy, especially if all the granddaddies signed by my colleagues kick the bucket at the same time. It's called the counterparty risk; professionals will tell you it's the most difficult one to quantify. Well, guess what: Osiris isn't exposed to it. Any idea why?"

I readily admitted my ignorance.

"Because should the insurer default, the states guarantee the payment of death benefits up to $300,000!" he screamed triumphantly.

He clearly expected me to greet this scoop with more enthusiasm. One of his sons came asking for help. For a while, Jean-Michel applied himself to the untangling of the kite string, on all fours in the sand. His children silently watched him work, showing no signs of impatience. Finally, the kite was ready to take flight again. The kids clapped their hands. Jean-Michel turned back to me.

"That's not all," he said as if he'd never been interrupted. "I'm wary of big policies. People who have the means to buy $10m of insurance coverage usually don't live hand to mouth. They take better care of their health; they take regular vacations; they eat more vegetables; and also, let's be honest, they value their life more…"

Panicked shouts resounded — the kite had crashed into the sea. Jean-Michel mumbled a few words of apology and made off like a jackrabbit.

I wonder what they talk about at the Jacques' around the dinner table?

*****

From: Vlad Eisinger <vlad.eisinger@wst.com>
Date: Thursday, July 12, 2012 9:07 P.M.
To: Dan Siver <danielgsiver@gmail.com>
Subject: The great American novel(s)

Sorry it's taken me a while to answer you. The paper's lawyers and I were reviewing my forthcoming articles with a fine tooth comb to make sure we can't be sued. The reason being that, contrary to some, we can't write just anything. Every name, date, and figure must be verified by at least three people. That's the price of writing about real folks, I guess…

Big kudos to you for the adventures of John D'Angelo and Matt Cosimano, which I found highly entertaining. I wish I could occasionally display that same degree of insolence. I took the liberty of showing your piece to my editor-in-chief — he was rolling on the floor.

"The characters and situations are what make those books so powerful," you wrote. You're right, of course. But without facts, without a solid economic or social backdrop, your characters will remain ectoplasms and your situations will fall flat. Your account of the Admiral's Club wouldn't do a thing for an economically illiterate reader. Why do we find ourselves liking D'Angelo, despite his blatant cynicism? Because he reminds us of uncles or older friends, whose over-the-top salaries slowly squeeze them out of the job market. Ditto for Marlowe, the university professor forced to sell his soul to the devil in order to pay his alimony. As for Cosimano, your readers will probably establish a correlation, from now on, between the size of Wall Street bonuses and the income of New Jersey prostitutes.

The economy rules and shapes the world, Dan. It constitutes both the foundation for social relations and the key to the progress of the human species. Without trade, you and I would still be dangling from branches like chimpanzees. Opponents of capitalism are quick to forget they owe it their brains.

Besides, the torments of the soul have long exhausted their novelistic potential. What's new on the subject of neurasthenia since Schopenhauer and Baudelaire? Nothing, or nearly nothing. Ah yes, pardon me — materia medica! If Flaubert were still alive, Madame Bovary's psychiatrist would be prescribing her some Prozac (a product that, by the way, would have never seen the light of day had pharmaceutical companies not turned depression into a market).

Take Tom Wolfe, DeLillo, Philip Roth: their characters have jobs, bank overdrafts, prostate cancer. Unlike you, I don't believe in the Holy Grail of the great American novel, and even less in its uniqueness. Each era gives birth to its share of masterpieces. Steinbeck's name is inseparable from the Great Depression. Tom Wolfe has produced imperishable pages about Wall Street. And what can we say today about oil that Upton Sinclair didn't articulate a century ago? It's no coincidence, in my opinion, that all three pursued dual careers as writers and journalists.

That's what I love about my work: I have a finger on the pulse of our time, more so than if I were pacing along Destin's beach every day.

P.S.: Indeed, few people are aware that Norman Drachydle, alias Raymond Chandler, had a byline in of the *Daily Express* for a brief period. Here's a telling detail: his exegetes ascribe his inimitable style, at once surgical and pictorial, melodious and edgy, to his experiences as a reporter.

P.P.S.: Hollis Alpern sends his regards.

*****

From: Dan Siver <danielgsiver@gmail.com>
Date: Thursday, July 12, 2012 9:50 P.M.
To: Vlad Eisinger <vlad.eisinger@wst.com>
Subject: The great American novel(s)

You really haven't changed. You express yourself more clearly than before (a consequence of the shrinking of your vocabulary required by your employer perhaps?), but you're wide off the mark as always.

The great American novel — which, I am certain, remains to be written — is the one that will capture the essence of the American psyche, that amalgam of optimism and candor, of cupidity and virtuous hypocrisy. The two authors who, I believe, almost nailed it are Mark Twain in *The Adventures of Tom Sawyer* and J.D. Salinger in *The Catcher in the Rye*. What role does the economy play in these two books? Virtually none (and don't you suggest that Holden Caulfield is too broke to treat himself to a hooker, or I'll flip my lid!). Who cares if one takes place in Missouri in the nineteenth century and the other in New York in the 1950s? Both are beautiful adolescent portrayals that reveal so much more about our country than the complete archives of your newspaper.

P.S.: What a strange fate, that of Ralph Ellison... A single novel — with which he wasn't satisfied — sufficed to secure his posterity. Did you know that he lost about 300 pages of a second book in a house fire?

P.P.S.: If economics ruled the world, Dan Ryan would have received the Nobel Prize in literature.

*****

From: Vlad Eisinger <vlad.eisinger@wst.com>
Date: Thursday, July 12, 2012 10:31 P.M.
To: Dan Siver <danielgsiver@gmail.com>
Subject: The insouciance of youth

You wrote it yourself: "two beautiful adolescent portrayals." No wonder the heroes of your favorite books are younger than 16. They don't have to earn a living, worry about their medical insurance, or buy a car. They don't trade the fruits of their labor. They live outside the world.

I wouldn't dream of criticizing those two jewels of literature; all I'm saying is that they couldn't possibly embody the great American novel, especially if, as you believe, only one book can aspire to that title.

Let's drop the subject, can we please? We fought about it 15 years ago; surely you don't want to have at it again, do you? I know you take this matter very much to heart. Not only did you devote your master's thesis to it, but you've become a writer so you could hunt your own white whale. I'm more pragmatic; I recognize a great novel when I see one, and I like *Wuthering Heights* as much as *The Bonfire of the Vanities*.

PS: You could also have said that Ellison had accumulated 2,000 pages worth of notes in preparation for his second novel. Apparently, I'm not the only procrastinator…

PPS: Ayn Rand, Nobel prize! And why not the National Book Award for Stephen King!

PPPS: I miss Lou Baswell.

*****

Dan's journal

Friday, July 13

Mark Hansen is dead! His car hit a tree in Sausalito, where he was traveling for business. He was 36.

I remember him, beer in hand, barely 10 days ago. We had a long talk with Ed Linkas, while standing around the barbecue. Mark had alluded to his upcoming trip to California. He was going to pay a visit to a few clients and, in his own words, "pop his head in at headquarters." If I understood correctly, his employer, a Silicon Valley firm, helps larger companies cut costs by relocating their call centers and administrative services to India.

The Hansens moved to Destin in 2008, when Jennifer decided that she wanted to live closer to her parents. He travels — or, rather, he used to travel — a lot, in the United States and Europe. She takes care of their five-year-old twins, a boy and a girl.

Thanks to the beer, Mark had confided in them on that day. Life was grand — he was driving an Audi, earning a six-figure salary, blessed with two beautiful children and a wife "who looked pretty good for her age," not to mention the occasional lucky encounter on the road. Of course, they were struggling a bit financially. They had paid too much for their house (the same model as mine) and their mortgage was burdensome, even though they were only paying interest for the first five years. Between the lease for the Cherokee, the children's Montessori school, Jennifer's new breasts, and their student loans, which they had yet to repay in full, they didn't have a penny left to save for a rainy day. But Mark wasn't losing sleep over it. His company had the wind in its sails and he expected to hit the jackpot when it went public. Donna Phelps had told him one of the mansions was about to go on the market. He was nagging Jennifer to walk over and take a look.

I'm pretty sure I've never exchanged a single word with Mark's wife. I run into her from time to time at the gym. She's part of a group I call the "ponytail gang" — those women between 30 and 40 who roam around the community, wearing yoga pants and sneakers, always carrying a bottle of mineral water. I feel sorry for her.

Saturday, July 14

News travels fast. Mrs. Cunningham is babysitting the Hansen children, Jennifer having left for California this morning, devastated by grief, to identify the body. Suddenly and unexpectedly widowed, she is obviously worried about her and her children's future. Like nearly all large-firm executives, Mark had life insurance worth two years' salary (Jennifer doesn't know whether or not that includes bonuses). She'll also receive $500,000, thanks to the policy Mark took out with Chuck. She won't be bathing in champagne, but it should allow her to retire their mortgage, repay her student loans, and begin anew.

(...)

Melvin Phelps, whom I ran into on the way back from the beach, was wearing a grieved look befitting the circumstances. He asked me if I wished to participate in the purchase of a wreath that the community has ordered for Mark's funeral. Rather stingily, I admit, I inquired whether such an expense shouldn't be covered by the association's general budget.

"Theoretically, yes," Phelps answered, "but we're as poor as a church mouse. As you know, some of our residents haven't paid their dues. I'm planning to raise the issue tonight at the homeowners' meeting. I can count you in, right? Kim's going to be there."

I promised I'd stop by, pretending not to have caught the allusion. With my crutches, I could hardly pretend I had other plans.

Phelps seemed in no hurry to go home. He unloaded against residents who pester him with petty matters (the amount of chlorine in the pool, dog turds, not being allowed to mow their lawns before 9:00 a.m. on weekends, etc.). But I'm no fool. I, too, would rather organize the trash pickup schedule than watch golf on TV with Donna, sipping ice tea.

I asked him how his daughter's business was progressing.

"All right — actually, better than all right. The *Wall Street Tribune* articles have somewhat harmed Chuck's reputation. Several of his clients have contacted Kim. Your neighbor, Mrs. Cunningham, for instance, has enrolled her to sell her life insurance policy."

Sunday, July 15

I don't regret having gone to that homeowners' meeting — my first ever. I still don't know what compelled me to attend, an inkling, perhaps, that Vlad's articles were still wreaking havoc in our small community.

Admittedly, the debates were heated — in every sense of the word. There were about 100 of us, squeezed together on folding chairs, waiting for latecomers, when the air conditioning unit produced a series of rattling noises before completely conking out. Manuel's best efforts couldn't bring it back to life, and, before long, the air was stifling. Susan McGregor suggested that we move outdoors, forgetting that the area is infested with mosquitos at this time of year. Donna and Kim drove to Publix to buy lemonade. Several old people returned home grumpily.

After a moment of silence in memory of Mark Hansen, Phelps reported on the accounts as of June 30. They're in pretty lousy shape: five homeowners (whom that dear old Melvin made a point of naming) have stopped paying dues, some of them over a year ago. Phelps harbors little hope as to the outcome of the ongoing court case. All five residences in question are indeed "under water," which means, he explained, that the unpaid balances of the home loans exceed their market values.

Blanche Patterson, Chuck's wife, deemed it "scandalous and immoral" that the families at fault are continuing to enjoy the amenities. As recently as yesterday, she ousted the Guerrero rug rats from the pool, asking them to please tell their parents that swimming is reserved for residents who pay their fees on time. A handful of men offered to take turns keeping watch around the tennis courts. They didn't say whether they planned on packing weapons or not.

Meanwhile, our dues are being raised by about $100 — an expense I would have gladly done without.

And as if that weren't enough, Susan McGregor proposed we exempt Jennifer Hansen from paying her fees for a year, "to give her a chance to get back on her feet."

"We're only talking about $20 or so per family," she argued, "but it will make a world of difference to her."

Her suggestion was met coolly, so to speak, considering the temperature was hovering around 90 degrees.

"We all know that Jennifer is about to collect $700,000," called out a couple of homeowners, all the more loudly since the person in question was a five-hour plane ride away. "Why should we save her two grand, when all of us are already forking out more than our fair share?"

The most emphatic attendees, waving the *Wall Street Tribune* article that reported on Osiris Capital's strong performance, stated that there was nothing stopping Susan from contributing the full amount of Jennifer's dues if she so desired.

During that exchange, a few of us were intently staring at the tips of our shoes. In an uncharacteristic display of tact, Phelps abstained from calling for a vote on the matter.

Different savings options were discussed — cutting back on annual pruning, reducing sprinkler run times in the common areas, postponing the renovation of the tennis courts until next fiscal year, and engaging, whenever possible, the services of Manuel and Rafaela, whose rates are more reasonable than those of local businesses. I wasn't the only one stunned to learn that, between painting jobs, regular cleaning of the clubhouse, and miscellaneous electrical and plumbing work, the Guttierez couple had billed the homeowners' association nearly $11,000 over the past six months.

Brian Hess's proposition that only residents with a view of the pond be made responsible for its maintenance fees sparked a rebellion among mansion owners. Lammons, who was wound up like a spring, asked Brian if he plays tennis. The latter confessed that, every so often, he does hit a few balls with Sharon on Sunday mornings.

"There you go!" the dentist exulted. "Melvin, take note to install a collection box at the tennis courts. I'm sure Brian and his sporty friends won't mind dropping in five bucks for every set they play."

Phelps, who lives in one of the mansions *and* plays tennis, muttered a couple of incomprehensible sentences about "the constraints of living in a community" and "a potential breach in the equal treatment of homeowners." The arrival of Donna and Kim bearing refreshments saved him.

After a short adjournment, Phelps announced that he intended to proceed with the renegotiation of several contracts, including the one with the Emerald Company. Chuck, who was quietly sipping his lemonade, nearly choked. He asserted that, over the six years since the contract took effect, none of the Destin Terrace residents had ventured the slightest complaint about Emerald's management.

Phelps replied that this was scarcely surprising inasmuch as the community hadn't experienced a single disaster in that span, during which it had paid Emerald the trifling sum of a quarter million dollars.

Chuck protested that this was precisely how insurance worked and that the day a swarm of locusts swept through Destin or some little kid drowned in the pool, we'd be pretty relieved to have chosen the Rolls-Royce of insurers. Phelps mocked Patterson's metaphor: "In these dire times," he said, "homeowners might consider settling for a Cadillac."

Chuck wouldn't drop the matter, however, claiming he wouldn't tolerate a call for new bids, "whose impartiality and transparency couldn't be guaranteed" — a barely veiled allusion to Phelp's conflict of interest. Fittingly, Kim came to her father's rescue. She suggested the bids be submitted, sealed, to an independent observer.

"Whom do you have in mind?" Patterson barked.

"Dan Siver, for instance," Kim answered.

People sitting in the first rows turned around to look at me. They must think we're an item — how embarrassing!

Chuck looked me up and down, as if to gauge my integrity.

"It's a deal," he finally proclaimed, sitting back down.

Clearly relieved, Phelps moved on to the next issue on the agenda, the excessive use of fertilizer in the yards, without waiting for my consent.

A little later, as he was about to bring the meeting to a close, Sharon Hess asked whether it was true that his grandchildren had been compensated for their participation at the barbecue last Wednesday.

Apparently I hadn't been the only one to notice that Rafaela had gotten stuck with all the work. Phelps didn't see it coming. His first reaction was to turn to Patterson, as if he suspected him of having orchestrated this leak. Then, suddenly getting up on his high horse, he launched into an incoherent tirade, shouting that he just couldn't believe his ears, that he was a volunteer for crying out loud, were we kidding him, and that he'd be tickled pink to let anybody take his seat if they were crazy enough to want it.

His words were met with an awkward silence. It was late; the meeting hall reeked of sweat; all of us were impatient to return to our air-conditioned homes and take a shower before calling it a night. Even Sharon seemed ready to put a sock in it. But Phelps, all hot and bothered, couldn't stop. He turned his pockets inside out and, throwing three crumpled $20 bills in Sharon's direction, bellowed, "There, here's your damn cash! Is that enough, or do you want more?"

Donna and Kim got up hurriedly, took Melvin firmly by the arms, and dragged him toward the exit, thanking us for coming. The whole scene lasted less than a minute.

We remained seated, dumbstruck, and no longer in such a rush to go home. A few people, like Susan McGregor and Michael Hart, offered excuses for Melvin: because he readily gave so much to the community, he couldn't bear having his probity challenged. Others, beginning with Sharon, deplored a ridiculous outburst, completely out of line with the issue at hand. After a while, realizing the Phelpses weren't coming back, people started to leave. Someone tried to grab the $60 lying on the floor, but Michael Hart beat him to it and slipped the bills into his wallet, promising to "pass them on to their rightful owner," failing to identify who that might be.

As I was helping myself to a glass of lemonade, I unwittingly overheard a conversation between Brian Hess and Anh Jacques. She was worried about "a childhood friend" who had just been diagnosed with bladder cancer. Could Brian estimate the chances of recovery? Gulping down a pistachio, Hess answered that there were different types of bladder cancer, but that, roughly speaking, the five-year survival rate was about fifty percent. Anh bit her lip to stifle a cry.

Week 4

Creative Destruction at Work

By Vlad Eisinger

The Wall Street Tribune, Tuesday, July 17, 2012

Thirty years ago, all was well for life insurance companies. Jim Robertson was singing the praises of their products on television. Three quarters of Americans considered life insurance "a staple of their investment strategy." Sales and profits were growing steadily.

Then life settlements cropped up.

In less than a decade, the practice of selling existing life insurance policies to third parties brutally exposed insurers' structural weaknesses: bloated overhead and exceedingly low payout ratios. It is estimated that only one in ten policies is held until maturity.

Insurance carriers call favor tighter controls on the resale of policies. Says Adam Connor, spokesperson for the Life Insurance Alliance, a consortium of 17 of the 20 largest insurance companies in the U.S.: "If left unchecked, the development of the life settlement industry could potentially ruin our economy."

Thousands of employees of the life settlement industry beg to differ.

One can get an idea of who they are by scanning the membership list of LISA, the association of life settlement professionals.

There are only a few dozen life settlement funds — or, in LISA's terms, financing entities. Typically staffed by just a few well-compensated professionals, they generally recruit from the ranks of insurance companies.

Susan McGregor is vice-president of Osiris Capital. An actuary by trade, she worked for Prudential for seven years, then interrupted her career to raise her young children. In 2007, she was contacted by an Orlando recruitment firm.

"I had a lot of preconceived ideas about life settlement," said Mrs. McGregor. "Jean-Michel Jacques, Osiris's founder, convinced me that they serve a valid and vital purpose."

Mrs. McGregor's husband, Jeffrey, is vice-president and chief actuary at Emerald, an insurer in Pensacola, Fla. He has repeatedly decried the dangers to which life settlement subjects the financial sector. How does he feel about his wife's career change?

"It was tough at first," admitted Mr. McGregor. "Susan took swipes at insurers all day long while I called her a vulture. Now we avoid the topic altogether. What's the point in arguing? We'll never see eye-to-eye on the matter."

Susan almost doubled her salary when she joined Osiris Capital. "Jeffrey accuses me of having sold my soul for a bag of peanuts," she joked. "At the same time, I know he enjoys our new-found affluence. Last summer, we spent 10 days in Europe, visiting London, Paris, Rome and Prague. We couldn't afford that type of vacation before."

The McGregors are also in the market for a bigger house. They've set their sights on one of Destin Terrace's mansions, that is currently in foreclosure. "Banks have a gun to the heads of those who default. The timing couldn't be better," Jeffrey gloats.

The vast majority of LISA members provide support services. In the metaphorical gold rush sparked by life settlement funds, they're selling picks and shovels.

Most of such suppliers specialize in traditional roles.

For instance, each life settlement transaction requires a broker and a provider. The broker is hired by the seller to help him maximize the proceeds from the sale of his policy; the provider advises the buyer. Both activities are highly regulated.

In 2010, there were 503 life settlement brokers in the state of Florida alone (source: Government Accountability Office). Some of these close only a handful of transactions per year. Their commissions typically amount to 6% of the face value of the policy, which, depending on the transaction, can amount to half the selling price.

Licensed providers (of whom there are 14 in Florida and 62 in Texas, according to the GAO) are paid between 1% and 3% of the face value of the policy changing hands. Funds in the business of acquiring hundreds of policies annually usually negotiate substantial discounts.

The growing number of life settlements has also proved a boon to the legal profession. The Tampa-based law firm of Magee, Stone & McDowell recently opened a new department dedicated to life settlement.

Norm Sullivan, head of the insurance practice, remembers his first case from 2001. "Our client sued an Atlanta pastor who had taken out policies on the lives of about 30 homeless people in his parish. For each of these, he would fill out the form, stuff a $100 bill in their pocket, and request a sample signature, which he later used to authenticate the transfer of the contract. By the time of his arrest, he had accumulated a stash of close to $6m. People said he had arranged for two of the hobos to me murdered by mafia hitmen, but the FBI couldn't prove it."

Over the years, Magee, Stone & McDowell has extended its reach as far as New York City. There's no shortage of cases in which "the insurers' modus operandi has been to mount a legal challenge to each and every premium finance contract," explains Mr. Sullivan. "It will take years to identify the thousands of policies that were underwritten during the bubble. At a minimum profit of $10,000 a pop, I'll let you do the math."

Audit firms are sharing in the bonanza.

Thirty-eight-year-old Ed Linkas has known Jeffrey and Susan McGregor since actuarial school. He moved to Destin Terrace a year ago. As a senior manager with Lark & Hopkins, a mid-sized accounting firm based in Panama City, he audits the books of insurance companies and pension funds. Over the past few years, life settlement funds have comprised an ever-growing share of his customer base.

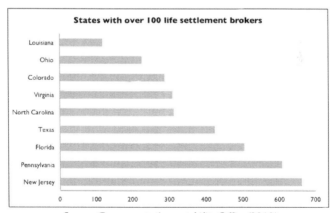

Source: Government Accountability Office (2010)

"We look at how they value policies to make sure they're not making overly optimistic assumptions," says Mr. Linkas. "Their perspective is the reverse of that of insurers. From an intellectual standpoint, it's absolutely fascinating, like sitting on both sides of a fence at once."

Other LISA members provide services most people don't even know exist.

Sellers and buyers sometimes turn to longevity consulting firms, which impartially estimate the life expectancy of a policyholder based on medical records. Market leader 21st Services, based in Minneapolis, books annual sales of about $30m.

Brian Hess, 36, works as a freelance consultant for one such longevity experts. After 4 years of medical school and 6 years of residency, and saddled with $230,000 in student debt, he opened an OB/GYN practice in Naples, Fla. in 2008. The following year, an expectant patient sued him for detecting too late that the child she was carrying suffered from a malformation. Emerald, Dr. Hess's insurer, reached an out-of-court settlement with the plaintiff and promptly raised Dr. Hess' monthly premium. His malpractice insurance would now cost him $77,000 a month, three times the pre-lawsuit rate.

Brian Hess

"It was ridiculous," said Dr. Hess. "Even working six days a week, I would start each morning $3,000 in the red. I called all of Emerald's competitors south of the Mississippi River. No one was willing to take me on for less than $60,000 a month. I had no choice but to close my practice."

While seeking another opportunity to practice his profession, Dr. Hess began producing life expectancy reports for Life Metrics LLC, a specialized firm based in Tallahassee, Fla. "It was fun at first," he recalled. "I deepened my knowledge of oncology, since most people who sell their policies have one form of cancer or another. This job requires a lot of discipline. You can't just write that a 75-year-old man with stomach cancer has an 80% probability of dying within 5 years. You must also consider the plight of the other 20%. Are such patients cured, and therefore back on standard mortality curves? Or are they just in remission?"

Dr. Hess bills between $90 and $300 per report, depending on the pathology and the number of records in the medical file. He sometimes spends an entire day on a single case. "I work 12 hours a day, six days a week, for a little over $80,000 a year. It's enough to cover the mortgage, but not to make a dent in my student loans. I've been paying only the interest so far."

Dr. Hess obviously regrets having closed his practice. "I used to save lives; now I'm reduced to guessing when people are going to die. How ironic," he said. At least he feels exempt from the current trend of having one's job exported overseas. Several longevity consulting firms have tried to reduce costs by outsourcing the production of their reports to India; every single one of them has reversed course.

Dr. Hess considers Indian doctors fully as competent as their American colleagues. "The problem is they have lower assumptions about outcomes. In their country, a man with pancreatic cancer has no more than six months to live. Here, we can prolong his life by three to four years."

The job of Rhonda Taylor, another Destin Terrace resident, didn't exist 20 years ago either. Mrs. Taylor works for Integrity Servicing, which manages thousands of policies on behalf of life settlement funds. Integrity notifies insurance companies of the changes in ownership, pays the premiums, and, when the time comes, collects death benefits.

Mrs. Taylor's job is to know at all times the locations of former policyholders and whether they're alive. When selling their contracts, policyholders usually provide a list of references — family, friends, employers, et al. — and promise to apprise the buyer of any change in their contact details. Some of them, however, fail to do so.

"The minute they receive the proceeds, their policy becomes a thing of the past. They don't understand why we need to keep in touch with them," Mrs. Taylor explained.

"Sometimes, locating them when they have moved or remarried requires considerable detective work. We call their relatives, posing as dentists or former colleagues. We tend to get better results when there's some kind of a freebie in play. I've never seen anyone decline a complimentary dental cleaning."

To hear Mrs. Taylor talk about it, AIDS patients are in a league of their own. "Most of them are single. They move a lot; their lives are complicated; and, more often than not, they've cut all ties with their families." To stay in the loop, Mrs. Taylor has created a fake Facebook profile, that of a 30-year-old bachelor who "likes to party" and is a dead ringer for Johnny Weissmuller in the early Tarzan movies. "Once they've accepted my 'friend' request, I can relax. If they fall ill, I know it before their mothers do. But if they keep quiet for a little too long, I start to worry," she said.

For here lies the second part of Rhonda Taylor's job: discovering who has died. The sooner she learns of a client's demise, the sooner she can collect the death benefit on behalf of her client.

Twice a year, Integrity writes to all its former policyholders, asking them to send back pre-stamped postcards to prove they're still alive. Sometimes the envelope comes back, unopened and marked "Deceased."

"Even if you receive the postcard, you're never 100% sure. Last year we heard that a man on our list had died. But his widow kept mailing the postcards. She was still mad at her late husband for selling his policy," recalled Mrs. Taylor.

Rhonda Taylor

90

Some people prefer to be contacted by phone, which can lead to awkward conversations. "From the moment one of them picks up the phone, we know that he or she isn't dead," said Mrs. Taylor. "Since we don't wish to imply that this is the only reason for the call, we make small talk for a while."

Surprisingly, not all deaths that occur on US soil are immediately recorded in a single national register. Mrs. Taylor considers Integrity's proprietary system more reliable than those of banks or even the Social Security Administration.

The local press has also benefited from the proliferation of life settlements. Integrity spends several thousand dollars annually on subscriptions to obituary databases, then redistributes a pertinent portion among local newspapers, such as the Northwest Florida Daily News.

In the absence of accurate data, Lawrence Johnson, professor at the Ross School of Business at the University of Michigan, estimates that approximately 10,000 jobs have been created directly or indirectly by the life settlement industry, one quarter of them based in Florida.

Insurance companies' head count has dropped by 27% over the past 10 years, from 470,300 in 2001 to 343,400 in 2011.

At the last congress of the American Council of Life Insurers, which took place in October of 2011 in Orlando, several speakers cited those two numbers — 10,000 jobs created in one industry, 127,000 destroyed in another — as justification for an outright ban of life settlement transactions.

Nathan Jacobson, professor of economics at the University of Chicago, takes issue with this argument, calling it "rhetorical" and "without any economic foundation." "There is no evidence that the two phenomena are related," he explained. "To me, new technologies and productivity gains are the main causes of those job losses. And, to be fair, they also sent insurers' profits and stock prices soaring.

"Established companies tend to consider their profits as an annuity and to characterize their attackers as corporate pirates. I have extensive acquaintances among financial executives and I don't think they're in a position to lambaste anyone."

According to Mr. Jacobson, the emergence of a secondary market for life insurance polices is a textbook example of what Schumpeter called "creative destruction." In the 1930s, this Austrian economist theorized that, in any market, innovative products and new manufacturing techniques destabilized existing players, strengthening the best performers and eliminating those unable to adapt.

Lawrence Johnson thinks that life insurers have created their own predicament. "Their outrageous overhead and ambivalence toward lapsing have paved the way for life settlement."

"If I were them," he concluded, "I'd stop whining and start rethinking my product entirely."

Write to Vlad Eisinger: vlad.eisinger@wst.com
Next week: *Why Life Settlements Are Rife With Fraud*

＊＊＊＊＊

Dan's journal

Tuesday, July 17

Vlad's fourth article is, in my opinion, the best of the series, probably because it doesn't contain so many statistics and puts real people front and center. I'm left full of compassion for Brian Hess, who can no longer practice medicine. I might actually forgive him for jogging on the beach in a fuchsia tank top, wearing headphones and belting out *Dancing Queen* at the top of his voice.

But the gem of the report is the character of Rhonda Taylor! Creating a profile of a hunk on Facebook was nothing short of brilliant!

I struck up a conversation with her by the pool earlier. She was flattered I had recognized her.

"They really joshed me at the office. The truth is they're jealous that my portrait is in the paper."

I jumped at the opportunity to listen to her talk about her work. She's full of juicy anecdotes, including some tragic ones, like that time she informed a mother of the death of her son (he had severed all contact with his family and she hadn't been previously notified of his passing).

She proudly told me that she manages a team of three people. She awards prizes to spur their competitiveness — such as a gift basket to the first one to report a death — since part of her compensation is tied to the amount of indemnities she collects. Mistaking my wonderment for disapproval, she defended herself: "Hey, I'm not the one killing them, all right? I'm just trying to do my job as best I can. After all, it's not my fault if that means finding out who's dead."

She dresses well and carries a designer handbag. I suspect she earns more than I do. She reminds me of La Gloïre, that character from Boris Vian's *Heartsnatcher*, who fishes out the villagers' shameful wastes with his teeth. He, too, makes good money.

As we were talking, she told me in confidence that she administers the policy of one resident in our community who is completely unaware of her role.

"I run into her on a regular basis at the Publix deli counter. When we greet each other, I try not to think about her fallopian tube cancer."

93

She introduced me to Melissa, her 16-year-old daughter, who had arrived home from school. The girl offered me her babysitting services. I told her that, in my situation, I doubted I would ever need her. She still handed me her card (made at Staples, $9.99 for a box of 250). She charges $8 an hour, "20 percent less than Rafaela," she pointed out. Competition truly is everywhere.

(…)

Also saw Chuck Patterson. He's back in the saddle after the news of his being pitted against Kim Phelps.

"There's nothing like a death to remind us how fragile life is," he proclaimed, all smiles.

For the moment, he's focusing on the settlement of Mark Hansen's case, having delivered Jennifer's request for the indemnity to Emerald Life headquarters himself.

"All the paperwork's in order. The payment should be presented at the signature as early as next week."

Chuck's dedication seemed a bit too purposeful to be altruistic. In fact, he's planning on paying Jennifer a visit to hand her the check in person.

"Every agent will tell you that it's the absolute best time to sell a new policy. She won't have the strength to resist. With two young children, not to mention grandparents in a retirement home, I'm going to stick her with at least $1m in coverage!"

He offered to drop me off at the beach in his new wheels. I politely declined. I'd never so badly needed to get some fresh air.

Wednesday, July 18

Sharon Hess came by to change my bandage. Out of pure mischief, I steered the conversation to last Saturday's homeowners' meeting. She was still marveling at Susan McGregor's chutzpah for acting as if she were Mother Teresa and we were all Scrooges.

"Not everybody's rolling in dough," Sharon railed, massaging my ankle to restore circulation. "Between her and her husband, they've got to bring in close to a quarter million a year, plus extras."

She stressed that last word just enough for me to inquire what she meant by it.

"Me? Nothing. Well, if you must know… Last year, I administered flu shots to their three kids. I do it every year: they supply the vaccines and pay me $30 for the three injections. It's supposedly cheaper than if they go through their insurance. Anyway, I overheard a conversation between Jeffrey and Susan. They had no idea I was listening — I mean, it's not like I was deliberately eavesdropping. They were talking about Ed Linkas, who had just bought in the community. Would you believe they pocketed a finder's fee of $1,000 for putting him in touch with the real estate agency? From what I gathered, your friend Ed has no clue about it. He is your friend, isn't he?"

(…)

Fatalitas! My air conditioning broke down at the worst time of the year. After trying in vain to repair it, I resolved to call Manuel, who dropped by in the evening and fixed the problem in a jiffy.

He refused any payment.

"Don't mention it. Now that you've seen what I'm capable of, I hope you'll hire me for a bigger job. Your window frames, for instance, could definitely use a coat of paint."

I promised I'd think about it.

I offered him a beer. He's a really nice guy, resourceful, hard-working, and clever. Bursting with pride, he confided that Rafaela is expecting. They don't know yet whether it will be possible for her to keep working (she babysits the McGregor children after school). His sister-in-law Lupita, who lives with them, might be able to help them out.

Shaken by Mark's death, Manuel is worried about what would happen to his loved ones if he were to meet his maker.

"Mr. Patterson told me the bank would force Rafaela to put our condo for sale. With the market being what it is, she wouldn't even get enough for it to pay off the balance."

Always ready to oblige, Chuck advised Manuel to take out universal life insurance, paired with a policy covering any remaining balance upon his death. Manuel solicited my opinion. Obviously, I had none, and recommended that he consult Susan and Jeffrey McGregor.

*****

From: Dan Siver \<danielgsiver@gmail.com\>
Date: Thursday, July 19, 2012 11:44 A.M.
To: Vlad Eisinger \<vlad.eisinger@wst.com\>
Subject: Raymond Andrew Wiggin

You may not have met Sir Ray Wiggin, who lives in one of the Destin Terrace's condos, during your investigation. Or if you have, you probably deemed him insufficiently interesting for your readers. Mistake, Vlad, big mistake.

Wiggin is in charge of the obituary section of the *Northwest Florida Daily News*, a rag whose local reputation rivals that of your journal. When he found out I was a writer, he insisted on showing me an invention he's been secretly developing for years.

Most submitters of obituaries write the death notices themselves. Sometimes, however, they leave that task to the paper. That's where Wiggin comes into play. He has designed a computer program that automatically generates a notice of the deceased, based on information provided by the kin (date and place of birth, names of children and grandchildren, profession, diplomas, honors and awards if applicable, etc.). The family can choose the length of the text (and therefore its cost), as well as — and I'll come back to that — the article's overall tone.

No sooner had I expressed an ounce of interest in his software than Wiggin launched into the tale of the circumstances surrounding its genesis.

Wiggin studied combinatorial mathematics at Loyola University, attending writing workshops in his free time. The biggest regret of his life: his mother, a respectable Missouri housewife, was unable to attend his graduation on account of a giant crane collapsing on the poor woman's car one week before the end of the school year, reducing her, in the matter of a multi-functional food processor, to mush.

Ray caught the first available flight to St. Louis. Once on the plane, between two announcements from the captain, he opened a copy of the *Washington Post* he had bought at the airport. The obituary of his mother, "Gertrude 'Trudy' Wiggin," was spread across the bottom of page 31. Ray read it a few times. His initial incredulity was succeeded by a combination of anger and despondency.

"You have to believe me, Dan," he implored with tears in his eyes. "It was a total disaster. Everything was wrong — events, dates, even the spelling of her surname. I first thought it was a mistake, some kind of homonymy, but the cause of death, sadly, left no room for doubt. 'Squashed by construction equipment in her fifty-third year.' Honestly, Dan, how can anyone write something so horrible? It was like killing my mom a second time."

As soon as he arrived, he put one and one together. Devastated by grief, Daddy Wiggin had entrusted Morris, Ray's brother, with the writing of the death notice.

"Morris isn't a bad guy," Ray told me, "but he's lazy as a sloth and just about as comfortable with words as I am with a monkey wrench. When a green intern at the *Post* offered to do the job for him, he jumped on it. My father should have proofread the text, but the paper called while he was buying a black tie at J.C. Penney. The notice was dispatched to the printer's unedited."

The *Post* apologized to the family and published a new notice for free. Ray showed me a copy of it — despite my insistent requests, he refused to let me have a look at the original version.

"It didn't do any good. The harm was already done. During the laying-out ceremony, the minister used the term 'construction equipment' while talking about mom. Evidently, he had read the same obituary. I thought: 'Never again.'"

Back from the funeral, Wiggin jotted down the basis for NecroLogos, the first semi-automatic software for writing obituaries. In order to broaden his knowledge as much as to make a living, he tried to find a job within the "Announcement Section" of a major newspaper. He received 500 rejection letters, until one day his telephone rang: the *Northwest Florida Daily News* was looking for a staff journalist. The following Monday, Ray moved to Destin with a suitcase and three computers. One year later, he could have shown a thing or two to the writers at the *New York Times*, the field's leading experts.

Yet his work wasn't progressing as rapidly as he had hoped. In the euphoria of invention, he had underestimated the difficulty of the program's semantic dimension. According to him, popping out grammatically correct sentences is a fairly easy matter of comparing them with an extensive corpus of millions of literary, journalistic, and academic texts. The question of meaning is an entirely different challenge. An ordinary entrepreneur would throw together a rudimentary prototype, and plan to enhance it later. Wiggin, on the other hand, never forgets — how could he? — that his users aren't ordinary customers. They're mournful widows and widowers, inconsolable children, families shattered by grief, for whom the slightest mistake is an added source of pain, all the more unbearable since it could have been avoided. Mourners are not placing an announcement in the press out of decorum or convenience. No, they're trying to pay a final tribute to someone dear whom they have loved passionately, and whose memory will, in time, blend with the printed words: "revered spouse," "beloved son," "exemplary father," etc. A well-chosen epithet, a thoughtful phrase, a beautiful metaphor will pacify them more surely than a litany of names and dates, hence the extreme care — some might say excessive — Wiggin takes in creating his lexical algorithms.

Take an adjective like "rich," which has at least a dozen connotations, depending on the context in which it is used or the name beside which it is placed. Thanks to the billions of neural connections in our brain, we know that "rich soil" refers to a fertile ground (and not one covered with gold coins). Do you grasp the magnitude of Wiggin's task? He has to fashion a software that will not characterize as "generous" a 300-pound matron, as "brilliant" a scientist struck by lightning, or as "hot-blooded" a grandfather felled by an overdose of Viagra! To further complicate things, this loony is committed to offering his clients several options (three initially) — "factual," "lyrical," or "sentimental." (He asked my opinion of these designations, which he founds insufficiently catchy. I could suggest nothing better.)

After 12 years of research, Ray is finally nearing his goal. He's currently negotiating with his employer for the right to submit NecroLogos solutions to the newspaper's clients as a real-life test that should identify the software's remaining glitches. Once he fixes those, he'll either seek distributors or create his own website.

While he waits for the *Daily News'* green light, that rascal has somehow managed to use Bruce Webb and Patricia Cunningham as unwitting guinea pigs.

Of course, he demanded that I lend myself to a demo — a macabre experience to be sure. After I had answered about a 100 questions, he pressed a button on his keyboard and the printer started to sputter. One minute later, I was reading three different versions of my own obituary. I'm only too happy to forward the files (see attached). You'll have to tell me what you think; I'd be lying if I said they were bad.

Back at home, I pondered the implications of Wiggin's invention. Automatic writing — or should I say "automated," to distinguish it from the surrealists' attempts — is a writer's recurring fantasy. Queneau composed one version with his *Hundred Billion Poems*, but the development of computer science opens breathtaking possibilities. You must have read, as I have, that several press groups have already automated the production of sports news ("*Bautista hits a home run and the Cardinals are back in the lead at the top of the third inning*") or of stock market roundups ("*Procter & Gamble advances 0.3% in heavy trading*"). But obituaries? How long before IBM publishes the eighth tome of Harry Potter's adventures? Or before Google releases a *Complete Version of The 120 Days of Sodom, based on the notes of the Marquis de Sade*?

I also couldn't help wondering about Wiggin's motivation. The unfortunate affront inflicted on his mother certainly called for redress, but devoting 12 years of one's life to such a project is taking it a bit far. He treats me as a peer, which leads me to believe that he considers himself a writer. Money doesn't interest him. Still, at the rate of 60 million deaths in the world every year, it wouldn't take but a minute proportion of families using his software to make a rich man out of him.

No, I believe his is at once a deeper and nobler purpose, probably closer, in fact, to a vocation. Wiggin is a modern crusader, the champion of greater cause than personal gain. He is the spokesperson of the dead. As far as he's concerned, even the worst kind of villain deserves a final homage, whose quality shouldn't depend on the eloquence of his relatives. My hat's off to him.

PS: Lou Baswell = Saul Bellow. Be honest now, Eisinger: did the name of the author of *Humboldt's Gift* spontaneously flow from your pen or did you choose it to make fun of me? Could it be you're comparing me to Humboldt, a writer true to his ideals, who believes in the power of words and literature and passes away penniless?

PPS: Mark Stober.

*****

Dan's obituary (factual)

Daniel Gerry SIVER, writer, died of a heart attack on August 12, 2012, in his Destin, Fla. home. He was 40 years old.

Born on April 2, 1972, in Cincinnati, to Owen Siver, railroad employee, and Lydia Ayers, primary school teacher, Dan graduated from Columbia University (Masters in French Literature in 1993, PhD in Comparative Literature in 1997).

He is the author of five novels and a collection of short stories, published by Polonius Editions. His first novel, *Wrong Move*, was nominated for the Los Angeles Times Award in 1999.

Between 1989 and 2011, Dan resided in New York. He moved to Destin upon the death of his parents.

Dan Siver is survived by a sister, Rebecca, a nephew, Edwin, and a niece, Julia. May his soul rest in peace.

*****

Dan's Obituary (lyrical)

Daniel "Dan" Gerry SIVER, writer, critic, essayist, succumbed to a heart attack on August 12, 2012, in his Destin, Fla. home. He was barely 40.

Death overtook Dan at his work table, just as he was putting the finishing touches on his novel, *Camelia Van Noren*, much awaited by his fans and heralded by critics as one of the significant events of the current literary season.

Siver was born on April 2, 1972, in Cincinnati, in the state famous for Neil Armstrong and Toni Morrison. His father, Owen Siver, was a stationmaster at the Cincinnati Southern Railway. His mother, Lydia Siver, née Ayers, was a primary school principal.

From a very early age, Siver demonstrated a natural talent for literary subjects. In 1988, he received the highest grade ever assigned for a Latin composition in the history of Jefferson High School. The same year, he ranked third in a regional spelling bee.

In 1989, Siver landed a scholarship from the prestigious Columbia University. In classrooms haunted by the ghosts of Barack Obama, Allen Ginsberg, and Paul Auster, he studied French literature, all the while

100

maintaining a correspondence with several key figures of the *nouveau roman*, especially Claude Simon and Nathalie Sarraute. He received his first diploma in 1993, a second, with honors, in comparative literature, four years later. His PhD dissertation about the Great American Novel can still be found at Columbia's Butler Library.

Entering the world of literature as one enters Holy Orders, Siver was quickly noticed by a publishing legend, Christian Polonius, who released Silver's first novel in 1999. *Wrong Move* received rave reviews from the critics, who recognized in Siver a "singular and promising voice." With three reprints to date, commercial success followed just as briskly.

This master stroke was followed by five books. *Clandestine Passengers* (2004, translated into Italian in 2006), *The Doppelgänger and his Double* (2007), and *The Usurper* (2009) reflect the author's obsession with schizophrenic characters who take refuge in imaginary worlds in order to escape from the tyranny of daily life. They are sketched in a humorous and fluid style comparable to Calvino's or Vonnegut's.

After a 20-year love affair with Manhattan's Upper West Side, Siver had recently settled in his late parents' home in Destin, joining on the Emerald Coast another best-selling author, John Grisham. He won his new neighbors' admiration with for sense of humor, nonchalance and phlegm.

A man of heart as much as a man of letters, Dan Siver is survived by an inconsolable family — his sister, Rebecca, his nephew, Edwin, and his niece, Julia — and he leaves millions of disconsolate readers throughout the world. He now rests in the paradise of giants.

*****

Dan's Obituary (sentimental)

Daniel "Dan" Gerry SIVER, beloved brother, exemplary uncle, and admired writer, left us on August 12, 2012, as he would have wanted to: at his desk, surrounded by pictures of those he loved.

He was the adored son and pride of Owen "Buzz" Siver (†2010), stationmaster and volunteer ice hockey coach, and Lydia Siver (†2011), educator, doting mother, cook, and happiness maker, as well as the little brother of Rebecca "Becky" Siver-Doyle.

Born on April 2, 1972, at the Good Samaritan Hospital in Cincinnati,

Dan was blessed with a joyous and carefree childhood. He combined his love of literature with the hobby of assembling airplane models, and he enjoyed meandering with his dog Puck, the family mascot. As a teenager, he exhibited a taste for chocolate ice cream, a fondness for the scent of cut grass, and a habit of spending long evenings by the fire. He eschewed meanness, rising early and brushing his teeth after dinner.

At the age of 17, Dan followed his star to New York. He showed great courage when it came time to leave his loved ones. Notwithstanding his schoolwork and exams, he returned to his home state of Ohio as often as possible. He was a brilliant and conscientious student, reflecting the values his family had instilled in him.

His first novel, *Wrong Move*, over which the shadow of Puck, taken away by cancer in 1994, is hovering, touched the hearts of thousands of readers, especially in the Midwest, where Dan has always enjoyed an outpouring of public affection.

He published many other books, but there was much more to his life than writing. He devoted many hours to his friends in Manhattan. For vacations, he would hike alone in the Adirondacks, the tranquility and wild beauty of which fed his inspiration.

He settled in Destin in 2011 to honor the memory of his parents. He won the affection of his neighbors with his conviviality, kindness and altruism.

His all-too-rare visits to Cincinnati were the occasion for memorable parties with his family. Dan was a role model for all of us, especially to his niece Julia, who was accepted at Columbia University, and his nephew Edwin, who also prefers chocolate ice cream. He encouraged us to pursue our dreams, whatever the cost may be. We miss him already.

Rest in peace, darling Dan, in the knowledge that we shall meet again.

*****

From: Vlad Eisinger <vlad.eisinger@wst.com>
Date: Thursday, July 19, 2012 1:22 P.M.
To: Dan Siver <danielgsiver@gmail.com>
Subject: The voice of the dead

Outstanding! I really like *"In 1988, he ranked third in a regional spelling bee"* and *"He was a role model for his nephew Edwin, who also prefers chocolate ice cream."*

Joking aside, I am stunned by the quality of the result. The impeccable grammar doesn't impress me so much as the relevance of the selected information (including the death of Puck, a detail that sheds new light on your work) and the subtle variations among the three versions. I confess to a preference for the "lyrical" rendition, which makes you an Allen Ginsberg disciple and the equal of John Grisham. Did you really answer only 100 questions?

I'm, of course, well aware of the various attempts to automate the writing of articles. National newspapers' editors-in-chief all swear that they'll never resort to it — which doesn't stop them from periodically mentioning that threat in house as a means of containing their journalists' demands for higher salaries. Indeed, some of my colleagues content themselves with fleshing out news wires by moving commas and changing epithets here and there. Those guys should definitely be worried.

PS: Too easy. Mark Stober = Bram Stoker. Any news from Carlo Stumper?

PPS: Tell me more about *Camelia Van Noren.* Are you really in the process of wrapping it up?

*****

From: Dan Siver <danielgsiver@gmail.com>
Date: Thursday, July 19, 2012 6:48 P.M.
To: Vlad Eisinger <vlad.eisinger@wst.com>
Subject: NecroLogos on the test bench

I would have answered sooner if I hadn't become stuck on that damn anagram. Carlo Stumper = Marcel Proust. Good move, your picking a foreign author. Makes me think of the late lamented Marcel Staub.

I agree with you: Wiggin has created a truly phenomenal invention. I took the trouble to analyze all three of his texts to understand where his algorithms still err.

Grammatically, the product is almost perfect. I spotted only one trivial mistake. In the following passage: "Clandestine Passengers, The Doppelgänger and his Double, *and* The Usurper *reflect the author's obsession with schizophrenic characters who take refuge in imaginary worlds in order to escape from the tyranny of daily life. They are sketched in a humorous and fluid style…"* I can't tell whether "they" refers to the novels or to the characters.

Although the facts and dates are correct, Wiggin doesn't always cite them judiciously. Admittedly, Grisham has a house in Destin (I forgot to tell you that NecroLogos resorts to online searches for some of the required information). As for suggesting that I sell as many books as he does… Ditto for the affiliations with Obama, Ginsberg, and Auster (please note, however, that from the hundreds of glorious alumni from Columbia, the software chose the three most appropriate ones), and for the reference to Neil Armstrong and Toni Morrison, just a smidgen over the top.

Wiggin's predilection for flattering details sometimes backfires by underlining the insignificance of my curriculum vitae. You quoted that dreadful third-place finish in a regional spelling bee. Similarly, mentioning the existence of an Italian edition of *Clandestine Passengers* is tantamount to admitting that my other books were never translated. As for describing Christian Polonius as a "publishing legend," and as "public success" a book that sold ten thousand copies, it's an invitation to ridicule.

Wiggin sometimes stretches the truth. For example, the sentimental version conjures an idea of a Siver family united like the five fingers of a hand (including Puck). Not quite. I hated that frigging mutt from the day he took a piss on my Faulkner, my sister annoys the crap out of me, and I don't know of a single reader of my books in the Midwest. As for Edwin, he's a world-class moron and fat as a porpoise, thanks to his immoderate love of chocolate ice cream, donuts, and fried chicken wings.

PS: You misread. I will finalize *Camelia Van Noren* on August 12, before dramatically raising my hand to my heart and collapsing, head first, onto my keyboard. Until then, mum's the word.

*****

From: Vlad Eisinger <vlad.eisinger@wst.com>
Date: Thursday, July 19, 2012 8:51 P.M.
To: Dan Siver <danielgsiver@gmail.com>
Subject: The bones and the meat

Returning to our discussion last week: essentially, Ray Wiggin needs only a single raw material to generate his obituaries — the facts. He can program his software to glean its words from such or such a register, or prohibit it from using adverbs, but he can't escape reality. A life is an aggregation of facts, figures, and dates, before being a collection of words, no matter how carefully chosen. You know where I'm going with this, don't you? It's the same with books. Some day, perhaps, computers, loaded with the complete works of the great masters, will be able to embroider a given framework, to add the flesh; but the skeleton will always emanate from the novelist's mind.

PS: You could have included a dire tendency to exaggerate in the list of Wiggin's software's flaws. It credits you with millions of readers, when everyone knows that the number of your fans doesn't exceed the hundreds of thousands.

PPS: I doubt you'd be interested in my opinion, especially after that sarcastic remark, but if you're looking for a proofreader for *Camelia Van Noren*, I'm game.

PPPS: And so we find ourselves among the French at present. Unlike Marcel Staub = Albert Camus, Alcofribas Nasier had no chance of killing himself at the wheel of a Facel-Vega.

*****

From: Dan Siver <danielgsiver@gmail.com>
Date: Friday, July 20, 2012 8:33 A.M.
To: Vlad Eisinger <vlad.eisinger@wst.com>
Subject: Baloney

I'm used to your BS, but man, you're outdoing yourself!

So, according to you, facts constitute the irreducible essence of a novel. Pardon me for laughing, but allow me to remind you of the plot of *A Life* by Maupassant. "Jeanne leaves convent school. After a brief courtship, she marries Julien, who soon cheats on her, first with the maid, then with a neighbor. She gives birth to a boy, Paul, aka Poulet, who will be a constant source of disillusionment." Even more concise is the journal, *Gil Bas*, which published the novel as a serial, advertising it to its readers as the tale of "the life of a woman, from the moment her heart awakens to her death."

Only a genius like Maupassant could transfigure that dull story into a hymn to little people, anticipating the way Proust will later transform a chronicle of high society into a reflection on the passage of time.

I believe a novelist possesses simultaneously an original sensitivity — a unique prism through which he sees the world — and a capacity to share that singular experience through words.

My all-time favorite authors all fall within that category: Proust, Maupassant, Kafka, Faulkner, Salinger, Auster, Mishima, Céline, Foster, Wallace, and so many others.

Because your profession compels you to stick to the facts, you have come to confuse reality with truth. When you write that Alexander Pope was "a short man" or that he measured 4'-6", you're stating a truth but not THE truth. To describe such a relative midget, I can draw from a repertoire that goes from runt to homunculus to knee-high to umpa lumpa. How very superior!

Do you remember when Birocheau gave us a famous quotation from Céline to analyze in our literary theory class?

"The story, my God, it's very incidental. Only the style matters. Painters have done away with the subject, a pitcher, or a pot, or an apple, or anything — the way one renders it is what counts. Life has made it so I found myself in circumstances, in situations that were delicate. So I tried to render them in the most amusing way imaginable, I had to become a memorialist, so as not to bore the reader if at all possible. And this with a tone I thought different from that of others, since I can't do it exactly like others."

"With a tone I thought different from that of others" — such humility!

Check this out. I've been toying with a passage from *Journey to the End of the Night*. After the war, Bardamu lands in New York. Here are his first impressions of Manhattan.

"As if I knew where I was going, I put on an air of choosing and changed my directions, taking a different street on my right, one that was better lit. "Broadway" it was called. I read the name on a sign. High up, far above the uppermost stories, there was still a bit of daylight, with sea gulls and patches of sky. We moved in the lower

lights, a sick sort of jungle lights, so gray that the street seemed to be full of grimy cotton waste.

That street was like a dismal gash, endless, with us at the bottom of it, filling it from side to side, advancing from sorrow to sorrow toward an end that is never in sight, the end of all the streets in the world.

There were no cars or carriages, only people and more people.

This was the priceless district, I was told later, the gold district: Manhattan. You can enter it only on foot, like a church. It's the banking heart and center of the present-day world. Yet some of those people spit on the sidewalk as they pass. You've got to have your nerve with you.

It's a district filled with gold, a miracle, and through the doors you can actually hear the miracle, the sound of dollars being crumpled, for the Dollar is always too light, a genuine Holy Ghost, more precious than blood.

I found time to go and see them, I even went in and spoke to the employees who guard the cash. They're sad and underpaid."

Here is what would become of this in your wretched jargon.

"Ferdinand Bardamu is one of those French citizens, demobilized after World War I, who moved to New York hoping to build a better life. He discovered Manhattan on foot, strolling along Broadway, from North to South, all the way to Wall Street, the temple of global finance. The bank clerks Mr. Bardamu came across gave him the impression of being 'sad and underpaid'."

Speaks for itself, doesn't it?

PS: Thanks for the offer but, for now, *Camelia Van Noren* needs an author more than a reader.

PPS: Alcofribas Nasier = François Rabelais. For your information, the author of *Gargantua* also hid behind the pseudonym Serafino Calbarsi. Will you be able to identify Bertrand Noe?

*****

Dan's journal

Friday, July 20

Had dinner at the Jacques' tonight. They're my first and, to be honest, my only friends in the community. Anh had prepared an assortment of Vietnamese dishes and I feasted like a king.

We talked about politics, cinema, literature, and, of course, life settlement. Jean-Michel proved bitterly hostile toward life expectancy consultants.

"Smooth talkers, if you want to know what I think. They sell 10-year predictions after having been in business for no more than half a day. I think Brian Hess is a great guy, but I'd never rely on his recommendation to buy a policy. Let's not forget that the poor boy was still inserting IUDs just three years ago."

Jean-Michel knows Rhonda Taylor well, and for good reason: Integrity Servicing processes all of his policies. I candidly asked if he wasn't afraid to put all his eggs in the same basket.

"On the contrary," he answered. "I benefit from rock-bottom rates, guaranteed for two years. In my situation, that's key, even though administrative costs are small potatoes in relation to a $10m policy. But otherwise they're a substantial budget item for me, since I own mostly small contracts. According to my calculations, I represent 50% to 60% of Integrity's business volume. When I get to 80%, I'll threaten to go to a competitor and then offer to buy them out for cheap. They'll cry foul, I'll raise my offer by a few percent, and I'll close the deal. Chances are, a year from now, Mrs. Taylor will be working for me."

Seeing my shocked reaction, he decided to clarify that boast.

"Oh, don't worry, she's got nothing to fret about. She might even be better off. I'm planning on expanding Integrity's client base by marketing to European funds."

That chap doesn't cease to amaze me. Behind his debonair appearance hides a formidable businessman. When he smiled, as he was explaining his Machiavellian plan, his pointed canines made him look like a miniature vampire.

At home, I found a message from Julia. She just found out, a month before enrolling at Columbia, that she'd have to share her room with a Korean girl. I sensed she was upset ("At least you guys had individual dorm rooms."). She's thinking about coming down to Florida in early August. Keep your fingers crossed.

*****

108

From: Dan Siver <danielgsiver@gmail.com>
Date: Friday, July 20, 2012 11:52 P.M.
To: Vlad Eisinger <vlad.eisinger@wst.com>
Subject: More baloney

I reread your email and, once more, I measure all that separates us. So much crap in your words!

How do you account for Queneau in that little theory of yours? What about his 99 different ways of telling the same anecdote? Seriously, take another look at my three obituaries and tell me if they all appear to honor the life of the same guy.

Perspective, Vlad, it's all about perspective. Yours is sad and cold, like death.

*****

From: Vlad Eisinger <vlad.eisinger@wst.com>
Date: Saturday, July 21, 2012 4:12 P.M.
To: Dan Siver <danielgsiver@gmail.com>
Subject: Cease-fire?

Let's drop the abuse, shall we? It's never moved the debate forward.

You gave me your definition for the art of the novelist: an original sensitivity paired with the capacity to share his experience through words. Here's mine: "A novelist is an observer who, through the depiction of a milieu or period, revisits universal questions such as the human condition, love, death, etc.." My personal heroes are Balzac, Zola, Greene, Orwell, and Le Carré on the European side; Melville, Hemingway, Lewis, Nabokov, Pynchon, DeLillo, and many others on the American side.

Without taking anything away from your authors of choice, their plots are relatively thin: "A teenager escapes from boarding school and goes to New York for a joyride," "A man wakes up one morning to find himself turned into monstrous vermin," etc. As for me, I prefer writers who rely on more complex architectures.

In a nutshell, you put the author in the center, I place him on the side.

PS: Don't think for a second that the reason it took me so long to answer was that I found your anagram challenging. Bertrand Noé = André Breton. Have fun with Carmella Pong.

*****

From: Dan Siver <danielgsiver@gmail.com>
Date: Saturday, July 21, 2012 4:17 P.M.
To: Vlad Eisinger <vlad.eisinger@wst.com>
Subject: Peace of the braves

I think you're right. That's what I feel when I read your articles: you keep to the sidelines of the subject. You describe something, without ever taking a stand. I'm personally incapable of remaining neutral. Even if I didn't have the right to express my opinion, I'd find a way to have it seep through, one way or another.

Have a nice weekend.

PS: Carmella Pong = Marcel Pagnol. The French anagrams are too easy. Back to the American ones?

*****

Dan's journal

Sunday, July 22
Decided on a whim to follow through with my Wikipedia plan this morning. There isn't a shadow of a doubt in my mind as to the kinship between Broch and Perutz. My discovery solves too many unanswered questions — Broch's sudden conversion, the suspicious lack of a relationship between the two men, etc. — for me to keep it a secret. The world needs to know the truth.

Just need to figure out how to go about it.

Supposing all sites prove as easy to modify as Wikipedia — which I doubt — I can probably falsify 10 to 20 separate sources. Even then, I will have dealt with only an infinitesimal portion of the electronic channels that refer to Broch or Perutz — not to mention dictionaries, encyclopedias, and

110

other textbooks in circulation.

It seems both simpler and more efficient to present my story for what it is: a theory, astounding to be sure, but one that can't be offhandedly dismissed. I don't expect anyone to accept it at face value. Quite the opposite — may historians and relatives conduct a bit of detective work! May they comb through Perutz's and Broch's correspondence; examine portraits of both men under a microscope in search of an undeniable sign (a matching dimple, a similarly prognathous jaw, identical hairlines); shout themselves hoarse at colloquiums, round tables, and seminars. Let them prove me wrong.

Obviously, I can't afford to appear to be in the forefront. I'm not a historian; I barely speak German; and I haven't set foot in Europe in 10 years. Besides, the few people who are both familiar with my work and aware of my fondness for trompe l'oeil might very well smell a rat.

So I'm going to hide behind a fake nose, or rather a bunch of fake noses — scholars from the four corners of the world, joined together by their love of German literature from the inter-war period. First in line: Thorsten Böhm, a young research fellow in Austrian history from the Institute of German Studies in Copenhagen (I resisted the temptation to call him a professor emeritus of a top-notch university like Heidelberg or Cologne). Böhm leads (remotely) a small group of aficionados: la signorina Paolita Dampieri from the Goethe Institute in Bologna; Klaus Kühn from the Thomas Mann Foundation in Venice; Ericka Kirchenmeister, PhD in comparative literature at the College of Humanities in Lausanne; and Lena Mirafuentes, professor of literary theory at the National University of Córdoba. Those four have co-authored an article, currently awaiting approval from an internationally renowned journal (the *German Studies Review*? The *Österreichische Literatur Zeitscrift*? To be decided), and have posted an English translation of their collaborative effort on a website created for the occasion (friendsofbrochandperutz.net? vienneseletters.at?).

I have a long day ahead of me.

Monday, July 23
Plugged away for 12 hours straight. I hadn't worked so diligently since composing the final chapters of *Double Play*. After putting the finishing touches to my website around midnight, I was so elated I had to take a calming walk along the beach.

I had underestimated the scope and complexity of even a small-scale project such as this one.

The writing of the article itself wasn't much of a hurdle. I've read so many of those verbose papers that I can just as easily spew out on Sartre's grandmother (conceited like Jean-Paul) as on the role of punctuation in Tom Wolfe's works (prominent).

The biographies of the group members required hardly more effort. I lavished special attention on Böhm, on paper the veteran among them. The others vanished from my memory as fast as they had materialized from my pen. At most, I remember feeling a slight giddiness when I realized that Lena Mirafuentes had graduated from Columbia two years after me.

Giving a face to everyone on that nice little crew should have been the easiest part of the exercise, but it turned out to be the most difficult. Strangely enough, I had a pretty good idea about what each of them should look like. Böhm, for instance, is 35 years old, with big bright eyes, an onset of baldness, and a thin blond mustache. I scanned through thousands of headshots on Google before finding his look-alike in the person of the production manager of a Columbian rubber plantation. The others didn't take so long. Ericka Kirchenmeister is the spitting image of some New Zealand porn star.

I then tackled the construction of the website. Trying to put myself in Böhm's shoes, I selected a template from hundreds of options. I'm afraid the poor fellow has questionable taste. Against the advice of his peers, he has designed his home page with the most unpleasant mustard-colored background and a fancy font, both intended to convey his excitement at the spectacular revelations contained in the article. Under the purple title "More than a Friendship," he showcases two sepia portraits of Broch and Perutz, both carefully selected to create an illusory resemblance.

Spent an obnoxious amount of time on a thousand tiny details, from the shape of the browsing buttons to the tone of Böhm's editorial (triumphant and lyrical) to the five acolytes' email addresses.

Finally satisfied with the result, I published the site. When I woke up this morning, I noticed with a shiver of delight that it was already indexed on Google and came up in twenty-fifth position in the search "Hermann Broch Leo Perutz."

I then eagerly referenced my sources on Broch's page. Let's see what the Wikipedia editor makes of this.

Week 5

Why Life Settlements Are Rife With Fraud

By Vlad Eisinger

The Wall Street Tribune, Tuesday, July 24, 2012

When Drug Enforcement Administration agents seized the submarine of Javier "El Tigre" Escobar, they found the typical trophies of drug kingpins: weapons, cash, Treasury bonds — and life insurance policies.

The reputation of life settlement — the resale of existing life insurance policies to third parties — has suffered a great deal from this kind of revelation. All financial products have had their share of scandals over the past few years, but the life settlement industry has made headlines more often than any other. This article will attempt to illustrate what makes the secondary market for life insurance so conducive to fraud.

Part of the explanation lies in the large number of parties involved in every transaction. The policyholder who wishes to sell his contract typically turns to his financial advisor, who refers him to a broker. The broker contacts one or more life settlement funds, which appraise the policy based on their internal criteria and sometimes commission longevity experts to produce life expectancy estimates. Then the fund with the highest bid must hire a provider to finalize the transaction.

All such parties are in a position to cheat, and many have repeatedly yielded to the temptation to do so.

In 1987, then 23-year-old AIDS patient Bruce Webb put his $400,000 life insurance policy on the block. To attract higher offers, he managed to look sicker than he actually was. During the week before his medical examination, he slept an average of two hours per night and consumed an excessive amount of tobacco, alcohol and other prohibited substances.

"I looked like a zombie," recalled Mr. Webb. "My lymphocyte count had dropped below eight hundred. One month later, it shot back up to fifteen hundred."

Based on Mr. Webb's blood test, life settlement fund Sunset Partners bid $255,000. "They thought I'd be dead within two years. Obviously, they were wrong," joked Mr. Webb who, 25 years later, works as a flight attendant for Southwest Airlines and leads a quasi-normal life.

The integrity of brokers isn't beyond reproach either. Some of them exploit the weaknesses of their clients, who are often old and ailing, to dupe them into signing extremely disadvantageous contracts.

Last year, Betsy Archambault, a retired shopkeeper from Duluth, Minnesota, hired Ned Sanders, a state-licensed broker, to help her sell her $2m policy in return for a 6% commission. "That percentage didn't seem excessive," recalled Mrs. Archambault. "It's more or less what you pay when selling a house."

Had Mrs. Archambault read her contract more carefully, she would have realized that the base for the 6% rate wasn't the selling price, but rather the face value of the policy. In other words, Mr. Saunders was guaranteed to collect $120,000 — 6% of $2m — regardless of the amount of the transaction.

"It didn't dawn on me until the provider handed us our checks. Mine was hardly bigger than Ned's! I also understood why he had insisted that I accept the first offer," said Mrs. Archambault who subsequently sued Mr. Saunders for breach of trust.

Neither Mr. Saunders nor his attorney was available for comments.

Jeremy Fallon, spokesperson for the Life Insurance Brokers' Association (LIBA), while regretting the misunderstanding, refuses to condemn Ned Saunders. "It's not my place to comment on a contract negotiated by two parties in good faith. We can only urge people trying to sell their policies to read all the documents thoroughly before they sign," said Mr. Fallon.

Though to a lesser degree than Mrs. Archambault, many sellers are surprised by the raft of fees and commissions deducted from the transaction price. Between the broker's and the financial advisor's cuts, the provider's fee, and miscellaneous expenses (life expectancy report, stamp duty, etc.), it's not uncommon for the seller to receive less than half of the price paid by the buyer. And it is worth noting that the portion of the proceeds that exceeds the accumulated premiums is taxed as ordinary income, unlike death benefits, which are usually tax-free.

Rick Weintraub, president of the Insurance Consumers' Association (ICA), says he receives several letters every week from seniors disappointed by the lack of transparency that pervades the sale of their policies. "A couple from Pasadena recently told me their accountant thought he could get $300,000 for their policy. The deal ended up closing around $260,000, of which only $140,000 found its way into their pockets. They were left with just $100,000 after taxes. They're not blaming anyone but it's obvious they wish they could undo the sale."

Complaints filed with state regulation authorities in Florida, Texas and Pennsylvania reveal other practices that are downright illegal.

In 2007, Nick Santorelli offered to personally buy back a policy he had sold six months earlier to a life settlement fund in Philadelphia. Intrigued, the fund manager did his homework and found out that the original owner of the policy had passed away the previous week. Having learned of the death before the fund did, Mr. Santorelli was trying to collect the death benefit.

In 2009, Texas regulators revoked the licenses of Wayne Johannsen and Scott Prideaux for accepting bribes from life settlement funds. "Instead of reaching out to as many potential buyers as possible, they would contact only a limited number of funds, which could then conspire to submit very low bids," explained Mr. Weintraub.

Mr. Johannsen and Mr. Prideaux are awaiting trial.

According to Jeremy Fallon, "such cautionary tales shouldn't sully the reputations of thousands of honest and trustworthy agents who, day after day, help seniors maximize the value of their policies in full compliance with the law."

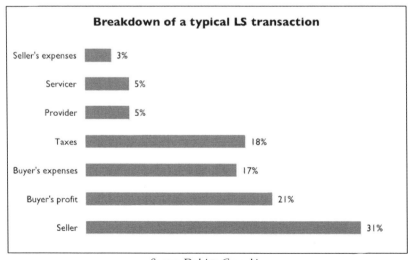

Source: Deloitte Consulting

Life settlement funds are not to be outdone.

Lifetime Opportunity LLC, a fund that went bankrupt in 2003, was notorious for manufacturing in-house its own ad hoc life expectancy reports. A high life expectancy helped to justify a low offer, whereas a low one served to pique investors' interest. Likewise, Life Partners used to promise its investors annual returns of 16% to its investors, based on what appear to have been bogus medical reports. The Waco, Texas firm is currently entangled in complex lawsuits with former shareholders.

Brian Hess works as a consultant for several longevity experts. His biggest client, Tallahassee-based Life Metrics, never tells him who commissioned the reports he writes.

"What I don't know can't influence me," he explained. "If I were to discover that the client is an old lady seeking to sell her policy, I might be tempted to find her a little sicker than she actually is." Mr. Hess wasn't born yesterday, though. "My boss recently scolded me for being too conservative in my estimates. I don't know what to make of that. Is it an invitation to be more lenient?"

The most spectacular instances of fraud have to do with money-laundering. Drug traffickers are constantly looking for ways to make their money legal, so that they can spend it in broad daylight. A classic technique consists in playing roulette and betting the same amount on red and black. Whichever color comes up, the player loses his bet on one side and doubles it on the other. By reporting his winnings to the IRS without mentioning the corresponding losses, he has turned ill-gotten gains into legitimate cash.

Over the past ten years, life settlements seem to have supplanted roulette as the stratagem of choice in drug traffickers' bag of tricks.

According to Raul Garcia, DEA special agent: "Drug lords have become addicted to life insurance. They love being able to recycle millions of dollars from the safety of their yachts without having to worry about casinos' CCTV cameras. They purchase mammoth policies, report the ones that mature quickly and dump the others."

A certain category of intermediaries specializes in sourcing such huge policies for Columbian investors. They are lavishly compensated for their services — in cash, of course.

Sunset Partners, the Panama City fund that acquired Bruce Webb's policy, started to draw the DEA's attention in the late 1990s. Nearly half of Sunset Partners' investors were South American. They would buy policies with face values running into the millions of dollars and never repatriate their gains, reinvesting them instead in commercial real estate in Orlando or Miami.

After a one-year investigation, DEA agents had gathered enough evidence to indict Tony Babbitt, Sunset's president, and his cousin Charly Babbitt, head of sales and marketing. The two men had developed a well-oiled machine over the years. Tony showered sellers and brokers with cash to acquire all the policies available on the market, while Charly's role was creating shell companies in Panama and the Cayman Islands and then organizing fund transfers from Columbia.

Tony and Charly Babbitt are currently serving prison terms of fifteen and thirteen years respectively.

The DEA wasn't able to build a case against Robert "Bobby" Babbitt, known in the business as Big Bobby, in reference to his imposing build. Mr. Babbitt, who is Tony's younger brother, wasn't officially employed by Sunset, although he had a consulting contract worth $60,000 annually with the company. Since he didn't have his own office, he usually sat in the conference room where, according to former employees, he sometimes entertained prostitutes after lunch.

Several people whom we interviewed — but who prefer to remain anonymous — describe Mr. Babbitt as a hot-tempered and even brutal man, "the mastermind of the family," "Sunset's real head honcho."

Robert "Bobby" Babbitt

Bobby Babbitt testified in several cases over the past ten years. He's also being audited by the IRS on suspicions of tax evasion.

Between 1996 and 2010, Mr. Babbitt reported a total income of $1,487,901. He lives in a 13,600-square-foot mansion, registered under the name of his brother Tony, overlooking the Gulf of Mexico, on Destin's most prestigious avenue. Local realtors whom we contacted estimate the value of the house to be at least $8m, given its unique situation on the Emerald Coast. They calculate that real estate taxes and basic maintenance costs on a residence of this size run around $15,000 per month.

Bobby Babbitt and his attorneys declined our repeated requests for comment.

Locally, though, Mr. Babbitt is well-known for his generous philanthropic contributions.

Last March, Lynn Huffman invited Mr. Babbitt to the annual gala of the Make-A-Wish Foundation's regional chapter. "He replied that, unfortunately, he couldn't join us. But he had attached a $25,000 check 'for the kids,'" recalled Mrs. Huffman.

Mr. Babbitt's residence in Destin, Fla.

According to his tax return, Mr. Babbitt donated a total of $1,123,000 to fifty-six different causes in 2010. The list of beneficiaries includes the Girl Scouts of the USA ($2,500), the National Breast Cancer Foundation ($100,000), the Save The Manatee Club ($5,000), the Veterans Jobs Alliance ($20,000) and the Coalition for Better and Swifter Justice ($250,000). The last-mentioned association defines itself in its bylaws as "a think tank of judges and prosecutors dedicated to accelerating the pace of justice."

For years, Mr. Babbitt also gave the maximum amount permitted by law, i.e. $2,500, to all candidates running for local office. Among the recipients was Michael Hart, Destin Terrace resident and Republican state senator in the Florida legislature. In 2010, pressured by the association of Sunset Partners' victims, Mr. Hart's campaign announced they would return the donation.

Public records show that, in the following month, Mr. Babbitt made a $5,000 donation to the Republican political action committee supporting Mr. Hart's candidacy.

Other, far more subtle forms of deception rooted in the difficulty of accurately evaluating any life insurance policy.

The price of a stock or a bond is determined by the market every day. Similarly, homeowners have a good sense of what their houses are worth. According to Susan McGregor, vice-president of fund Osiris Capital, evaluating a policy is anything but an exact science. "It's the result of complex calculations, based on multiple variables, each subject to interpretation. Add to the mix the fact that the seller always knows something the buyer doesn't, and you'll understand why two funds can be so far apart in their valuations."

Ed Linkas, senior manager at the accounting firm Lark & Hopkins, couldn't agree more. "It's what I call 'Excel magic': the slightest change in a single hypothesis has enormous repercussions. Take a life settlement fund who banks on an average life expectancy of seventy-eight years. On paper, they appear to be doing a great job: they're on track for 12% annual gains, managers are being praised to the skies, and collect multi-million-dollar bonuses. Now imagine the same fund with a life expectancy of eighty years: performance would go down the toilet, managers would be called failures and shown the door. That's why fudging numbers can seem so compelling."

In 2011, the financial group SunAmerica, which holds $4bn worth of life settlement assets, took a $100m write-off following a change in its internal evaluation methodology.

Insurance companies are not immune to the temptation, either. According to Ed Linkas, "they're constantly tweaking their hypotheses, upward when they need to boost profits, and downward when they've achieved their quarterly numbers and want to set money aside for a rainy day."

More worrisome still, the gap between the projections of insurers and those of life settlement funds keeps widening. Either insurance companies are misleading their shareholders or life settlement funds are promising returns that they will be unable to deliver.

Ed Linkas

Ed Linkas, who splits his time between both industries, witnesses such divergences on an almost daily basis. "One of my insurance clients recently raised its life expectancy assumptions for AIDS patients, citing a study by the Pasteur Institute. A week later, another client, this one a life settlement fund this time, referenced the same study as its basis for shaving eighteen months off the longevity of its portfolio!"

How does Mr. Linkas reconcile such conflicts? "I try to understand my clients' logic, while warning them of the dangers of excessive optimism. It's not always easy."

Kenneth Courtney, professor of securities law at the University of Chicago, belongs to a group of experts who advise President Obama on financial regulatory issues. He believes the life settlement industry suffers from a fundamental flaw: the very long time horizon of its investments.

"You can't determine the exact performance of a policy until the death of its original owner," explained Mr. Courtney. "In the meantime, everybody takes their cut: the seller, of course, who receives a check; the broker; the provider; the servicer, the life settlement fund, which bills management fees year after year; and even managers who earn cash bonuses on paper profits. By the time the policy matures in a quarter-century, all those players will have retired."

Mr. Courtney goes one step further. "It's the perfect market for the next Bernie Madoff. You take investors' money, allegedly to buy policies; you call them for more cash every year, claiming the original policyholders aren't dying; and if they ask to withdraw their funds, you tell them they've lost everything."

Several European countries are considering whether to regulate the trading of life insurance policies more strictly. The British Financial Security Authority (FSA) is even considering banning the retail sale of life settlement products altogether.

Jean-Michel Jacques, president of Osiris Capital, supports the FSA's initiative.

"There's no doubt in my mind that life settlement transactions should be restricted to accredited investors [i.e. those with extensive market experience and a minimum of $2.5m in investable assets]," he said. "Individuals don't stand a chance against the sharks who rule this industry."

Write to Vlad Eisinger: vlad.eisinger@wst.com
Next week: *Should The Life Settlement Industry Be More Regulated?*

Dan's journal

Tuesday, July 24

Ran into Lammons who was walking his pooch on the beach. Afraid that he might ask for the $100 I owe him, I slowed my pace and hunched over, as if engrossed in profound thought. That was hardly enough to shut him up.

"Really, can you believe that crap? That damn faggot finally admitted that he played us for fools! No wonder the doctors gave him only two years to live — he hadn't slept in a week, and he was high as a kite! And he makes a joke of it, like 'it's water under the bridge now.' What the hell is she thinking, Miss flight attendant? That because 25 years have gone by, I'm going to kiss my money goodbye and slap myself on the knee? No way, Jose! Now that he's been stupid enough to publicly confess, my lawyers are going to take him to the cleaners."

Poor Webb. I hope he didn't land himself in a big mess.

*****

From: Dan Siver <danielgsiver@gmail.com>
Date: Tuesday, July 24, 2012 3:15 P.M.
To: Vlad Eisinger <vlad.eisinger@wst.com>
Subject: Crime against humanity

I know we said we would "drop the abuse," but enough is enough! You know what makes me puke about that profession of yours? The implacable formatting of your articles. You think I haven't noticed your tricks? Every other article opens with some catchphrase, promising a juicy anecdote that never comes: *"When Citibank threatened to foreclose on her house, Cynthia Tucker, 77, pored over her finances one more time."* And this week: *"When Drug Enforcement Administration agents seized the submarine of Javier "El Tigre" Escobar, they found the typical trophies of drug kingpins on board: weapons, cash,* **Treasury bonds** *— and life insurance policies."* It's all in the dash. Bravo! What a brilliant way to captivate your reader! I nearly wet my pants.

Same deal for the last paragraph, invariably a quote, if possible a slightly

124

provocative one. *"Life settlement transactions should be restricted to accredited investors. Individuals don't stand a chance against the sharks who rule this industry."* Or: *"Should we discover a cancer vaccine, I hope my investors will be wise enough to think about the years they've come out ahead, rather than the millions they've lost."* My goodness, move over, Michael Crichton — here comes Vlad!

And don't get me started on the rest of the article. Actually, do get me started: adverbs are banned; sentences never exceed twenty words; and a quote's plugged in every time the reader threatens to doze off. Help!

Honestly, Vlad, aren't you ashamed of yourself?

*****

From: Vlad Eisinger <vlad.eisinger@wst.com>
Date: Tuesday, July 24, 2012 5:36 P.M.
To: Dan Siver <danielgsiver@gmail.com>
Subject: True obedience is true freedom

You don't know the half of it, old sport. It goes way beyond anything you could imagine. All the paper's rookies have to gnaw their way through a 500-page manual, which is updated every year: *The Associated Press Stylebook.* On the menu: editing rules (use of the dash, writing of a number with numerals or letters, etc.); a plethora of lists (common abbreviations, kosher bad words…); vade mecums on accounting or nuclear physics (just to save the halfwits that we are from the embarrassment of writing big foolish things); the proper way to report tennis scores or survey results (never forget to include the sample size and margin of error); etc. It's the Bible of newsrooms — we're supposed to know it by heart, or, at the very least, to know what's in it. Woe to those who stray from it! I once used "holiday" instead of "holy day." I was hauled over the coals! My skin's still burning.

But that's not the worst of it. We also take our orders from another breviary, the inescapable *Elements of Style* by the illustrious William Strunk and E. B. White, which enumerates 21 principles that writers ignore at their own risk. Here are some of them in no particular order: "Stay in the background;" "Use as few adjectives and adverbs as possible;" "Refrain from exaggerating;" "Beware of complicated words;" "No imagery;" and, finally, that edifying guideline (I'm quoting from memory): "A sentence should not contain any superfluous words, nor a paragraph unnecessary sentences, for the same reason that a drawing should not contain useless lines nor a machine extra parts." (I beg you not to roll your eyes to the high heavens.)

To top it all off, over the years every newsroom has developed an "in-house" style, by which its journalists have to abide. The *Wall Street Tribune*'s rules in regard to first and last paragraphs didn't escape you. That catchphrase, which, as you said, is "a promise to a juicy anecdote that never comes," is called a "lead." There are two different types of leads: those that reveal the article's main information from the get-go (the most famous: "Two men have landed and walked on the moon") and those, better suited to an investigative series such as mine, which sets the scene or tells a story in order to pique the reader's interest.

We use other methods, some of which quickly become second nature. Quotes, for instance, fulfill a dual role. First, they break the monotony of the reading by offering a refreshing counterpoint. Second and more importantly, they instill an element of subjectivity (a "different prism," to use your phrase) in articles that are theoretically devoid of it.

Take my article about the infamous lunch at the Admiral's Club. My status as a reporter forbids me to put forward any judgment about Professor Marlowe, even though, deep down, I liken his presentation to prostitution. Hence the importance of being able to lend my mic to one of the guests, in this case El Señor Gonzales, who was shocked by Marlowe's proselytism. How many times have I been tempted to create an expert or an average Joe as a mouthpiece for a point of view that I felt was missing from the debate. Rest assured, I've never yielded to such an urge.

Jayson Blair, a colleague from the *New York Times*, didn't have such scruples. He was fired in a huge uproar, when his superiors discovered that he was quoting witnesses he'd never met and describing places he'd never visited. Not a single soul in the profession ventured to defend him.

Journalists who cover the news — which, as you've gathered, isn't my function — frequently resort to another technique, known as the reverse pyramid. They lay out the main facts in an often indigestible first paragraph, then distill the rest of the information in descending order of importance. If, say, a Los Angeles real estate agent has killed his entire family, you'll find out in the sixth paragraph that he was a Lakers fan, and, in the last few lines, that he slept in a jersey signed by Kobe Bryant. The advantage: the article can be truncated almost anywhere without requiring editing.

126

As obscene as these rules may seem to you, you get used to them. Queneau, Perec, et al., claimed that formal constraints stimulate the imagination. Though I don't go as far as writing in alexandrines or avoiding the letter "E", I've noticed that my prose has gained in vigor since I've imposed those standards on myself. You should give it a try.

*****

From: Dan Siver <danielgsiver@gmail.com>
Date: Tuesday, July 24, 2012 10:06 P.M.
To: Vlad Eisinger <vlad.eisinger@wst.com>
Subject: Get a hold of yourself!

I ordered your *Associated Press Stylebook*. Seriously, what a load of manure! How can you yield to those idiotic directions, when you, Vlad, had such a lovely way with words? Not being allowed to use expressions? Dear God, kill me now!

As for your reverse pyramid, you can shove it up your ass, starting with the tip!

*****

From: Vlad Eisinger <vlad.eisinger@wst.com>
Date: Tuesday, July 24, 2012 10:07 P.M.
To: Dan Siver <danielgsiver@gmail.com>
Subject: From one poet to another

You too, Dan, have a lovely way with words…

*****

Dan's journal

Wednesday, July 25
Whoopee sessions at lunch time, witnesses willing to talk on condition of anonymity, donations to the Make-A-Wish Foundation — no doubt about it, Vlad nailed his Bobby Babbitt portrait. Could it be that my piece

on the Admiral's Club helped pull the stick out of his derrière?

Realized that the shack of Sunset's "head honcho" is no other than that ultramodern blockhouse, protected by an electric fence, in front of which I pass every day when I walk along the beach. This morning, for the first time, I noticed two armed guards, positioned on the terrace. Is Babbitt afraid of retaliation following Vlad's article? He must have no shortage of enemies.

(…)

Dropped by Manuel's to return the screwdriver he had left at my place. He followed my advice and spoke to the McGregors about his quandary. A close look at his mortgage contract revealed that he already has coverage through his bank and therefore doesn't need any additional insurance. Susan said there's no way Chuck could not have known this. Jeffrey, who works in the same shop as Patterson, laid the blame of his colleague's overzealousness on Emerald's big marketing campaign to promote that type of insurance. The agents who sign the most policies between now and the end of the year will receive two tickets to the Super Bowl!

Susan advised Manuel to take out a 30-year term life insurance policy, which, if I understood correctly, won't cost him as much as if he were to buy whole life insurance. Obviously, Manuel refuses to deal with Chuck. I recommended that he contact Kim Phelps (and I'll make sure to claim a referral fee in due course).

Manuel introduced me to his sister-in-law, Lupita, who lives with them while studying to become a dental hygienist. I told her all about my squabbles with the despicable Lammons. She said that the inter-professional organizations of dentists and hygienists have been embroiled in a protracted legal battle. Hygienists are asserting their rights to set up shop, to offer basic care (fillings, prophylaxis, etc.), for prices two to three times lower than those charged by traditional practices, whereas dentists, defending their monopoly for dear life, are lobbying the legislature to preserve the status quo. I was only half-surprised to learn that Lammons sits on the board of the Florida Dental Association, and that Michael Hart has publicly ruled out any reform project.

Thursday, July 26

Had coffee with Jean-Michel at Starbucks this morning. He finds Vlad's articles hugely entertaining. He's so thrilled to see Wall Street's ploys exposed that he's ordered reprints to send to all of his clients. I asked him if he agrees with Vlad's analysis.

"Absolutely. He hit the nail on the head. His articles are incredibly instructive. He should be awarded a medal."

"Wait a second. He's not painting a very flattering picture of the life settlement business. Aren't you worried that he might scare your clients away?"

"Not at all," he answered. "I don't have that many investors, barely a few dozen. I know all of them personally. Most of them are entrepreneurs. They like that I'm heavily invested in my own funds. I'm completely transparent with them. They know they can drop by my office any time, ask to see any one policy and contest its appraisal in our books. I limit administrative fees to 1.5% a year, versus an average of 2% for other hedge funds, plus a performance bonus if we exceed specified returns."

He made sure to add that he won't collect such performance incentives until the final liquidation of the funds. His competitors, on the other hand, regularly re-evaluate their portfolios to account for recent deaths and for the latest trends in life expectancies. If the value of the funds has risen over the course of a year, the managers help themselves to their bonuses without delay.

"That's classic Wall Street," he thundered. "Paper gains leading to the payment of real bonuses. Bottom line: the manager drives a Maserati, and the day it all comes tumbling down like a pack of cards, the investor is left holding the bag. I may have to wait fifteen years before I receive my bonus, but at least no one can accuse me of having paid myself before my investors."

He brought his cup to his lips and, not realizing it was empty, gulped an imaginary swig. In the heat of the discussion, his French accent was back with a vengeance. The girl behind the counter was watching us, clearly amused.

"Between you and me, Dan, it's the entire ecosystem that needs to be fixed. Too many middlemen; too many pseudo-experts whose words you can't trust; the rampant greed that justifies every base act…"

I teased him a little: "Come on, Jean-Michel, are you telling me that European financiers work for pleasure?"

"Of course not. They're trying to earn a living, like everybody else. But they still have a semblance of principles, unlike their Wall Street counterparts, who pretend not to grasp the distinction between what's ethical and what's legal. Listen to this: A few years ago, the American bank that employed me devised a complicated strategy to take advantage of some anomalies in the copper futures market. I showed my boss that at least one of the components of the scheme violated securities regulations. Our lawyers provided us with the solution: to notify the market authorities of the infringement ourselves and then to pay the maximum prescribed fine of $1m, versus $40m in profits. My boss didn't think twice…"

Another swig. This time he realized his mistake, and stared at our neighbors warily, as if he suspected them of having drained his cup on the sly.

"Let's take the case of your friend, Ed Linkas. No, no, hear me out. I know you enjoy his company, understandably so by the way — he's a very nice fellow. He's been auditing our accounts for two years; in other words, he checks our valuation methodology and makes sure we're not overly optimistic in our assumptions. What Ed forgot to tell the *Wall Street Tribune* is that he bills us additional fees for, I quote, 'taking the time to review the validity of our hypotheses.' "

I wasn't following; Jean-Michel explained.

"You understand, don't you, that the value of a fund is the result of a negotiation? With an average life expectancy of 80 years, Osiris's portfolio is worth $120m. At 79 years, it flirts with $130m. At 90 years, it isn't worth a hill of beans. Personally, I don't mind these variations, since I plan to keep my policies all the way to the end. My competitors, however, harass their auditors until they obtain the figures that work for them. Careful now, I'm not saying I could bring Ed to validate a 10% increase in Osiris's book value. But 2 to 3%? Easy as pie. I can even tell you how much that would cost me, give or take $1,000."

And to think I considered Ed a decent man! How depressing! The expression "Money rules the world" had never rung so true.

Jean-Michel leaned toward me and confided he's going under the knife next Wednesday. He hopes the surgeon will successfully remove his tumor, or else he's headed for chemo, which will mean the end of the last couple of hairs on his noggin.

In the meantime, he's acquiring policies of bladder cancer patients like there's no tomorrow, motivated by a strategy at once cynical and perfectly sound.

"If there's a revolutionary cure, I'll lose money on my policies, but I'll have the consolation of still being alive. Otherwise, Anh and the children will make a nice little bundle."

I didn't bother pointing out that he's forgetting the case where he dies and other patients pull through. He's too smart not to have thought about that. I guess studying other patients' files helps him keep the disease at bay.

Remembered after parting that he doesn't have medical insurance. The cost of his treatment must run in the tens of thousands of dollars. How will he able to pay?

(…)

The homeowners' board had set the deadline for proposals for the Destin Terrace insurance contract renewal to eight o'clock tonight.

Kim came by first. She gave me a thick envelope, joking that she'd sealed it with some nail polish that would withstand any attempt to open it with steam. Despite her apparent nonchalance, I sensed that she was quite nervous. She told me she'd worked like crazy on that offer, securing exceptionally favorable rates from her superiors in exchange for reducing her own commission by half. As neutral as I try to be, I couldn't help but wish her good luck.

She ran into Chuck Patterson at the door. He informed me without preliminaries that he had decided not to submit an offer.

"Your little friend must have pulled out all the stops for that bid. Now why in the world would I jump through hoops for pocket change? You've got to know when to let a deal go."

So as not to leave empty-handed, rather than out of true conviction, he offered to match my current home insurance policy.

"It won't cost you a dime, and I'll take care of all the paperwork," he promised.

"No thanks, Chuck."

"Geez, Dan, you do realize that every year some stranger cashes in more than a few coins thanks to your contract, don't you? Wouldn't you rather that money find its way into your neighbor's pocket?"

He didn't have the gall to say "your friend."

"No, not really. Of course, it'd be a different story if said neighbor was a fan of my work…"

He left, slamming the door behind him.

I called Kim, who instantly saw how she could take advantage of the situation. She pretended she had mistakenly given me an interim version of the contract.

"I'm coming over to bring you the final bid, all right? After all, it's only 7:30."

I had to explain to her that it really wouldn't be fair to the homeowners. As I was saying this, however, I was mostly thinking about myself. I've figured out that each percent of savings on the existing policy translates into a drop of about $2 in my annual fees.

Friday, July 27

Hooray! The Wikipedia editor has approved my revision! Better yet, he's proposing that I enhance Hermann Broch's page with a section devoted to the matter of his presumed kinship with Leo Perutz.

Quoting him: "*The website you steered me to suggests a relationship between the two men that extends well beyond a mere friendship. Naturally, we must proceed with caution, inasmuch as the works of Böhm, Mirafuentes and company, though they seem perfectly reliable and serious, have yet to be approved by the biographers and the Broch and Perutz families. So I recommend that you initially include the usual caveats in your contribution, and that, as soon as it's been endorsed, you copy it verbatim to Leo Perutz's page. At my end, I shall notify my German counterparts, through Wikipedia's internal channels, so that they can add these new elements to the pages for which they're responsible. Editions in other languages will follow suit within a few weeks. Thank you in advance for your cooperation.*"

I keep reading that message over and over again — it's almost too good to be true. Holy Moses, I did it! Today marks the beginning of a new golden age for Austrian studies, bogged down for the past thirty years in endless debates about Stephan Zweig's European sensitivity and the influence of the suicide of Wittgenstein's three brothers on his philosophy. Truly virgin territories, in which a promising researcher can hope to make a name for himself, are few. I'm willing to bet that, within one year, a Ph.D. student from the University of Graz will publish a *Case for a new interpretation of the father figure in* The Death of Virgil. Unless the dean of the German department at Yale beats him to it with a *Broch, Perutz: Blood Brothers, Soul Brothers.*

When I think of the trolls of the *New York Times Book Review* who deemed Mark and Minnie "improbable characters without any bearing in reality…" It would warrant my sending them Thorsten Böhm's biography, or, better yet, a video of Ericka Kirchenmeister hard at work.

In the evening

As the day progressed, my elation gave way to anxiety. The thought that other editors, German ones at that, will be looking into my falsification terrifies me. For the first time, I'm forcing myself to consider the legal implications of my hoax. All kinds of charges, real or imaginary, are flying through my mind: identity theft, defamation, offense to the memory of a deceased person, violations of copyright law. Are my actions liable to a fine? To a suspended jail sentence? Would I be granted extenuating circumstances by reason of my occupation as a writer? Would the Wikipedia foundation file a civil case?

Saturday, July 28

Fought all night against the temptation to confide in Vlad, who's probably a lot more knowledgeable about these subjects by virtue of his profession. With any luck, he might even be able to discreetly consult the *Wall Street Tribune* attorneys.

I'm giving myself 48 hours to think it over.

(...)

At the gym I ran across Bruce Webb. I told him about Lammons' threats while he was taking a breather after bench-pressing 180 lbs.

"He's already carried out his threat," he said, wiping his forehead with a towel. "He's suing me for fraud, misrepresentation, and two or three other trifles. Between legal fees and interest, he's asking close to $1m."

He didn't seem overly concerned, and for good reason — the statute of limitations expired years ago.

"I don't see how his lawyer failed to realize that," said Webb, gathering his belongings.

"It might be the same one who is representing him in his lawsuit against Emerald. Are you going to answer him?"

He broke into a wide grin.

"Why the rush? I'm going to let his meter run."

I was coughing my lungs out on the treadmill when Jennifer Hansen entered, wearing tight black yoga pants and a white t-shirt, her ever-present water bottle in hand. Since we were alone, and even though I had never exchanged a word with her, I felt obliged to extend my condolences.

She confessed that she comes every morning, while the children are at school, to ride the exercise bike, "so as not to lose her mind." Taking (mistakenly so) my nod for an invitation to elaborate, she randomly unloaded her troubles: the higher-than-expected cost of the funeral (she initially had her heart set on a wooden coffin, but her in-laws insisted on a steel model); Mark's salary, which stopped coming in; a delay in receiving Emerald's check.

She worries (rightfully so, in this case) about her future. An experienced press agent, she stopped working six years ago, after she became pregnant with the twins. She has no idea of her value on the job market; she's wondering if she should go back to school (but then who would watch her kids?); she hasn't decided whether to sell the house and to buy a smaller one, etc. Not wishing to give her the impression that her agonizing indecisions were a bore, I extended my jogging session way beyond reason, throwing in an "I understand" dripping with sweat and compassion every now and then between two wheezing gasps.

The conversation took a slippery turn, in every sense of the word, when Jennifer inquired whether I thought she would find a new partner someday. I climbed off my torture apparatus pretending I had an appointment, and advised her to try and take her mind off her troubles. Later, I dropped off my last three books on her doorstep.

Unfortunately, that's about all I can do for her.

*****

From: Dan Siver <danielgsiver@gmail.com>
Date: Saturday, July 28, 2012 11:58 P.M.
To: Vlad Eisinger <vlad.eisinger@wst.com>
Subject: Melvin Phelps

You'll never guess what's causing havoc in our little community. This evening, Melvin Phelps, president of the homeowners' association, knocked on my door. He wanted to discuss the deplorable effects of your articles. After such enticing preliminaries, I hastened to invite him in. Obviously, he has no idea that you and I are in contact; as you can imagine, I don't boast about being counted among your friends.

Apparently, several of my neighbors have complained that your weekly compositions are infringing upon their private lives. One could argue (and I was happy to oblige) that they knew the rules of the game when they agreed to meet with you. Phelps wouldn't hear of it; he claims that you're going too far and taking perverse pleasure in depicting Destin Terrace residents in the worst possible light. That last argument staggered me. Admittedly, Bruce Webb and Brian Hess wouldn't do their mothers proud in your last article. Yet I have the feeling they confided in you of their own free will, even that they were grateful for the platform you provided. Who is being panned exactly? Babbitt? But why would Phelps defend some crook who doesn't even live in Destin Terrace? And so what if two or three residents came crying on his shoulder — why should he care? He sure didn't make such a big hoopla when you exposed Chuck Patterson's misdeeds in broad daylight... Could it be that you've uncovered some ghastly secrets about the man?

For your information, he tried to have me sign a petition threatening the *Wall Street Tribune* with a lawsuit if you guys don't immediately discontinue the publication of your articles. I told him I'd sleep on it. Phelps seemed disappointed.

"I thought I could count on you, Dan," he whined.

I was shocked by his reaction. Surely a man of his standing knows that such pantomimes won't accomplish anything.

PS: Let's give the anagram game another go with Lupe Baslow.

*****

From: Dan Siver <danielgsiver@gmail.com>
Date: Sunday, July 29, 2012 00:33 A.M.
To: Vlad Eisinger <vlad.eisinger@wst.com>
Subject: Donna Phelps

I just waded through your last article, looking for what could have compelled Phelps to come out of the woodwork. I think I found it. When I read that Babbitt donated $20,000 to the Veteran Jobs Alliance, I remembered that Donna Phelps, Melvin's wife, heads a charity for the benefit of retired military personnel. I checked, and it is indeed the same organization.

*****

From: Vlad Eisinger <vlad.eisinger@wst.com>
Date: Sunday, July 29, 2012 09:06 A.M.
To: Dan Siver <danielgsiver@gmail.com>
Subject: Good eye

Shame on me for missing that! In my defense, Babbitt contributed to more than 50 charities last year alone — a typical move for white-collar criminals awaiting trial. They shower the community with donations, hoping that the jury will include the parent of an autistic child, a breast cancer survivor, or any other recipient of their largesse. It comes out cheaper than hiring big shot lawyers or multiplying second opinions. Besides, is there any greater delight than to look generous with other people's money?

Nice work in any case; you'd make an excellent journalist. Would you like me to inquire whether we offer summer internships?

P.S.: Lupe Baslow = Paul Bowles, a talented composer but an overrated author. Here's an easy one: Pearl Lehr.

P.P.S.: I just remembered a little something about your friend, Ray Wiggin. Every evening, he sends Chuck Patterson the list of obituaries for the following day, in exchange for an annual invitation to a baseball game. From what I've gathered, that clever Chuck has similar arrangements with dozens of forensic pathologists, funeral directors, and every professional in between.

*****

Dan's journal

Sunday, July 29
Mrs. Cunningham practically broke into my house this morning to share the latest gossip: the reason Jennifer Hansen has yet to receive her check is that Mark's policy supposedly contains some irregularities. I find that unlikely, since Chuck himself processed the case from beginning to end.

Out of respect for poor Jennifer, I changed the subject, and asked Mrs.

136

Cunningham if she was making any progress with the resale of her policy. She was only too happy to report that she had negotiated an unbeatable commission rate with Kim.

"She needs my business a whole lot more than I need her," she shrewdly explained. "And since she has but a handful of clients, I can rest assured she'll take good care of me."

On another note, Mrs. Cunningham is amused by the attentiveness of her daughter, who visits every day and accompanies her to the doctor's.

"I wasn't born yesterday! I know she's hankering after my policy and that she'll stop coming to see me the moment I sell it."

I once again took Ashley's side, jokingly this time.

"Come on Patricia, why won't you admit that your daughter adores you?"

She burst out laughing.

"Well, I guess your mother was right — you don't know anything about life. Now I see why your books aren't flying off the shelves."

I'd be lying if I denied having felt a pang at these words.

(…)

Saw Susan McGregor in the frozen food section at Publix. I knew right away that something was wrong. She was stacking trays of lasagna in her shopping cart with a suppressed rage that seemed out of place in a supermarket. She didn't need to be asked twice why she was so upset. Apparently, Jennifer Hansen has approached Rafaela to ask whether she'd be interested in watching the twins if she were to go back to work. She'd pay the same wages as the McGregors for one hour less of work per day. Rafaela claimed that she turned down the offer, but still felt the need to discuss it with her employer. Susan sought my support, but I prudently abstained. Being very fond of Rafaela, I merely noted that she has to defend her own interests.

"It's the law of supply and demand," I asserted. "In that respect, the babysitters' market is no different from that of life insurance policies."

Susan opened her mouth, then walked away abruptly. I'm afraid she might have missed my point.

(…)

Jotted down a few drafts of the paragraph on Broch and Perutz after dinner.

I've decided not to talk to Vlad at this juncture. After all, Sade and

Soljenitsyne did their best work in prison.

Monday, July 30

It's Dad's birthday today. He would have been seventy-seven years old.

He was preparing to climb Mount McKinley along with some former colleagues. But as a precaution, he had decided to have an appendectomy first. At 20,000 feet, peritonitis is not an option. He checked into the hospital on Monday. According to the doctors, he caught some nasty bug during the surgery. On Wednesday, he had a fever of 104. By Friday, he was dead.

(…)

I invited Kim over for a drink as she was leaving Mrs. Cunningham's. She told me the old hag is driving her crazy.

"I warned her that I wouldn't be able to sell her policy without a life expectancy report, which costs around $800. She's already squeezed my commission so much, there's no way I'm taking on that additional expense. So now she's taken it into her head to deal directly with Brian Hess. I've tried to explain to her that a report from a freelancer wouldn't be worth much, but she refuses to listen. Had I known, I would have gladly let Patterson deal with her."

While she was talking, I remembered that Mrs. Cunningham is currently embroiled in a lawsuit with her stockbroker. In early 2009, as the market was collapsing, she liquidated her retirement savings on a whim. When the stock market trend reversed, she blamed her broker for letting her give in to panic. The advisor, one of Otto Cunningham's childhood friends, explained the difference between a broker and an asset manager, and gave her a stainless steel toaster, usually reserved for the bank's new customers. Railing that they wouldn't silence her with the gift of a kitchen appliance, Mrs. Cunningham hired a lawyer nicknamed Clark the Shark, who, in exchange for one third of the recovery, subpoenaed all of the financial establishments with which the Cunningham family had ever held an account. Last I heard, justice was running its course.

For some reason, I didn't deem it appropriate to share that anecdote with Kim. The poor girl confessed she's having a hard time finding her niche in the field. Her father's friends aren't turning out to be the easy prey she expected. They're already insured up the wazoo. As for the few who still don't have the whole shebang, they all have a cousin or a niece vying for their business.

To date she has signed only three contracts in the community: a car insurance policy for Ed Linkas (whom I suspect isn't entirely disinterested); a boat insurance policy for Michael Hart (who prides himself on fueling the local economy); and, of course, the contract with Destin Terrace, on which she fears she won't make a living. Chuck watches over his clientele with an eagle eye. I described to Kim the network of informers that he has patiently put in place over the years, and this information discouraged her even more.

She promised to invite me to dinner if she strikes a deal with Manuel. I took the opportunity to ask her how in the world Chuck could have offered him a policy that serves the same purpose as his mortgage contract. Kim explained to me that what I consider a mistake is a common practice in the industry. The last time she rented a car, she mindlessly signed up for the optional renter's insurance, before realizing she already was protected by her personal car insurance and by the company that issued her credit card.

"Had I been in an accident," she said, "all three parties would have divided up the repair costs. That's how insurance agencies manage to keep increasing their profits in a saturated market."

Week 6

Should The Life Settlement Industry Be More Regulated?

By Vlad Eisinger

The Wall Street Tribune, Tuesday, July 31, 2012

The life settlement market — the resale of an existing life insurance policy to a third party — emerged in the 1980s, in a total legal vacuum.

Then lawyers got involved.

Today, the life settlement industry is regulated in varying degrees in all but nine of the fifty states. New legislation is being considered in additional states. Lobbying firms on retainers from insurers and life settlement funds are besieging Congress, not to mention the dozens of associations with more or less respectable motives that seek publicity on the Web.

Has the life settlement industry become too regulated?

Before answering this question, let's take a look at the historic forces at play.

For two centuries, insurance companies denied their customers the right to sell their policies, invoking the precedent of eighteen-century England, where unscrupulous businessmen purchased insurance on the lives of strangers only to have them killed. In 1911, the U.S. Supreme Court ruled that policyholders were free to dispose of their contracts as they pleased.

The AIDS epidemic that struck America in the 1980s prompted insurers to rally again. In a matter of a few months, thousands of HIV-positive individuals sold their policies to newly created entities. In the grand scheme of things, the amounts at stake were negligible; besides, few terminally-ill patients stop paying their premiums. Nonetheless, insurance companies tried to forestall the development of an industry potentially threatening to their interests.

Rather than vilifying their customers, which would have tarnished their public relations, insurers turned to such lobbying organizations as the National Association of Insurance Commissioners (NAIC), the Life Insurance Settlement Association (LISA, founded in 1995), and consumer associations. These groups' combined efforts led to the passage of the Viatical Settlement Act in 2001.

According to Kenneth Courtney, a professor of securities law at the University of Chicago, the Viatical Settlement Act contains several major breakthroughs. "First, it provides a blueprint upon which states are free to model their own laws. It also calls for a moratorium of at least two years, during which policyholders cannot sell their contracts. Last, but not least, it allows terminally ill patients to collect between 25% to 95% of their death benefits while they're still alive." According to Mr. Courtney, the only reason insurance companies agreed to this concession was to discourage their clients from shopping their contracts to third parties.

After this much-needed clarification of the legal landscape, each side returned to the drawing board.

Insurers set about convincing state legislatures to transpose NAIC directives to the local level, while life settlement funds devised sophisticated schemes to increase their purchases of policies while fully complying with the law (see our July 10 article, *The Cut-Throat Fight Between Insurers and Premium Finance Funds*). The market expanded at a brisk pace, reaching some $13bn in 2008.

But the fund managers' hopes were quickly dashed. As the first maturities arrived, insurers refused to pay death benefits whenever a policy was tainted by the slightest irregularity.

According to Jean-Michel Jacques, president of Osiris Capital: "the fund managers realized that insurers wouldn't do them any favors. If the application forms contained a single mistake, the insurers would deny payment and sue the policyholder for fraud."

Mr. Jacques believes life settlement funds didn't take their opponents seriously. "They viewed life insurance as an antiquated, slow-to-adapt industry. They couldn't have been more wrong. Insurers are shrewd, greedy, and extremely well-organized. They can endure blows, but they also know how to return the favor. You underestimate them at your own risk."

The main life settlement players eventually counterattacked on the legal front. They also formed a new professional society in 2007, the Institutional Life Markets Association (ILMA).

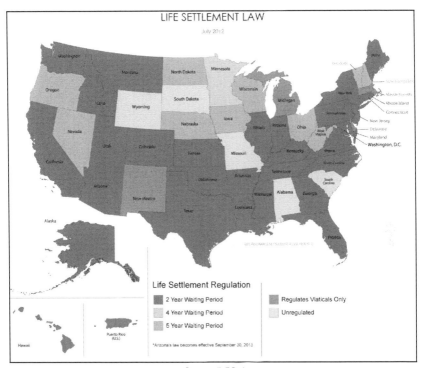

Source: LISA

Until then, big Wall Street firms had stayed on the sidelines of the life settlement debate — for instance, JPMorgan Chase, one of the leading financial institutions in the country, was not even a member of LISA — but a few firms had quietly entered the market.

The presence of Goldman Sachs, Bear Sterns, Credit Suisse, and UBS among ILMA's founders speaks to the association's ambitions, which are reflected in its mission statement: "To apply capital market solutions in life insurance, to educate consumers that their insurance may be a valuable asset, to expand consumer choices about how to manage it, and to support the responsible growth and regulation of the industry."

According to Mr. Jacques: "The creation of ILMA marks the first step toward Wall Street's ultimate goal: the launching, through securitization, of a death derivatives market."

Securitization is the technique of pooling a large number of loans (mortgages, credit card debts, auto loans, etc.) into one bond and marketing it to investors. Between 1999 and 2007, Wall Street firms generated billions of dollars in revenue by packaging subprime mortgages into tradable securities. By buying or selling those bonds, investors could speculate on the direction of real market prices. Some of them won, such as John Paulson, whose eponymous fund recorded profits of $15bn in 2007; the vast majority lost. As for brokers, they made money on the way up and on the way down.

ILMA's timing proved catastrophic. "After the 2008 financial crisis, no one cared to hear about securitization anymore," recalled Mr. Jacques. "But it's only a matter of time. People like Goldman Sachs don't give up at the first hurdle."

A few years behind insurers, it's now the turn of life settlement professionals to call for more transparent rules.

Evidently, the two parties have contrasting visions of what those rules should be.

Insurers use guerilla tactics, somewhat reminiscent of those employed by pro-life activists. Although they're officially no longer pursuing a ban on life settlement transactions, they're doing everything in their power to make such transfers more costly and time-consuming. For example, ten states, including Ohio and Oregon, have already extended the ineligibility period from two to five years.

Rick Weintraub, president of the Insurance Consumers' Association, also denounces the intimidation maneuvers to which certain insurers subject their clients. "Their contracts list all the risks a customer incurs by selling his policy. They're clearly trying to discourage the less motivated candidates."

Insurance companies are waging another internal battle. It's common knowledge that some general agents — sales people who work for a single carrier — moonlight as life settlement advisors. Insurers, feeling betrayed, are trying to stop this practice.

Jeremy Fallon, spokesperson for the Life Insurance Brokers' Association (LIBA), which represents general agents, says LIBA is ready to dialogue with insurance carriers, provided they pledge to compensate agents for the negative impact of any future legal restrictions on their scope of intervention. "Our members will do anything to please their employers — except reduce their income," he explained.

Some agents go to great lengths not to tarnish their reputations. The *Wall Street Tribune* has discovered that at least four of general agent Chuck

Patterson's clients sold their Emerald life insurance policies during the past two years. They all retained Byron Meeks, Mr. Patterson's brother-in-law, as their broker.

Mr. Meeks runs U-Break-It, I-Fix-It, an odd-job business based in Niceville, about ten miles from Destin. He took his life settlement broker's examination in February, 2010. One month later, he completed his first transaction. To our knowledge, Mr. Meeks has no other clients than those referred by Mr. Patterson.

Mr. Patterson denies having influenced his brother-in-law. "Byron is a Jack of all trades. That one-stop handyman gig doesn't work for him anymore. He became a broker, but he could just as well have learned Italian, or trained for a marathon."

Life settlement funds have their own hobbyhorses.

They oppose the extension of ineligibility periods, which reduce the number of policies available.

They also call for streamlining procedures. Today, a transaction typically takes between two to six months to complete.

Last, they seek to clarify the period during which insurers can challenge the validity of a policy. "That's the biggie," said Mr. Jacques. "When we buy a ten-year-old policy, we need to be sure that the carrier won't nitpick because the original owner had failed to report, say, that he's into hang-gliding or that his grandmother was a hemophiliac."

The battle extends to spokespersons. Insurers bet on soap opera star Gloria Suarez to woo Latinos, who are generally keen on financial protection products. Life settlement professionals have contracted the services of former Green Bay Packers quarterback Kenny Jennings. In commercials broadcast every night before *Wheel of Fortune*, Jennings, now seventy, proudly boasts that he used the proceeds of his policy to buy a condo for each of his two daughters.

One voice is strangely absent from the cacophony. Lawmakers, who are brimming with ideas on topics such as renewable energies or farm subsidies, seem reluctant to become involved in the life settlement debate.

Stephanie Welsh, associate director at WGA Consulting, a firm specializing in regulatory affairs, worked in Washington as a congressional staffer for twelve years. White papers commissioned by both insurance and life settlement trade associations usually landed on her desk.

"They were never shorter than one hundred fifty pages, which left me with two options," Mrs. Welsh recalled. "I could either read the executive summary and agree 100% with the author, or I could spend my entire weekend trying to wrap my head around the report, to feel even more clueless in the end. And yet, I have a business degree, unlike most of my colleagues who majored in political science."

Kenneth Courtney isn't really surprised by Mrs. Welsh's recollection. "It's the sad reality of our western democracies. We can't expect our representatives to be experts at once in public health, nuclear safety and bank accounting. Since they're required to vote on the bills that come before them, they delegate most decisions to party committees composed of a handful of individuals who'll likely end up working for the industry that they're currently regulating."

After thirty years of studying securities law, Mr. Courtney has come to question the very concept of regulation. "Last year, the Supreme Court invoked the First Amendment to prohibit the government from restricting political expenditure by corporations or lobbyists [Citizens United v. Federal Election Commission]. Because money wields influence, in the long run, laws will no longer reflect the common good, but just the point of view of the richest camp. It's quite depressing."

According to the Center for Responsive Politics, the insurance industry spent $1.77bn— or $14,000 hourly — on lobbying since 1998, second only to the pharmaceutical industry.

Not included in this figure are contributions to political candidates. Over the last electoral cycle, these amounted to $42.6m, 60% of which went to the Republican party or directly to its candidates. The biggest donor, New York Life Insurance Company, dished out $2.5m among several hundred candidates.

Insurers are especially generous to congressmen who are most likely to affect their industry. As an example, seven of the twenty senators who received the largest contributions from Wall Street are members of the U.S. Senate's Finance Committee.

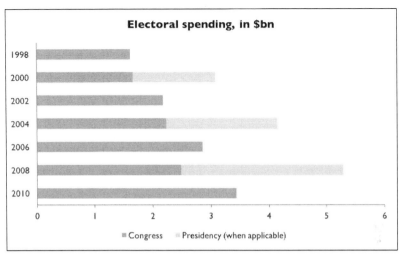

Electoral spending, in $bn

Source: Center for Responsive Politics

However, most life settlement battles are fought at the state level, where regulation is passed and enforced.

In Florida for instance, insurers spent $12.2m during the 2010 local elections. Again, they directed a disproportionate share of their contributions toward a few strategic candidates, such as Jeff Atwater, the state's chief financial officer and insurance commissioner, as well as several members of the Florida Senate Banking & Insurance Committee.

Michael Hart, a Destin Terrace resident and senator of the Florida's First District, has chaired the Banking & Insurance Committee since 2009. His official web page describes him as "an expert in financial services, securities law, and life settlement transactions."

In 2010, insurers contributed $140,000 of the $266,000 spent by Mr. Hart in his successful campaign for reelection. Emerald, a Pensacola-based insurance carrier and a vocal opponent of the life settlement industry, donated $25,000 both directly and indirectly. Matthew Fin, Emerald's president, personally gave $5,000.

Public records show that Kaplan, Hatcher & Boggs, the law firm in which Mr. Hart is still a partner, billed fees totaling $1,180,000 to Emerald between 2008 and 2010.

Kaplan, Hatcher & Boggs declined to comment.

Contacted by phone, Mr. Fin went on record to say: "It's Emerald's policy always to seek the best professional advice. The attorneys of Kaplan,

Hatcher & Boggs rank among the most competent in our fields of interest. We are fully satisfied with their services."

In an email, Mr. Hart wrote that he no longer has any functions within Kaplan, Hatcher & Boggs, and denied any conflict of interest. "I have no other lord and master than the constituents of the First District," he added.

Michael Hart

In 2011, Mr. Hart's share of the profit of Kaplan, Hatcher & Boggs amounted to $195,000.

Since the beginning of the year, Mr. Hart has introduced three bills in the state legislature in Tallahassee aimed at restricting life settlement transactions.

All life settlement players indulge in doublespeak at one point or another. Insurance companies claim an obligation to offer reasonably priced policies to thrifty householders, but never mention the related profits. And life settlement funds' insistence that they are trying to return power to the people would almost have you forget that they strive for annual yields of 15% or more.

Two examples illustrate this hypocrisy.

In the 2000s, AIG, one of the largest insurers in the country, repeatedly attacked the life settlement industry even as it was purchasing huge quantities of policies on the market through its secretly financed Coventry fund. By the time AIG was bailed out by the government in 2008, it controlled approximately 40% of the life settlement market worldwide.

On a different note, *The Wall Street Tribune* obtained a copy of a document prepared by the Manhattan public relations firm Vox Dei for the Society of Life Settlement Professionals (SLSP). This report, entitled *Life After Life*, "lays out various strategies to make the general public, and especially seniors, more comfortable with the idea of selling their insurance policies."

The first section, *Understanding Misgivings in Order to Overcome Them*, presents the results of a series of focus groups conducted by Vox Dei's consultants. After listing the myths and clichés associated with life settlement transactions, the authors evaluate the reputational damage caused by the repeated scandals that have rattled the industry.

The second section, *Elements of Language*, suggests a few semantic adjustments. The term "pass away" is declared preferable to "die" ("too brutal"), to "maturity" ("too technical") and to "liquidity event" ("too obscure"). The preliminary medical exam becomes a "check-up," and the act of transfer, a turn of phrase considered ambiguous by some seniors who think they still own the policy, is called a "bill of sale."

The third section, *New Horizons*, introduces several themes powerful enough to energize a global communications campaign. Among the proposed slogans: "Who knew you were so rich?", "You can't take it with you," and "Isn't it time you thought about yourself?"

Life settlement funds, which have an answer to all legal and economic arguments, rarely feel the need to justify themselves on philosophical grounds, and with good reason — their opponents (religious organizations, ethical societies, et al.) have insufficient resources to hire lobbyists.

Luke Coleman, president of Christians Against Death Betting, laments: "Once a year, the SLSP's head of communications agrees to meet with us. Her message is always the same: 'We understand that you don't like this market. Nobody is forcing you to partake in it.' "

Write to Vlad Eisinger: vlad.eisinger@wst.com
Next week: *Are Life Settlements Useful? Are They Moral?*

Dan's journal

Tuesday, July 31

Seeing a crook get knocked off his pedestal is a delight in itself — but two in the same week! In a handful of paragraphs, Vlad's article delivered the *coup de grâce* to both Chuck Patterson and Michael Hart.

We knew that Uncle Chuck cheated his clients by selling them contracts they didn't need and pocketing ginormous commissions on policies that would lapse after a couple of years. Now we find out that he was underhandedly buying back the insurance of grannies, pulling a fast one on his employer. The man has no shame!

I naively expected Patterson to lay low today. Far from it. Although he hates gardening, he spent the entire afternoon pruning his rose bushes with a smile on his face, as if daring anyone to ask him for an explanation. I hope for his sake that he has clients outside Destin Terrace because his career here is as good as over.

Hart has even less panache. He still hasn't shown any sign of life. According to Phelps, the Republican Committee will meet next week to rule on his nomination for the upcoming elections. I wouldn't pin much hope on his chances.

Phelps expressed his gratitude for my help in the call for bids won by his daughter.

"Thanks to you, we're going to save $9,000 per year. That's almost $40 per household."

Shocked by the size of the amount, I asked Phelps how he accounted for such a gap.

"Well, for starters, Kim agreed to a huge dent on her commission. But mostly we played with the coverage. That money-grubbing Patterson had us insured against anything and everything — earthquakes, radioactive clouds, killer bee invasions, etc. We kept the insurance for the most common risks — hurricanes, tsunamis, fires — and dropped everything else."

(…)

A new rumor is making the rounds: the reason Jennifer Hansen has yet to receive her check is that Marc allegedly lied when he purchased his policy. He stated that he had never smoked so that he would qualify for a lower rate. Apparently, Emerald has unearthed several photos on Facebook, showing him puffing away. Mrs. Cunningham says Jennifer claims she never saw the medical evaluation form. Now the case is said to be in the hands of Emerald's "mediation" department, headed, if I'm not mistaken, by one of our neighbors.

(...)

Praise the Lord for allowing me to be in the right place at the right time! Here is the scene I just witnessed.

I was strolling around on the beach around 10:00 P.M., when I glimpsed of a silhouette crouching in the bushes, not far from Big Bobby's blockhouse. Pretending I hadn't noticed anything, I lay down facing the sea, spying on that scallywag out of the corner of an eye. Dressed in camouflage gear and wearing dark face paint, he was surveying through binoculars the comings and goings of the security guards as they crisscrossed the terrace, Tommy guns over their shoulders. The moment the gorillas had their backs to him, he made his move and came out of his hiding place on all fours. The light of the moon briefly illuminated his face. Imagine my surprise when I realized that this Rambo wannabe was none other than the one and only Lammons! I should probably have sounded the alarm (he may well have been planning to murder Babbitt), but my curiosity got the better of me.

Sylvester Lammons crawled like a lizard toward the shed where Babbitt stores his beach equipment. When he reached his destination, he inspected the surroundings for a long while. He must have thought I was asleep because he pulled a bolt cutter from underneath his jacket and proceeded to sever the padlock on the door, making a barely audible clack. One last look around, and he slipped into the shed, pulling the door shut behind him.

About thirty seconds went by, during which I tried to imagine what treasures — diamonds, gold bars, sentimental relics — Babbitt's shed was housing that would prompt such an expedition. Suddenly, I had a revelation: Big Bobby must have built a secret passageway between the house and the beach, in anticipation of the day when the police would come to arrest him. Chuck Norris Lammons had learned about it, and was at this very moment demanding that Babbitt compensate him for his losses, lest he see his dirty little secret revealed.

I was so certain that I walked to the shed and abruptly opened the door, expecting to find stairs disappearing deep down into the bowels of the

Earth.

Lammons started like a teenager caught with his wiener in one hand and *Playboy Magazine* in the other. Speaking of bowels, he was squatting, pants around the ankles, in a position that left little doubt as to his intentions. I just had time, while he was finishing dropping his load, to pull out my phone and capture this Kodak moment for eternity. Lammons jumped, pulled his pants back halfway up his ass, and scurried off like a bunny rabbit, chased by the Spanish curses of Big Bobby's bodyguards.

Wednesday, August 1

My work is moving along well. Broch's and Perutz' Wikipedia pages now both contain this paragraph.

The recent works of a group of German-speaking academics, led by Professor Thorsten Böhm, are suggesting that Hermann Broch and Leo Perutz are half-brothers — a theory that has yet to be verified. According to Böhm, Perutz' father had an extramarital affair with Johanna Schnabel-Broch in 1886, during a trade fair in Berlin. Perutz informed Broch of this in 1926, in a meeting arranged by their common friend, Franz Blei. Inspired by the example of his older brother, Broch put the family business for sale to fully devote himself to literature and to scientific studies. The two men are believed never to have met again, for fear of arousing the suspicion of Ida, Perutz' very religious spouse.

*****

From: Dan Siver <danielgsiver@gmail.com>
Date: Wednesday, August 1, 2012 10:27 P.M.
To: Vlad Eisinger <vlad.eisinger@wst.com>
Subject: In praise of Frances Gray

Really, after Ray Wiggin, I'm starting to believe that you've ignored **the most fascinating** personalities in our community. I just left Frances Gray, whom you quoted in your third article. It so happens that Jennifer Hansen, one of my neighbors you must not have met, recently lost her husband. He had taken out a $500,000 policy with Emerald, but had apparently omitted to indicate that he had smoked in his youth. It's now up to the mediation committee, chaired by Mrs. Gray, to determine whether his widow will receive the indemnity.

In a surge of altruism that may surprise you, I had planned on speaking in favor of my neighbor, who, I'm sure, knew nothing of her husband's deceit. Mrs. Gray stopped me the moment she understood the purpose of my visit.

"If I listen to you, you'll have no choice but to appear before the committee, since we must all have the same information."

Even so, she invited me to come in.

Have you ever found yourself in the presence of grace? That's how I felt as I listened to Frances Gray describe her profession. The woman oozes virtue from every pore — not that sickening and moralistic self-righteousness that has become the hallmark of our leaders, but rather a genuine goodness, rooted in virtually superhuman courage and empathy.

She and her team are responsible for resolving cases unforeseen by the law, such as those in which Emerald's employees have infringed on internal rules and regulations, and those likely to create a legal precedent. With every case, she attempts to unravel a tangled skein so as to uncover, beyond contingencies and inevitable similarities, what makes such a situation unique and therefore worthy of being heard. During this examination phase, which can take anywhere from an hour to a few weeks, she puts herself in the places of four different parties — the client, the employee who handled the case, the other clients, and, finally, Emerald's shareholders.

"Being able to consider those four angles one by one is within anybody's reach," she asserted. "The challenge lies in embracing them all at once. When I finally accomplish that, both the truth of the case and the appropriate decision become obvious."

She illustrated her story with countless anecdotes. One in particular made quite an impression.

Some years ago, Emerald refused to honor the payment of a $5m indemnity, on the ground that the policy had lapsed three weeks earlier. And for good reason — the day the annual bill had landed in her mailbox, the insured was in a coma as a result of a car accident. She succumbed to her injuries two months later, without ever regaining consciousness. The Emerald employee explained to the deceased's husband that, under Florida law, he should have petitioned the local court for guardianship. The judge would have then notified Emerald, which would have automatically granted the family a deferral of payment.

According to Mrs. Gray, Emerald's stance was legally ironclad. The policy had indeed lapsed, and the husband of the deceased hadn't complied with the state laws governing his contract. One might even argue that by neglecting to put his wife under guardianship, he had failed in his duty to behave, in the legislator's words, like a "good family man" — that last stipulation virtually eliminating the widower's chances of winning in court.

Nonetheless, Frances Gray authorized the payment of the indemnity.

"That was the right thing to do," she explained. "For two months, the husband had set up camp at his wife's bedside. He would sing lullabies to her, massage her feet, brush her hair; the nurses at the hospital had never seen anything like it. Had I even begun to suggest that this man wasn't a good family man, they would have scratched my eyes out."

"Given the amount, I had to present my decision to Emerald's board members. None protested. I insisted that a $2,000 bonus should be awarded to the employee who had frozen the payment of the indemnity. She had shown an exemplary rigor in her handling of the case; yet her written communications were models of humanity."

You have no idea how impressed I am with this woman, Vlad. To hear her describe it, her job isn't even difficult.

"Truth reveals itself to anyone who really wants to see it. All of us have a small, nearly inaudible, internal voice that drives us to heroism. Unfortunately, our interests scream so loud that our inner voice is easy to ignore."

I quoted a sentence from Renoir in *The Rules of the Game*: "The truly terrible thing in this world, is that everyone has their reasons." That seemed to resonate with her.

"Everyone does have reasons," she pensively agreed. "Unfortunately they're almost always bad ones."

*****

From: Dan Siver <danielgsiver@gmail.com>
Date: Thursday, August 2, 2012 1:42 A.M.
To: Vlad Eisinger <vlad.eisinger@wst.com>
Subject: Panegyric of Frances Gray

I can't sleep. I'm obsessed with Frances Gray. Dear God, what a charismatic woman!

As she spoke, I was trying to remember where I had already seen that fervent expression in someone's eyes, at once gentle **and unwavering**. I just figured it out: among the great resistance fighters — Mandela, Aung San Suu Kyi, Martin Luther King — those exceptional humans who stare truth in the face and are impervious to doubt, fear, flattery, or money.

Since we're on the subject of money, how about this: Frances Gray lives alone in a one-bedroom condo with low ceilings and windows that overlook the clubhouse's parking lot. She probably earns in a year what Lammons rakes in every month, and Matthew Fin, Emerald's big boss, every week. I know Gandhi was so poor he used to cut his saris out of his bedsheets (or is it the other way around?), but still…

OK, back to bed I go.

*****

From: Dan Siver <danielgsiver@gmail.com>
Date: Thursday, August 2, 2012 3:07 A.M.
To: Vlad Eisinger <vlad.eisinger@wst.com>
Subject: The other face of justice

I realized as I was tossing and turning in bed that I had left your last anagram unanswered. Pearl Lehr = Harper Lee, whose character Atticus Finch, a kind of Frances Gray from the Roosevelt era, did more for the prestige of the legal profession than all the public relations campaigns of the National Lawyers Association.

*****

From: Dan Siver <danielgsiver@gmail.com>
Date: Thursday, August 2, 2012 5:24 A.M.
To: Vlad Eisinger <vlad.eisinger@wst.com>
Subject: On the footsteps of Vlad Eisinger

All right, this night is shot.

I'm going to try, just for kicks, to transcribe my interview with Frances Gray, *Wall Street Tribune* style. I give myself 30 minutes and one pot of coffee.

In order to deal with situations lawmakers hadn't anticipated, most insurance companies have set up special committees in charge of assessing families' indemnity requests. Frances Gray, 48, a Destin Terrace resident since 2006, oversees the Emerald Life Committee, which handles about two hundred cases per year.

A testament to her independence, she reports directly to the president, and has no set objectives in terms of numbers or productivity. Her opinions are final and executory, and are scrutinized by observers with an intensity usually reserved for judgments of the Supreme Court.

"We're not serving the law; we're serving justice. That's very different," says Mrs. Gray. "I remember the case of a Jacksonville client who was claiming the $5m payment due upon the death of his spouse, even though the policy had expired. He explained that he had been too busy taking care of his wife, who had become comatose after a car accident, to think about paying the annual premium. Emerald's legal stance was ironclad. Yet, after checking with the hospital staff, we came to the conclusion that our client was sincere, and we authorized the payment in full."

What do you think? Wanna give me a job?

*****

From: Vlad Eisinger <vlad.eisinger@wst.com>
Date: Thursday, August 2, 2012 10:50 A.M.
To: Dan Siver <danielgsiver@gmail.com>
Subject: Corrections

Well, well, well, looks like someone had a long night...

It was indeed one of my regrets not to have been able to feature Mrs. Gray in more of a spotlight. I just couldn't find room for her — perhaps because she's first and foremost a fiction character.

A few comments on your prose.

You should have written, "*A testament to her independence, Mrs. Gray reports directly to the president,*" instead of, "*A testament to her independence, she reports directly to the president.*" You never begin a paragraph with a personal pronoun.

To which president is she reporting? The President of the United States? That of the Rotary Club? You should have specified "*to Emerald's president.*" I assume you wished to avoid the repetition, since you had mentioned "*the Emerald Life Committee*" in the preceding paragraph. In this line of work, you'll sooner be forgiven for lack for elegance than for imprecision.

In the next paragraph, you'd be better off replacing *"I remember the case of a Jacksonville client"* with *"A Jacksonville client"* — it's crisper. As a general rule, avoid piling up relative clauses.

Finally, my chief editor would never have let me get away with *"Her opinions are final and executory, and are scrutinized by observers with an intensity usually reserved for judgments of the Supreme Court."* Too pompous — and incidentally, untrue.

P.S.: Seems you're leaving me hanging. Here's another one, anyway: Corina Pinslut.

*****

From: Dan Siver <danielgsiver@gmail.com>
Date: Thursday, August 2, 2012 11:19 A.M.
To: Vlad Eisinger <vlad.eisinger@wst.com>
Subject: Corrections? You must be joking.

Duly noted, Obersturmführer Eisinger. I'm going to start reading the *AP Stylebook* in the john.

You reacted as I expected: by criticizing style rather than content. If I were to incorporate your changes, my text might be factually and syntactically correct, but it wouldn't be true.

The problem, Vlad, is you can't **nail** a character like Frances Gray in 150 words. You'd have to **convey** how thoroughly she investigates her cases (Brian Hess told me she sometimes calls him on weekends to inquire whether it's possible for an insured not to be aware of his or her state of health), how much she dreads committing an injustice, and how utterly incorruptible she is.

P.S.: Like you, I could never stand that yawn of Upton Sinclair. I'm guessing, you're not a fan of Brett Forros.

*****

From: Vlad Eisinger <vlad.eisinger@wst.com>
Date: Thursday, August 2, 2012 11:22 A.M.
To: Dan Siver <danielgsiver@gmail.com>
Subject: Poetic license

Why do you say that you can't nail a character like Frances Gray in 150 words? To me, the number of words is less relevant than the register from which you draw them. I don't have your freedom, pal. For better or for worse, my employer won't allow me to write that an insurance mediator has an Aung San Suu Kyi sparkle in her eyes, or that some hubby massaged the toes of his wife as she lay in her hospital bed. I don't think such limitations detract from my integrity.

P.S.: And stop insinuating that I'm impervious to the beauty of our language — I love Robert Frost (not to mention his four Pulitzer Prizes!). Are you still reading Arno Della Page?

*****

From: Dan Siver <danielgsiver@gmail.com>
Date: Thursday, August 2, 2012 11:37 A.M.
To: Vlad Eisinger <vlad.eisinger@wst.com>
Subject: Poe

Edgar Allan Poe is too important to be relegated to a postscript. Yes, I still read him. I believe I can even say that I always will. *The Purloined Letter* is one of the greatest literary works. Think of its richness of themes — Dupin, who solves the enigma put forth by G. without leaving his armchair; the truth that is never as well-hidden as when presented in broad daylight; the dialectic of the hunter and the hunted; the suggested brotherhood between Dupin and Minister D. I would give *everything* (and I say this all the more willingly as I own *nothing*) to have written a text of that caliber.

Back to Frances Gray. Who's going to talk about her, Vlad? Or about Ray Wiggin? You said it yourself: there's no room for them in the *Wall Street Tribune*. But ask yourself — and I'm serious —what will readers take away from your articles? That insurance agents are crooks? That politicians sell themselves to the highest bidder? As if they didn't know all that already…

They'll fold up their papers, confirmed in their prejudices. Their life won't have been changed; at most they'll be a little more circumspect about paying their insurance premiums on time.

*****

From: Vlad Eisinger <vlad.eisinger@wst.com>
Date: Thursday, August 2, 2012 11:40 A.M.
To: Dan Siver <danielgsiver@gmail.com>
Subject: And what about the stock market?

I agree with you, about Poe and the rest of it. I'd love to write a story about Ray Wiggin. But I can already hear my boss: "Jeez, Vlad, do you really think our subscribers pay $200 a year to read about some dimwit who fiddles around with obits in his kitchen?" Last I heard, the *Wall Street Tribune* was still a financial newspaper.

*****

From: Dan Siver <danielgsiver@gmail.com>
Date: Thursday, August 2, 2012 12:12 P.M.
To: Vlad Eisinger <vlad.eisinger@wst.com>
Subject: A platform for the nobodies

Listen Vlad, I'm going to make a painful confession: I enjoy your articles. Last Tuesday, I even snatched Lammons' copy from his doorstep. Your series introduced me to a brave new world! I now look at my neighbors differently. For example, I notice that Kimberly wears shorter skirts when she has an appointment with Manuel; that Sharon Hess doesn't offer receipts; and that Susan McGregor drives a car that is newer and fancier than her husband's.

I think I understand the point you're trying to make: all of us, including you, pursue our individual interests. You probably covet your boss's job, while I wouldn't mind selling a few more books, despite my tirades about the artist's independence. Your demonstration is convincing, if narrow. Lammons interests you because he made a bad investment; yet, for a novelist, he's a gift from above. (Two days ago, I caught him in the act of taking a crap in front of Big Bobby's house!). By reducing your characters to their financial dimensions, you're making the same mistake as Mrs. Cunningham, who'd rather believe that her daughter is hankering after her money than admit she might simply be terrified at the thought of losing her mother. As for individuals with no economic role, you dismiss them entirely, despite the fact that they are generally the most colorful, the most amiable, in a word, the most human.

You see, Vlad, Ray Wiggin and Frances Gray don't give a hoot about money. They may never even have read the *Wall Street Tribune*. Yet, in their own way, each of them is a hero on a quest for the Grail. And because no one's told them their goal is unattainable, they'll probably come closer to it than anyone else.

*****

From: Vlad Eisinger <vlad.eisinger@wst.com>
Date: Thursday, August 2, 2012 12:56 P.M.
To: Dan Siver <danielgsiver@gmail.com>
Subject: Olive branch

You're right.
Every day we devote one front-page article to a topic that is somewhat offbeat and non-financial. I'll talk to my boss, and offer to do a paper on Wiggin.

*****

Dan's journal

Friday, August 3
Julia plans to arrive on Sunday afternoon. Excellent.
(...)
I dropped by the Hesses' house earlier to return Sharon's crutches. For a change, Brian was having lunch with his wife in the kitchen (he usually takes his meals at his desk to enhance productivity). While he was preparing himself a tuna sandwich, I couldn't help but ask if he'd received a visit from

Mrs. Cunningham. He seemed reluctant to betray a confidence. Luckily, Sharon doesn't share his scruples.

Our three stooges have concocted a flawless little scheme: Brian will evaluate Mrs. Cunningham's life expectancy, and she, in return, will call on Sharon every time she needs the services of a nurse (which, knowing her, is likely to happen quite often).

Brian sought my approval, looking rather embarrassed.

"What do you think, Dan? Everybody wins, right?"

"Everybody except for Mrs. Cunningham's insurer," I answered. "Which company boasts the privilege?"

Sharon broke into a malicious grin. My question couldn't have pleased her more.

"Those Emerald bastards, the same ones who refused to insure Brian after his accident. That'll teach them to dump their clients the moment the going gets tough."

I was speechless. "Brian's accident?" The only accident I could recall was that of the poor woman who, because of her ob-gyn's professional negligence, had given birth to a handicapped child. As for Emerald allegedly having terminated Brian's contract, that, too, was inaccurate — the company had only raised his premium, taking into consideration the seven-digit indemnity that they had just paid to one of his patients.

I should have said something. I should have explained all that, and added that by signing his name to some phony report, Brian was further disrupting the financial markets, thereby hastening our collective demise. I could clearly hear my heroic inner voice, whose existence Frances Gray had revealed to me thirty-six hours earlier. It was begging me to enter the arena, don the armor of truth, and pounce on falsehood, as convenient and widespread as it might be.

But I couldn't. Was I afraid that Sharon would turn her wrath on me? Worried about telling Brian to his face that he'd been the victim of a misfortune but certainly not of an injustice? Scared of looking like an even bigger fool in Mrs. Cunningham's eyes? Maybe, but that's no excuse — I betrayed Frances Gray, as surely as Peter, in his era, denied Jesus.

(...)

Can't concentrate on *Camelia*. I keep thinking about the investor who will buy Mrs. Cunningham's policy based on Brian's report, and about Kim Phelps, who's unknowingly about to play a part in this farce. What a disgrace.

(...)

I called Jean-Michel Jacques to ask him how he was doing. He cheerfully invited me to come by his office. I convinced myself to abbreviate my afternoon session, which had yielded a grand total of 140 words, in favor of buying some groceries from Publix in anticipation of Julia's arrival.

Jean-Michel was perky as can be. His operation went without a hitch. The surgeon thinks he removed the entire tumor.

"So no chemo for now. Samson can keep his mane!" he said joyfully, pulling on all three of his stringy hairs. "That's not all. I received a phone call from my doctor this morning with additional good news: the test results are excellent. And just like that, my five-year survival rate shoots up to 90%, barely less than if I'd started bungee jumping! I gave Anh a goodbye kiss, left for the office, and guess what I found waiting for me here: three maturities! It's just one of those days, I guess!"

An empty bottle of champagne was sticking out of the trash can. I'm afraid I know which of those good tidings it helped him to celebrate.

Taking advantage of his euphoria, I asked him a question that had been nagging me: how did he pay of his surgery? My curiosity didn't seem to bother him in the least, although he did shut the door to his office.

"Susan McGregor lent me $50,000."

"I didn't know you were that close," I said, before remembering that Susan works for him. If anyone had better hope that Jean-Michel makes it, it's Susan.

My Belgian friend must have read my ratiocinations, for he clarified: "We drew up a proper contract — I pay Susan a standard interest rate, I give her my apartment as collateral, and we've agreed to settle any future differences through mediation. Would she have lent me the money if I weren't her boss? Probably not. But that doesn't make our agreement a bad one."

"And what's Jeffrey's take on all this?"

Jean-Michel shrugged.

"You'll have to ask him. I made a deal with Susan, not with the McGregor family. But every cloud has a silver lining: this predicament gave me an idea for a new product for Osiris. Instead of buying the policies of old or sick people at the end of their lives, we'll lend them money at a substantial interest rate, using their life-insurance policy as collateral. This way, we'll win no matter what: if the client stops paying us back, we'll seize his policy and carry it to term. I'm meeting with ad agencies on Monday."

Jokingly, I blurted out, "At Osiris, pay us back after you're dead!"

Jean-Michel froze and stared at me.

"Hold on a second, Dan. Did you just come up with that? It's absolutely perfect! To think I was about to shell out $50,000 to some agency! Here, I offer you $10,000 for your slogan."

"I couldn't, really. Consider it a gift."

"The real gift is the $40,000 you just saved me. Seriously, Dan, I insist."

"We'll see," I answered, suddenly rather embarrassed.

"It's a done deal," Jean-Michel exclaimed. "At Osiris, pay us back after you're dead! What a find!"

I then asked him about my moral dilemma: should I dissuade Mrs. Cunningham and Brian Hess from implementing their plan? Jean-Michel was tickled by my anguish.

"Didn't I tell you that whole field was rotten to the core! I love your story — everyone's looking after their own wallet, all the while acting like moral exemplars.

"Mrs. Cunningham sincerely believes that the percentage of Kim's commission leaves her no choice but to exaggerate the seriousness of her illness. Hess is willing to skew his professional opinion for a few hundred dollars, because he blames Emerald for the shutdown of his office. Sharon intends to pad her invoices in the name of marital solidarity. Finally, little Kim Phelps will rely on Brian Hess's report, pretending not to know it's bogus."

"Exactly. Shouldn't I blow the whistle?"

"Whom are you trying to protect? A Lammons who buys policies at random, without doing his homework as an investor? Insurance companies who squander half of their clients' premiums in operating costs? No, really, Dan, leave these fools to their diddling."

I asked him how he survives in this wicked world.

"It's very simple," he answered. "I don't trust anyone. Not the insured clients who, like Mark Hansen, brazenly lie; and not the intermediaries who care about nothing but maximizing their commissions. I rely solely on facts, statistics, and test results. If a policyholder claims to be sick, I ask for a copy of his doctor's prescriptions, or, even better, of his pharmacist's bills. And if I'm still not convinced, I assess his policy as if he were in good health. Too bad if he takes his business elsewhere. There are enough honest people around not to deal with thieves."

*****

From: Ulrike Richter <urichter@princeton.edu>
Date: Saturday, August 4, 2012 03:55 P.M.
To: Thorsten Böhm <t.bohm@gmail.com>
Subject: Danke!

Dear Thorsten,

Congratulations on your extraordinary publication tracing the kinship between Hermann Broch and Leo Perutz. I've taught Austrian humanities at Princeton University since 2004, and I can't remember any other contribution shedding such radically new light on the literary landscape of the Viennese interwar years. Broch is one of my favorite authors — if you're not familiar with my works, I invite you to browse the articles I've written about *The Death of Virgil*, on Princeton's website). I've always considered his Broch's appearance in literature at once late and sudden, an enigma that I think you may well have just solved.

I regret that our paths have never crossed. Did you attend Andreas Krüger's colloquium in Heidelberg? I couldn't find your name in the members directory of the German Literary Society. The dues are admittedly a bit high, but, in my opinion, fully justified by the quality of our debates. I would be happy, if you were so inclined, to sponsor your application.

I now come to the true purpose of my message. With the help of a female colleague from Yale, I'm organizing a seminar next spring on the birth of the modern novel. We would be delighted if you could come and present your research on Broch and Perutz, which, unless I'm mistaken, has yet to be the topic of an official lecture. We would, of course, cover your hotel and travel expenses (in business class). I might even be able, without getting too far ahead of myself, to offer you a speaker's fee of $5,000.

I hope you'll consider my proposition as the starting point of a fruitful cooperation. In the meantime, please allow me to reiterate my gratitude, as well as that of all my colleagues at the Princeton German department.

Ulrike

P.S.: I would have liked to write you in the language of Goethe. Unfortunately, even though my parents are German, I was raised in the United States, where English quickly became my dominant language. I wouldn't dare inflict my imperfect syntax upon an eminent Germanist.
Mit freundlichen Grüssen.

*****

From: Thorsten Böhm <t.bohm@gmail.com>
Date: Sunday, August 5, 2012 09:33 A.M.
To: Ulrike Richter <urichter@princeton.edu>
Subject: Your generous invitation

Dear Fräulein Richter,

Please believe me when I tell you that your message pleased me ever so much more because it was written in English! The opportunities to speak and to write in the language I so love are few and far between in Copenhagen, which explains the mistakes that will sprinkle my emails and for which I pray in advance for your forgiveness.

Your appreciation of my work is extravagantly flattering. For a pair of years I have been working on a book about Franz Blei, a superb mind unjustly forgotten, to whom his friend Kafka didn't do a favor by declaring that he was infinitely more intelligent than his books. I was peeling off Blei's correspondence, when a letter from Perutz captured my eye. I had no problem reconstituting the entire story whole, with the help of the article's co-signers, and especially that of Ericka Kirchenmeister who displayed her characteristic candor and spirit.

I wish I could have been present at Heidelberg, if only for the pleasure of attending your presentation on Musil. I don't travel as much as I should like, thanks to our institution's tight budget. My mentor, Doktor Eisinger, advises me to lift my nose from my books and to promote my work harder. That is why I fanatically accept your generous invitation to the United States. You will signal me the dates of the seminar at the suitable moment, will you not?

With cordiality,

Thorsten

*****

Dan's journal

Sunday, August 5

Phew, I nearly made a boo-boo. Last night, I was about to send Ulrike Richter my reply, when it dawned on me that it was four o'clock in the morning in Copenhagen. Workaholic as Thorsten Böhm may be, he shouldn't appear to have been carried away…

If my German weren't so rusty, I would gladly make the trip to Princeton. But I seem to recall that Vlad is virtually bilingual, as he used to speak German with his grandparents. He would make a far more credible Böhm than I. Besides, given his profession, butchering the English language should be a cakewalk for him. And we could split the five grand!

I must admit I wasn't expecting such a rapid reaction. I looked up Fräulein Richter's biography on the Princeton website. Thirty-four years old, *summa cum laude*, a Ph.D. from the University of Pennsylvania, several significant publications in journals of international standing, conquering chest, predatory smile — I'm obviously dealing with the killer queen bee.

In any case, the subterfuge in her email couldn't be more transparent. Why didn't she simply write:

Dear Thorsten,

I can't believe you managed to shed light on the family relationship between Broch and Perutz before I did. Since when do impecunious hicks supplant Princeton wunderkinds?

But enough with the chitchat, I've got a deal for you. You have Blei's correspondence, we have the cash. How about $5,000 to show your face at my colloquium? I might be able to stretch it to $10,000 if you let me co-sign your next article. We'd make one hell of a duo, you and I — have you seen my steely eyes and gargantuan breasts?

Ulrike

P.S.: I should have listened to my mother when she insisted I go spend the summer at her sister's in Mainz! I look like an utter fool, writing in English about Kafka and Musil. Scheisse!

I checked the mailboxes I created for Böhm's four sidekicks. They're empty. That makes sense: it's better to talk to the organ-grinder than to his monkey.

*****

From: Ulrike Richter <urichter89@gmail.com>
Date: Sunday, August 5, 2012 11:16 A.M.
To: Thorsten Böhm <t.bohm@gmail.com>
Subject: Hooray!

Dear Thorsten,

Wonderful! As soon as we set the dates, I'll let you know. You might wish to arrive a few days early. We could get to know each other better, and see how we could work together in the future.
Tschüss!
Ulrike

*****

Dan's journal

Sunday, August 5
I told Julia the whole story tonight over a bottle of wine. Ulrike's emails proved highly entertaining to her. She pointed out that my pen pal had changed addresses between her two messages.

"She's trying to move your relationship to a more personal level. Her choice of salutations is another telltale sign. 'Tschüss' means 'See ya,' doesn't it? What does she look like?"

I showed her the photograph on the Princeton website. My niece whistled in appreciation.

"Fine specimen — have you looked up her Facebook page?"

I hadn't even thought about that. Julia took control of the computer.

She found Richter in the blink of an eye.

"Status: single — what a surprise! Interested in men — you don't say! Born on August 9 — that's next week, isn't it? Five hundred and fifty friends — about average. Do you know any of them?"

I scrolled down the list. Lots of German names, among which I recognized a few Broch specialists whom I had quoted in Böhm's article.

"All right," said Julia, "I don't think we have much of a choice. We have to create a profile for Thorsten. Wanna help?"

We spent the evening doing just that. I gave my opinion on certain sections; Julia unilaterally filled out the others. Thorsten Böhm was born in Kiel on August 9, 1977 — two years to the day before Ulrike (Julia's idea). He grew up in Lübeck, studied German literature at the University of Hamburg, and spent one semester as an exchange student at the Scuola Normale Superiore in Pisa. He's been teaching at the Institute of German Studies in Copenhagen since 2009.

Agreeing on a suitable photograph wasn't so simple. I was in favor of sticking to the portrait of that Columbian rubber plantation owner, or possibly using Vlad's picture, since he'll be the one showing up at Princeton next year. Julia wouldn't hear of it. She feared Ulrike might not fall for Vlad's rugged charm (which I took as a quasi-personal offense, given the uncanny resemblance he and I share). Instead, she convinced me to use an androgynous charcoal drawing by Schiele, which leaves room for doubt about our buddy's sexual orientation.

As Thorsten began to take shape before us, I realized the madness of our plan.

"This is crazy," I said. "How do you explain that he's never posted anything until today?"

Julia told me that many Facebook members are inactive.

"What would be really odd would be for him not to have any friends. But we're not about to let that happen."

She sent a few messages from her cell phone. In less than 30 minutes, Thorsten had about 20 connections in Europe and the United States.

Perplexed, I asked Julia if her friends didn't mind opening their networks to someone they'd never met.

"Do you really believe Ulrike has 500 friends?" she retorted. "I personally accept everybody, provided their profile picture isn't too ridiculous."

It was almost midnight. I opened a second bottle of Malbec, aware that I'd regret it later, but I could vaguely sense there was an important lesson latent in our experiment.

"Give me the name of Thorsten's compadres," said Julia. "We're going to create pages for them too."

Leaning back in my chair, wine glass in hand, I admiringly watched my niece go from one window to the next, copy email addresses, paste passwords, expeditiously select pictures from galleries filled with millions of portraits. Obviously, for her, and most likely for the rest of her generation, the boundary between real and virtual doesn't exist. Paolita Dampieri, whom she knows sprang from her uncle Dan's imagination, is no less alive in her eyes than Elena Lombardi, an Italian from Boston whose daily Facebook feed she's been following for months, even though she can't exactly remember where, when, or even if she's met her.

"Done," Julia finally said, shutting her laptop. "They're all friends with one another. That's a start. Tomorrow, we'll expand their networks."

Monday, August 6

Slept very badly. Jean-Michel's offer of $10,000 is making my head spin.

Ten thousand dollars! The equivalent of 22,000 books sold — enough to replace the stucco on the house and purchase a second-hand scooter. And for what? For a three-second quip, seven words placed one after another, some lame one-liner any average Joe could have come up with?

But let's return to the matter of principle, before the size of the amount irreparably clouds my judgment.

An initial question arises: why did I instinctively turn down Jean-Michel's offer?

That an idea should be remunerated according to its immediate profitability doesn't shock me any more than the custom of compensating an athlete in proportion to the advertising revenues he generates, or that an entrepreneur's reward should reflect his contribution to the community. If I save Jean-Michel $50,000, one could arguably claim that I deserve half, or even two thirds, of that amount.

In hindsight, it seems obvious I had qualms about accepting money from a friend. That doesn't make much sense. After all, Jean-Michel would gladly pay $10,000 to a copywriter he doesn't know from Adam, so why shouldn't he compensate his neighbor for the same work, regardless of whether he enjoys his company?

No, the truth — and it's about time I face it — is that Jean-Michel's profession unsettles me. I wouldn't be so ambivalent if he were selling cruises or orthopedic inserts. I'm sheepishly realizing that I don't really have an opinion on life settlement. Vlad presents the facts, but conveniently refrains from judging. Much like all the *Wall Street Tribune* readers I guess, I've experienced contradictory emotions over the course of his articles — disbelief, amusement, indignation, jubilation, disgust — which were further heightened by Mark Hansen's death and Mrs. Cunningham's illness. Never have I been better informed, yet never have I felt so little qualified to rule on an industry simultaneously capable of saving the life of a Bruce Webb and engendering a Bobby Babbitt, of giving the power back to the insured and leading to the monstrosities of premium finance.

Is life settlement moral? I hope Vlad will answer that question in tomorrow's article.

(...)

I took a long walk on the beach with Julia this morning. She told me about how Rebecca and Edwin are faring. We mainly spoke about her imminent enrollment at Columbia, where, by her own admission, she's about to spend a quarter million dollars, without having the faintest idea of what she will do afterward. I marveled at her lucidity; I don't remember ever thinking about it in those terms. For the first time, facing the turquoise sea, I wondered whether my six years at Columbia had made me a better or worse writer. A poorer one, without the shadow of a doubt. An accomplished one? That remains to be seen.

Julia does hope to follow in my footsteps by becoming a novelist. I recommended she take Paxton and Caldwell's classes, in addition, of course, to Goodman's seminar on Poe. I was tempted to advise her to major in finance, land a well-paying job on Wall Street, and retire at forty, then seriously devote herself to writing. Destitution and literature don't make good bedfellows, probably because the gestation period for a novel exceeds that of a poem or a picture. Van Gogh revolutionized painting while living off of his brother; oddly enough, I can't imagine Proust undertaking to compose *In Search of Lost Time* with a student loan to repay.

For the first time since Emily left, I seriously discussed *Camelia Van Noren* with another person. I rediscovered the pleasure of telling a story while minding my timing and effects, of divulging my intentions to a receptive audience, and of sharing a particularly heartfelt scene. Julia listened attentively. She inquired about the sequence of events, laughed a lot, and rolled her eyes when one of the characters stepped over the line of what's tolerable. I could see that the complexity of my tale went a little over her head. That's understandable: at twenty, one hasn't learned to construct a novel.

Back at home, we connected to Facebook. Böhm received fifteen friend requests overnight. Next to that social animal, Mirafuentes, Dampieri, and especially Kühn, look like wallflowers. Thanks to her blonde highlights and plunging neckline, no doubt, Kirchenmeister has already attracted a horde of admirers.

Julia sent hundreds of invitations in their names, targeting in priority the Germanists of Ulrike Richter's network. Each positive response triggered a new wave of requests from our side, which had that much more chances of being accepted, Julia explained, now that both parties had acquaintances in common. Before the sun set, Lena Mirafuentes had acquired fourteen friends in her hometown of Buenos Aires alone, Klaus Kühn and Paolita Dampieri had joined a group of semiologists, all Luchino Visconti lovers, and Ericka Kirchenmeister had rejected the advances of a Schnitzler specialist.

It's my turn to feel out of my depth.

Week 7

Are Life Settlements Useful?
Are They Moral?

By Vlad Eisinger

The Wall Street Tribune, Tuesday, August 7, 2012

Over the past quarter-century, life settlement — the sale of an existing life insurance policy to a third party — has become an asset class of its own.

Does this demonstrate its economic utility? In other words, does it contribute to lifting the general welfare?

It's difficult to dispute that life settlement has improved the lot of policyholders. In the past, someone wishing to abandon a policy (either because they didn't need or could no longer afford the coverage) would simply let it lapse. If that person had overpaid during the initial years, the carrier would refund the policy's net cash position, known as its "surrender value".

Policyholders can now sell their contracts to whomever they please, after a waiting period of two to five years, depending on the state of jurisdiction. If their life expectancy appears relatively short, they can pocket a tidy sum.

As early as 2002, the Wharton Financial Institutions Center calculated that such sellers were earning an aggregate $240m annually.

The Life Insurance Settlement Association (LISA) claims on its website that the development of a secondary market for policies has freed up $8bn for seniors during the past four years. That's $7m per day, and approximately 700% more than the surrender value insurance carriers would have otherwise paid.

No serious study has been conducted to determine how sellers use this cash. Most of the professionals we talked to cite medical procedures (surgeries or treatments not covered by Medicare) and recreational activities, such as travels or cruises, as the primary motivations for such sales. Since the 2008 economic crisis, more and more seniors have also extended financial support to their children or grandchildren in difficulty.

By selling her policy, Cynthia Tucker, a retired school teacher from Columbus, Ohio, was able to save her house from foreclosure. "Realtors were circling my home like vultures. Now that I'm caught up with my mortgage, I hope they'll leave me alone."

This undeniable benefit has a less pleasant corollary: in order to maintain their profits, insurance companies raise premiums on the assumption that fewer policies will lapse.

Jeffrey McGregor, vice-president and chief actuary of Emerald Life, finds it only logical. "In a world with no life settlement, most of the policies acquired by investors would lapse, and no indemnity would be paid out. For us, this phenomenon generates a net loss for us, which we have no choice but to recoup from our customers."

Is increasing options for the few policyholders intent on selling their contracts worth higher rates for the overall population? The jury is still out.

Bruce Webb thinks so. In the 1980s, Mr. Webb auctioned his life insurance policy, as did thousands of other AIDS patients. With the $160,000 he netted, he was able to purchase drugs and receive heavy dental care.

"For some of my friends, selling their policies meant the difference between life and death," adds Mr. Webb. "Even those who didn't make it were grateful for the dignity it provided them."

Not everybody shares Mr. Webb's opinion. Adam Connor, spokesperson for the Life Insurance Alliance, views life insurance as an unparalleled planning tool, a natural supplement to Social Security pensions. "For as little as $30 per month, a 30-year-old head of the household can protect his loved ones with a bequest of half a million dollars, should he die before the age of 60. Widespread price hikes would deprive millions of their safety nets."

As for investors, at least those who haven't been the victims of swindles (see our July 24 article, *Why Life Settlements Are Rife With Fraud*), they have every reason to rejoice over the development of life settlement, as it is one of the few asset classes almost entirely decoupled from the economy. A portfolio made of a large enough number of policies is almost bound to rise steadily, without the usual bumps along the way.

Osiris Capital owns more than 6,000 policies. According to its president, Jean-Michel Jacques, the firm experiences four to five maturities per week, sometimes more in the winter. "When we have a slow month, I take solace in the fact that people have grown older and are a bit closer to death," Mr. Jacques says.

Institutional investors with a very long time horizon, such as pension funds or university endowments, value life settlement for its ability to offset, at leat partially, the fluctuations of stocks, bonds, and commodities in their portfolios.

The overall consensus is that, from an economic standpoint, life settlement is neither good nor bad : it just is.

Nathan Jacobson, professor of finance at the University of Chicago, sees little point in debating the utility of a market that has developed freely. "If life settlement transactions weren't useful, they would never have come about in the first place," he says.

Susan McGregor, vice-president of Osiris, couldn't agree more. "It's often said that the role of finance is to allocate capital across space and time. Products like life settlements or reverse mortgages clearly fit the second category."

The expansion of life settlement has ramifications that go beyond finance. It is, for instance, credited with enhancing the quality of life expectancy tables.

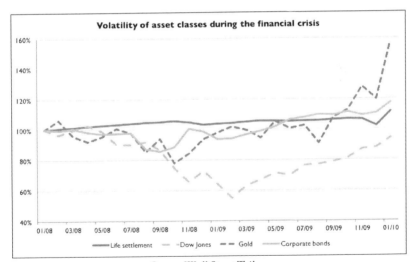

Source: Wall Street Tribune

In September 2008, 21st Services, the largest life expectancy advisory firm in the U.S., released new mortality tables that marked a significant departure from the figures published and regularly updated by the Society of Actuaries. The new data sent the small world of life settlement into a panic: it showed a significant increase in the life expectancy of healthy people, and a decrease in that of people with a serious medical condition.

Lawrence Johnson, professor at the Ross Business School of the University of Michigan, believes that better data benefit society as a whole, from public authorities to pharmaceutical companies (whose executives can decide where to allocate their research dollars), to — ironically — insurance carriers.

Jeffrey McGregor admits to having read 21st Services' report. "We, actuaries, revel in data. We can't get enough statistics," he jokes.

Once in a while, the mining of these statistics leads to discoveries in related fields, such as the dynamics of spousal survival. Many family doctors have noticed that elderly people often pass away shortly after the death of a spouse. Mr. Jacques has quantified this phenomenon with the help of mathematicians from the Massachusets Institute of Technology.

Jean-Michel Jacques

"I have since acquired hundreds of so-called 'last-survivor' policies (i.e. which pay an indemnity upon the death of the second spouse), recalls Mr. Jacques, who confesses he never would have looked into this matter without the lure of profit. "Making money for my investors while serving science: that's what I call a win-win!" he says.

However, the main criticisms of life settlement are of an ethical and moral nature.

Life settlement investors aren't alone in depending on death for their livelihood. So do coroners, undertakers, and gravediggers. The big difference is that these professionals don't hope for the death of a particular person. For them, any death will do.

In his recently published book, *What Money Can't Buy: The Moral Limits of Markets*, Michael J. Sandel, professor at Harvard University, dismisses the notion that trading life insurance policies is a business like any other.

"If it's morally comparable to life insurance, shouldn't it have the same rights to lobby on behalf of its interests? If insurance carriers can lobby for their interest in prolonging life (through mandatory seat belt laws or antismoking policies), shouldn't life settlement firms be allowed to lobby for their interest in hastening death (through reduced federal funding for AIDS or cancer research)?" Mr. Sandel asks.

"Life insurance has always been two things in one: a pooling of risk for mutual security, and a grim wager, a hedge against death. These two aspects coexist in uneasy combination. In the absence of ethical norms and legal restraints, the wagering aspect threatens to swamp the social purpose that justifies life insurance in the first place."

This duality is not new.

England, where the subscription of policies on the head of third parties had always been legal, reversed course in 1774, when it became apparent that bookmakers were using life insurance to bet on trials involving the death penalty. Interestingly, the bill that put an end to this practice is known both as the Assurance Act and the Gambling Act.

At about the same time, in France, jurist Jean-Etienne-Marie Portalis wrote: "Man is priceless: his life shouldn't be a matter of trade, nor his death the object or mercantile speculation. The greed that speculates on a citizen's lifespan is often only one remove from the crime that can shorten it."

In America, the life insurance industry faced fewer obstacles in its development. People started by insuring themselves, then their spouse, business partners, and even employees. In 1911, the Supreme Court confirmed once and for all the legality of a practice still forbidden or severely restricted in many other countries.

Today, life settlement has relatively few detractors in the U.S., other than insurance carriers, whose impartiality can hardly be trusted.

Luke Coleman, president of Christians Against Death Betting, blames this apathy on Wall Street's proverbial lack of interest in moral issues. "They think everything is for sale, including death. Alan Greenspan [former chairman of the Federal Reserve] sees no difference between speculating on the death of an elderly person and betting on the price of orange juice. I pity him."

According to Lawrence Johnson, life insurance is not the first financial product to have deviated from its original purpose.

"The commodity futures market, too, started as a simple idea. Oil companies would sell part of their production in advance in order to lock in a minimum price. Gas stations and airlines welcomed this opportunity to hedge against brutal price swings. But little by little, speculators have taken over this market, accounting for an ever greater share of transactions. Today, a barrel of oil changes hands dozens of times before being even extracted. Is it illegal? Of course not. Does this trading frenzy still benefit the original players? That's a good question."

Anita Cox, professor of ethics at the University of Notre Dame, finds no fault with the life settlement business, "as long as all parties are free and properly informed."

On the other hand, Ms. Cox lambastes companies who insure the lives of their employees without their consent. In a series of articles published in 2002, the *Wall Street Tribune* reported on the case of 29-year-old Felipe Tillmann. When Mr. Tillmann died of AIDS, his family didn't collect anything, but his employer, Camelot Music, pocketed $339,302.

In the 1990s, multinationals such as Nestlé, Procter & Gamble, and Walt Disney secretly insured thousands of their staff members, using Corporate-Owned Life Insurance (COLI) programs, also known in the industry as "janitor's insurance" or "dead peasant insurance".

Melvin Phelps is the president of the Destin Terrace Homeowners' Association. Until his retirement in 2009, he was vice-president of human resources at Bank of America, where, according to our estimates, he insured about 100,000 employees over the course of twelve years.

Mr. Phelps resents the term "janitor's insurance," which he finds derogatory. Employee consent is a non-issue for him. "We don't ask them to pay the premium, so why should we inform them of the insurance?"

In the 1990s, Wal-Mart took policies on the lives of about 350,000 workers. The death benefits, typically ranging from $50,000 to $500,000, were supposed to help the grocer recoup the cost of training the subsequently deceased employees.

According to recruitment specialist simplyhired.com, the annual salary of a greeter at Wal-Mart is about $14,000.

Wal-Mart would offer $5,000 of free coverage to employees in exchange for their written consent. The company claims that no more than 500 people rejected the offer.

Michael Sandel views janitor's insurance as a "morally corrosive practice. Creating conditions under which workers are worth more dead than alive objectifies them. It treats them as commodity futures rather than employees whose value to the company lies in the work they perform."

Wal-Mart stopped insuring its workforce in 2000. Other companies, such as Bank of America and JPMorgan Chase, still do so. According to a report compiled in May 2012 by consulting firm Michael White & Associates, banks currently hold life insurance policies with a combined face value of $143bn.

Mr. Jacques can't help but notice that, unlike the life settlement industry, the COLI market has developed with the blessing of insurance carriers, despite an apparent lack of moral justification. "I can understand why Disney would choose to insure their top executives. But the hot dog vendor in Orlando?"

What does Mr. Jacques say to those who call for banning life settlements?

"No market is reprehensible *per se*. There is no dirty business, only dirty ways of conducting business. A life insurance policy is a saving and estate-planning vehicle, just like a house or a 401(k). Why should it be the only asset that cannot be sold or tapped when the need arises?"

"Life settlement is yet another market that has been corrupted by Wall Street. Every day, I try to prove to my investors that it's possible to do my job in a way that is both respectful to the deceased and beneficial to society. However, there is a real risk that the inconsiderate acts of a few reckless individuals will destroy an entire industry, thereby reducing the financial options of millions of Americans."

Write to Vlad Eisinger : vlad.eisinger@wst.com

*****

Dan's journal

Tuesday, August 7

And to think I was counting on Vlad to answer my $10,000 question, I guess I'm on my own.

I still highlighted a few passages on Lammons's copy.

Nathan Jacobson, professor of finance at the University of Chicago, sees little point in debating the utility of a market that has developed freely. "If life settlement transactions weren't useful, they would never have come about in the first place," he says.

In other words, something that exists eludes judgment by the very fact of its existence. I'm no philosopher, but it seems we're bordering on circularity here.

And, of course, Jean-Michel's final words: *"No market is reprehensible* per se. *There is no dirty business, only dirty ways of conducting business."*

Although I'd like to believe him, I'm wary of that human tendency he himself warned me about: to call virtue what is nothing but our looking out for our own interests. Who can better judge the morality of the life settlement market? Those who, as active participants (Jean-Michel, Susan McGregor, Mrs. Cunningham, maybe me tomorrow), have an objective interest in its survival? Or those who demonize it and cover their ears when Bruce Webb explains that Bobby Babbitt saved his life.

I need to ponder all this.

*****

From: Dan Siver <danielgsiver@gmail.com>
Date: Tuesday, August 7, 2012 10:52 A.M.
To: Vlad Eisinger <vlad.eisinger@wst.com>
Subject: Bravo

Congratulations on your last article. *In cauda venenum*! Now I see why Melvin Phelps was trying to prevent its publication. Insuring the life of cleaning ladies in order to fatten up Bank of America's stockholders, that's pretty despicable...

You'll be happy to know that Michael Hart has decided not to run for

184

Congress. According to local papers, your revelations weighed heavily in the debates of the Republican campaign committee. That is a testament to the power of the press. Had I shouted from the rooftops that Hart is a scumbag, nobody would have listened to me; whereas you, a reporter on the *Wall Street Tribune*'s payroll, knocked him into oblivion in three paragraphs.

I still think it's a pity you don't write fiction. However, I now understand what you meant when you claimed that journalism offers a unique window on our times. I was thinking earlier about the way I would have treated the whole life settlement issue in a novel. I imagine I would have had to call on questionable experts, indulge in long, technical digressions, and bore my readers stiff with numbers and percentages. Perhaps with a topic such as this one, the journalistic approach is indeed the most effective.

*****

From: Vlad Eisinger <vlad.eisinger@wst.com>
Date: Tuesday, August 7, 2012 11:43 A.M.
To: Dan Siver <danielgsiver@gmail.com>
Subject: Thank you

Thanks for the compliments, old sport, too rare not to touch me deeply. I'm glad you recognize the merits of journalism — I'm not talking about rewriting news wires, but about true investigative journalism, which exposes lies and overthrows dictators. Yet I must confess that your initial criticism hit home. Your country club vignette, and your thoughts on Ray Wiggin and Frances Gray struck a chord with me. It's been so long since I've strayed from reality, I have no idea whether I'm still capable of imagination. My job is but a series of constraints… I can't write anything that hasn't been triple-checked. I'm sick of seeing my articles edited by lawyers or truncated to make room for IBM's quarterly results.

All this to say the time may have come for me to revisit my first love by reverting to what you've been doing for the past fifteen years.

P.S.: I had learned of Michael Hart's misadventures. I bet he won't sit in Tallahassee for much longer. The Florida Chamber was only a stepping-stone. Without the prospect of national office, he'll go back to practicing law, where he can exploit his knowledge of the inner workings of the legislature to promote amendments that will earn his clients millions.

*****

Dan's journal

Wednesday, August 8

Frances Gray delivered her verdict: Emerald will not honor the payment of the indemnity to Jennifer Hansen. The general terms and conditions were crystal-clear: lying in any form on the medical questionnaire voids the policy.

Mrs. Cunningham, who has kindly taken it upon herself to spread the news throughout our community, couldn't refrain from snide comments about Mark Hansen.

"If he was going to cheat, he should have stayed under the radar (*sic*). How dumb do you have to be to leave pictures floating around on the Internet…"

Unaccountably, I felt a need to comfort Jennifer. She showed me Emerald's letter. "*Feel free to contest this decision through the legal channels at your disposal. Please be aware, however, that on several occasions this case has consistently been decided in favor of the insurer.*" Enclosed with the letter was a check for $420, corresponding to the premiums Mark had paid before his death.

My attempts to cheer Jennifer were met with a litany of complaints about the unfairness of life, but mostly about the carelessness of the deceased.

That's how I learned that Mark Hansen used to manage his money on MyBudget, the same personal finance software to which I entrusted my existence for a while.

Three or four years ago, I was pacing the aisles of the Upper West Side's Staples store, searching for that ruinous elixir, more precious than the Wise Men's myrrh, known as printer ink, when my eyes fell on a message that would briefly but deeply change the course of my life.

"Are you in control of your finances?" asked the cardboard effigy of an accountant seemingly straight out of *1984*, pointing an accusatory finger at the potential customer. Having no choice but to admit that I was not, I purchased — for the ridiculously modest sum of $19.99 — what promised to be "my personal accountant and most trustworthy advisor for all my financial decisions."

The myth of the man-machine fusion, so dear to cyberneticists, perhaps never came so close to becoming a reality than during the first weeks of our short life together. I would record the tiniest of my expenses with a fanatic zeal. No sooner had the two-dollar tip for the pizza delivery guy left my pocket than it was entered in the section "Take out," subcategory "Italian cuisine." As a reward, MyBudget would on the fly generate bar graphs and multicolored pie charts at which I would stare for hours on end. Each report delivered its share of astounding revelations. I consumed more in air conditioning than in heating. I spent less than one dollar per day to clothe myself. Reducing if only by half the number of my visits to Starbucks would save me the equivalent of a New York-Paris, round-trip ticket every two years.

True to its publisher's promise, MyBudget was much more than a mere accountant. Its expertise spread over a variety of related subjects, in which it indicated, lay the key to my financial salvation. For instance, it would suggest I print on both sides to reduce my paper consumption. It also regularly drew my attention to the extravagant cost of my visceral aversion to subscriptions of any kind. Buying the *New York Times* every day impoverished me at the alarming rate of $150 a year, or $3,750 over 25 years. (Indeed, MyBudget would as a rule calculate savings and squanderings over the span of an entire generation, programmed no doubt to jolt my mind with staggering figures and impart a sense of urgency to my decisions. Who would have thought that deferring the installation of low-energy bulbs in my apartment would eventually hack $9,000 off my finances or that my daily latte would wind up costing me thirty-four grand?)

I ineluctably changed my habits.

I let my hair grow out, reduced my visits to the bookstore, canceled a dental appointment (a decision that would come back to haunt me). I stopped going to the movies, except for the half-price matinees, swapping knowing glances with the rare spectators sitting next to me. I'm ashamed to admit that the thought of the next moviegoer to occupy my seat paying twice as much often thrilled me more than the film itself. I would trot home, as much from impatience to resume work as from a desire to save an aggregate $5,500 in bus fare.

I also began to buy my groceries at Costco, the official supplier for local delis and Mormon housewives, where the promise of unbeatable prices comes with the obligation to buy bulk-packaged goods. The booty from my first expedition — which included 12 rolls of paper towels, 1,800 Q-tips, 6 tubes of toothpaste, 16 cans of corn, and 2 pounds of Cheerios — wouldn't fit in the trunk of the cab I had chartered for the occasion. Back in my apartment, calculator in hand, I compared the unit cost of my purchases with what I would have paid at the corner grocery store. I had saved 44% on cup noodles, 57% on my 60 slices of prosciutto, but only 21% on my favorite cereal bars. I spent the rest of the evening planning my next outing, cramming my cupboards, and composing menus consisting of tuna and rice.

Strangely, this all-consuming discipline was slow to bear fruit. My expenses weren't declining.

"That's normal," answered MyBudget, to which I had candidly posed the question, "The growth of your stock of food products is exerting temporary pressure on your treasury, but that will ease as you begin to reap the rewards of your frugality." (That technocratic language, far from irritating, had soothing effects on me. Such a clearly superior mind, I thought at the time, couldn't stumble for long over such insignificant problems.)

My quality of life, however, was taking a turn for the worse. I wasn't sleeping as well as I used to, now that the washing machine would switch on at three in the morning to take advantage of lower electricity rates. I shivered in the bathroom, hated the pallid light of my office, and, by the end of each afternoon, found myself craving for caffeine. My closets were spewing corn, and my ass-wiping needs were covered until 2017, but the simplest of pleasures — unfolding the newspaper at the breakfast table, treating myself to a hot dog on the street, buying a book the day it was released without waiting for the paperback version — were off-limits.

My rising irritation left MyBudget cold. Convinced, like a good moralist, that virtue is its own reward, the program demanded total commitment and invincible resolution, which, since I am made of flesh and blood and not of zeros and ones, I was unable to muster.

An incident revealed the magnitude of my shortcomings. One day, MyBudget took the liberty of circling on my credit card bill the $14.37 I had paid for a bottle of Malbec. It reminded me that I had vowed a few weeks earlier to forgo my daily glass of wine. At the stiff and Jansenist tone of his answer, I understood I had been taken literally to mean that I would never drink another sip of alcohol for the rest of my life. In the cyberworld, a door is either open or closed — but never ajar.

My partner's fundamentalism wouldn't have bothered me so much had I not suddenly discovered the true reason behind it. Various advertisements were now scattered over MyBudget's reports, praising the merits of a new razor with moisture-rich blades or touting whatchamacallit smartphone plan. I didn't pay much attention to it until the day when, noticing an advertisement offering 30% off a Cincinnati-La Guardia flight, I wondered who in the world could have tipped the ad department to my ties to Ohio. I had never browsed the *Enquirer*'s website or watched a Bengals game on pay-per-view. I did, once in a while, call Rebecca or my uncle Marty from my cell phone, but who knew about it, apart from the phone company? No one. Unless…

I reached for MyBudget's package box. Under the text "Proudly designed in the United States, Made in China," a message in tiny print disclosed: *"Creative Consumer Solutions reserves the right to use any and all information directly or indirectly provided by its consumers, as a means to present third-party special offers likely to help them to attain their financial goals."*

The publisher's plan then revealed itself in all its ingenuity: he undercharged for the software to ensure the widest distribution possible; MyBudget, half-snitch, half-Trojan Horse, collected all the data about my consumption habits I had been stupid enough to provide, then urged me to cut down on items that didn't yield anything to the publisher, so as to maximize my discretionary revenue he would then sell to the highest bidder. If I weren't careful, MyBudget would progressively reallocate my expenditures toward products and services less and less in line with my actual needs. From plane tickets to fondue sets, it would bleed me to my last dollar, before slipping me the address of a law firm that would be happy to assist me in my personal bankruptcy proceedings.

That evening, I paid for a round at Starbucks. I blew in one shot what my nighttime laundry was supposed to save me in a decade. The sensation of freedom I felt, however, was priceless.

I could imagine only too well the damage MyBudget must have caused to the finances of a guy like Mark Hansen. Then Jennifer reminded me of one of the software's options that allows the user to simulate the impact of an increase in revenues over the next several years. Given the irregularity of my royalties, I had thought it wise to disable that feature, called the Accelerator. Mark Hansen had set the cursor to 15% — a rate that, without being totally absurd in the high-tech sector, is almost impossible to sustain over the long run. According to Jennifer, the couple had felt an illusory sense of affluence.

"Mark wanted to enroll the twins at the Montessori school, a $12,000 hit per year. I told him over and over again that we couldn't afford it, but he kept bringing it up, MyBudget's projections in hand. He would argue that what seemed unreasonable today would be an ordinary expenditure in three years and a rounding error in ten. The school was offering financing programs. I let him convince me. It was for the kids, after all. You understand, don't you?"

"Of course," I said, thinking that it was quite a bit of cash for play dough sessions.

"The following month, my old Camry conked out. I'd had my eye on the Tucson, Hyundai's little SUV. It started at around $250 a month. Mark wouldn't hear of it. He said his princess deserved better than some Korean shoebox. Since German cars were out of our league, we fell back on the Grand Cherokee. MyBudget protested that it meant an extra $400 a month, plus a $3,000 down payment, since Mark insisted on the full safety package — airbags galore, automatic locks for the back doors, parking assistance, etc. Even if we raided the kids' piggy bank, we couldn't make ends meet. After spending the weekend tweaking the numbers, Mark finally found a winning combination. By raising the rate of the Accelerator to 17%, we could scrape by; at 18%, we'd be living large.

"Was it realistic?"

Jennifer thought about it, as if she were considering the question for the first time.

"Yes, fairly. Mark was doing great at work. At the time, he was also negotiating with some cable operator from Dallas who sought to outsource his customer service to India. He was talking about 3,500 jobs at first, 10,000 over time. Mark pocketed a huge commission when they sealed the deal."

"But he didn't stop at 18%, did he?" I asked, thinking about Mark's self-congratulatory speech on the Fourth of July.

"Oh, no. Every time he wanted something he didn't have the money for, he'd bump up the Accelerator by one or two points. It was magical. Our credit card bills were getting longer month after month and MyBudget kept telling us everything was fine."

"How far do you think he would have gone?"

"I'd rather not think about that. I put my foot down at 25% — to no avail. Mark had gotten his hands on another of the software's features, which allowed him to anticipate an inflow, as long as it had some degree of certainty — inheritance, donation…"

"Initial Public Offering," I suggested.

"Exactly," sighed Jennifer. "Since he had been named vice-president, part of Mark's bonus came in the form of stock options. We would have hit the jackpot the day the company went public — $500,000, or even $1m."

I asked Jennifer why she had used the past tense. Last week, she found out that OutSourceIn has canceled Mark's options on the ground that, per his contract, they weren't technically his until three years had elapsed. Jennifer consulted a specialized attorney, who proposes to drag OutSourceIn to court to have Mark's skidding off the road requalified as a work-related accident. His fee: forty percent of all monies recovered.

Jennifer is hesitant — and I would be too — about launching a protracted legal procedure with an unpredictable outcome. She contacted Michael Hart, who refused to help her.

"I can't decently stand up for someone who lied," he had the nerve to give her as an excuse. It's the pot calling the kettle black.

Thursday, August 9

Julia looks peaked. She spent the better part of the night breathing life into the pages of our European characters. The moment Thorsten rose from his bed in Copenhagen, he wished Ulrike a happy birthday, marveling at the coincidence of their being born on the same day. As for Klaus, he updated the list of his favorite movies and expressed his admiration of Yo-Yo Ma's interpretations of Saint-Saëns' cello concertos. Finally, Ericka turned yet a few more heads with pictures taken at a country fair, showing her successively firing a rifle, jumping into a bumper car, and biting into a candied apple.

I logged onto Facebook, while Julia, completely out of it, drowned her pancakes in a flood of maple syrup. Alleluia: Ulrike had already replied. She thanked Thorsten, and wished him "einen ganz besonderen Tag" in a mischievous tone that hardly leaves any doubt as to her intentions. I answered her pronto, sharing with her my latest discovery — which, naturally, I begged her not to leak. It seems that, following a bet, in 1928, Franz Blei wrote an entire episode of *Little Apple*, the serial published by Perutz in the *Berliner Illustrierte Zeitung*. In my pidgin English, I explained to Fräulein Richter that Blei's half-faded scrawl prevents us from determining exactly which of the eight chapters he may have composed. I promised to keep her informed of my progress.

I was in the middle of posting lewd comments on Ericka's pictures, when Ulrike's answer came in.

"Dear Thorsten, my, oh, my, you truly did hit a gold mine. How was it again you came into possession of those letters? Did you know I'm one of the most prominent living experts on Blei's work? Let me reread *Little Apple* this weekend. If I manage to identify the chapter in question, perhaps you and I could co-sign an article in the fall? What do you say?"

"What you say is that she can go fuck herself," said Julia who'd been reading over my shoulder. "Does she think you're about to let her steal your scoop? Please."

(...)

I ran across my idol, Frances Gray, on the beach tonight. She summed up Emerald's position in the Hansen case.

"It's quite straightforward. Mark lied on two occasions: first on his medical questionnaire, and then to the physician who administered the check-up. Although I'm perfectly inclined to believe his wife knew nothing of it, the facts remain. No reputable lawyer will ever take her case."

I asked her how she deals with occasional smokers who light a cigarette every now and then, without really putting their health at risk.

"They benefit from an intermediary rate, which reflects the limited but real damage they inflict on their lungs," Frances Gray answered with the patience of an angel. "We're not monsters, you know. Mark Hansen could have lit up a cigar to celebrate the birth of his niece without getting into trouble. Unfortunately, my colleagues gathered countless pictures, taken over the course of the last five years, which show him, cigarette in hand, in the most diverse circumstances."

"Couldn't you at least pay the indemnity corresponding to the smoker's rate?"

"Certainly not. That would send a deplorable message to the consumers of tobacco, alcohol, and drugs of all types, who would suddenly have everything to gain and absolutely nothing to lose by lying. In the end, and at the risk of repeating myself, that would result in an increase in rates for all our clients who play by the book and never cheat."

Cheating — there's the big bad word, I thought, as I strolled. We Americans don't toy with rules. On Christmas Eve, a property owner can evict a single mother whose rent is fifteen days overdue, because he has the law on his side, but the most insignificant mistake on his tax return could send him to jail.

Travelers who enter the United States and scoff at the questions on the immigration forms (Are you addicted drugs? Do you belong to a terrorist organization?) don't understand the logic of the American judicial system. The questions themselves are less important than the text directly below the signature: *"I understand that any misstatement, falsification, or omission of information contained in this declaration will subject me to deportation, imprisonment, and/or a fine of up to $250,000."* At the first misdemeanor, the jihadist will find himself behind bars, not because of his political opinions (which would violate his right to free speech), but because he lied.

Friday, August 10

Not everyone has bad news. Chuck Patterson informed me via a mass mailing that he has changed employers. He now sells policies for Serenity, a Denver-based insurance company that I remember hearing him bad-mouth just a few weeks ago. His letter is a model of hypocrisy. He looks forward to "expanding his clients' options by giving them access to a wider range of services." Yuk!

At first, I naively believed that Emerald, appalled by Chuck's repeated ethical breaches, had given him the boot. Ed Linkas (who by the way has landed a date with Kim Phelps) laughed in my face when I let him in on my theory.

"No way, Jose! Serenity just bought him out. They're growing like weeds in the South-East. Knowing Chuck, he must have cashed in big time — eyeballing it, I'd estimate $500,000 to $600,000. And of course, he'll keep earning commissions on his former Emerald contracts."

Half a million less for Jennifer Hansen, half a million more for Chuck Patterson. Where's the logic in all of this?

(…)

Rafaela had her first ultrasound today: she's expecting twins. Manuel is talking about increasing the policy's coverage. So much the better — when Kim invites me to dinner, I won't have any qualms about ordering the lobster.

(...)

Lammons' secretary called to ask for my second $100 payment.

"Would you be so kind as to tell Dr. Lammons that he can wipe his ass with my bill," I said in my most amiable tone.

I hope he'll comprehend — I'd hate having to send him the picture I took with my phone.

I had just hung up when a tearful Ashley Cunningham came knocking on my door. Her mother had told her about the plan she's devised with Brian and Sharon Hess. Ashley assured her she wouldn't need a nurse, as she was herself was willing to move to Destin Terrace to lend her a hand. Mrs. Cunningham rebuffed her, stating that she didn't see why she'd go through all that trouble since the insurance would pay for it.

I tried my best to comfort her.

Saturday, August 11

I stopped by the Jacques' this morning, to return a book that Anh had lent me.

Jean-Michel opened the door, eyes red with grief. He had received a phone call from Belgium announcing the death of his mother (71, lung cancer). He tried humor ("Now there's one maturity I could have done without"), but his heart wasn't in it.

Considering the circumstances, he's postponed indefinitely the launching of his new loan service indefinitely. Dare I write it: shit.

(...)

Dramatic turn of events — Mrs. Cunningham is cured! Or, more exactly, she was never ill. Brian Hess examined her this morning in his basement (I've been trying very hard not to picture the scene...). He happens to have a lot of experience treating uterine cancer. He's positive: Mrs. Cunningham's lesion can be treated with laser surgery, because it doesn't touch the endocervix (he was about to elaborate, but I stopped him right there).

Apparently Mrs. Cunningham was quite upset. She can kiss her dreams of cruises and Vegas getaways goodbye. If she wants to live the high life, I guess she'll have to mortgage her house like everyone else.

Brian, on the other hand, is ecstatic. He feels useful again for the first time in years. He's talking about reopening an office, but first, he must find an insurer. I referred him to Frances Gray. It's not her area of practice but I have absolute faith in her powers.

(…)

Julia left earlier. God, do I love that kid! She's going to keep our puppets' Facebook pages hopping, at least until school starts. As she was climbing into the taxi (which she shared with Jean-Michel, who's flying to Europe to bury his mother), she made me promise not to cave in to Ulrike Richter's intimidation maneuvers.

"She needs your imagination more than you need her dollars," she said, with the carefreeness of the adolescent who has never paid a single bill.

(…)

I called Julia to read her the too-good-to-be-true email that I had just received. I caught her as she was boarding the plane.

"Dear Daniel, you may have noticed that Hermann Broch's and Leo Perutz' Wikipedia pages are being modified little by little, in all languages, to reflect the facts contained in your August 1 contribution. Slovenian and Ukrainian editors are typically a bit slow to react, so please be patient with them.

Let me take this opportunity to ask for your advice on a recent change made by a user from Princeton, New Jersey (screen name: urichter0809), on the page of another Austrian writer, Franz Blei. According to that contributor, Blei wrote the entire fifth chapter of Leo Perutz' novel, *Little Apple*. May I ask whether you're aware of this information, of which I can find absolutely no other trace on the Web?

Cordially, etc."

"That bitch, she's trying to beat you to the punch!" Julia exclaimed. "Man, I hope you put her through the wringer!"

"We'll see," I answered, smiling. "I haven't decided yet. Have a good flight, kiddo."

Hard as I try, I can't feel anything but pity for Richter. After all, who, after having spent a decade and half a million dollars to organize a seminar entitled "Vienna, Cradle of the Modern Novel," wouldn't give in to a baseness or two to see their name listed in the table of contents of the *Journal of Austrian Literature*?

I answered the Wikipedia editor.

"No, I've never heard that Blei may have written a line, let alone a whole chapter, on behalf of Perutz. Do you know under what circumstances the two men could have agreed to such an arrangement? Could it be a bet of some sort?

The theory isn't completely ludicrous, nonetheless. According to Lena Mirafuentes's work, Blei harbored an inferiority complex vis-à-vis his literary friends, all of them more famous and, let's face it, more talented than he. He could very well have submitted a pastiche of *Little Apple* to Perutz, who may have passed it as his own for all sorts of reasons (to help a friend, to fool the Viennese establishment, etc.).

Between you and me, I think we're dealing with a scholar who, by pre-publishing on Wikipedia, is trying to establish a precedent for his or her work. I believe it would be most prudent to delete that contribution, pending more tangible evidence."

Then Thorsten wrote Ulrike.

"Dear Fräulein Richter, what a brilliant idea! I reread *Little Apple* too in its entirety today. A wonderful book, isn't it? I would bet my life that it was Blei who wrote the fifth chapter, but I doubt I can succeed to prove it. Your help would be infinitely appreciated, if you were kind to give me some."

All right, I suppose I'll have to do some serious brushing up on Blei before I can dive into his correspondence.

*****

From: Dan Siver <danielgsiver@gmail.com>
Date: Sunday, August 12, 2012 10:35 A.M.
To: Vlad Eisinger <vlad.eisinger@wst.com>
Subject: Christmas in August

You'll never guess who had the honor of Ray Wiggin's first lyrical obit — Big Bobby! That fat bastard croaked two days ago, while he was celebrating his birthday with a couple of babes. It seems none of his family members volunteered to offer a tribute (admitting they can write).

You'll see, Wiggin outdid himself. His text is perfect, with the exception of one mistake, which I challenge you to find.

Northwest Florida Daily News
Sunday, August 12, 2012

Robert "Bobby" BABBITT, consultant, investor, man of vision and action, succumbed to a massive heart attack on August 10, 2012, date of his fifty-third birthday, in his Destin, Florida residence.

Death surprised Babbitt as he was enjoying the company of two very dear friends, Charlene LaVigne, 18, student, and Shaniqua Richardson, 21, actress.

Babbitt was born on August 10, 1959, in Camden, New Jersey, the home state of Joe Pesci and Frank Sinatra, from the union of Mike "Bugsy" Babbitt, public works contractor, and Rita Babbitt, née Esposito, housewife. He was the youngest of five boys, two of whom survive him.

"Mens sana in corpore sano": no one lived by that precept as earnestly as Babbitt who, throughout his studies, distinguished himself in various sports, including boxing, Greco-Roman and freestyle wrestling, and weightlifting. To this day, he remains the only student from Christopher Columbus High School in Camden to have lifted 120 kg in the clean and jerk technique — a performance that made the headlines of the *New Jersey Herald*'s sports section, and that sparked off fierce competition among local universities eager to recruit him. Babbitt chose to join the Benedetti Institute, a Catholic school in Elizabeth, famous for its accounting curriculum and boxing coach, Aldo Fontanella, a former sparring partner of Joe Frazier and a well-known figure among Atlantic City bookmakers.

Between 1978 and 1981, under Fontanella's guidance, Babbitt won a string of amateur championships, earning several colorful nicknames in the process, like "Camden's Butcher," "il Toro," and "the Anvil." He would have most likely turned professional if his mother, who had already lost a son (Ricky, killed at knifepoint in a fight in 1980), hadn't been so vehemently opposed.

In 1982, Babbitt joined the family construction business as a sales representative, a position that seemed tailor-made for his tenacity and force of persuasion. In five years, he won all of the fourteen calls for bids that he had submitted. Among his most memorable projects are the Teamsters Center of Hoboken, Camden City Hall, the Bridgeton north interchange, and the four-lane widening of a section of the Garden State Parkway, to name only a few.

Love entered Bobby Babbitt's life in 1987, in the form of Consuela Villablanca, daughter of wealthy Columbian ship-owner Hector Villablanca. The two young people met in Coney Island, during a party given in honor of Frank Sinatra's seventy-second birthday. Six weeks later, they were married and moved into a penthouse on Park Avenue.

With his father's blessing, Babbitt joined the Villablanca empire. His first mission consisted in negotiating a new contract with the dockers of the Newark Port. He did so with astounding finesse, reducing the average time for unloading ships by thirty percent and cutting merchandise theft in half. Saying that Babbitt discovered a passion and a genius for business during those years is no exaggeration. A devoted son-in-law and tireless worker, he traveled each month to Cali, the group's birthplace, to promote the commercial opportunities offered by the American market to local businessmen. Before flying home, he always found a few hours to retreat to his oasis, an organic coffee plantation, whose location he never disclosed to anyone, and to which access was gained through a narrow mountain pass, guarded by former soldiers of the Columbian army.

In 1992, Consuela divorced by mutual consent. The couple had borne no children. Babbitt moved to Miami to regroup, settling in a modest apartment that contrasted sharply with the flashy opulence of the Villablancas. He was free to travel, to resume competitive weightlifting, to build highways and orphanages. However, the call of family again proved stronger. Never stingy with his time, Bobby agreed to advise his eldest brother, Tony, president of Sunset Partners, a company that came to the aid of terminally ill patients. Over time, he took on a larger role in the organization's strategic orientations, but never accepted more than a token remuneration for his efforts. Sunset remained Tony's project, and Bobby had no desire to steal his brother's show, especially now that he had finally found his life's purpose: philanthropy.

Since his public donations represented only a tiny fraction of his largesse, it's difficult to determine exactly when or in what circumstances Bobby Babbitt began to disperse his fortune. The first transaction on record dates back to 1995, when, at Coach Fontanella's request, he underwrote the expense of renovating the boxing gymnasium, which had been the scene of his youthful feats.

The donations grew year after year, as if Babbitt were in an increasing hurry to rid himself of the money burning a hole in his pocket. In 1996, following the death of his father, he donated $200,000 worth of life insurance policies to the Prostate Cancer Research Foundation. In 1998, he pledged up to $750,000 to a fund intended to finance the Miss South Beach annual election. Love and generosity making good bedfellows, it came as no surprise when Babbitt walked down the aisle with Amanda Lauer, the lovely laureate of the 2000 contest. Their union ended in 2003, the year Bobby announced he was planning to dedicate even more time and energy to the management of his foundation.

Soon afterward, Babbitt was plunged into a deep dejection by the imprisonment of Tony and his cousin Charly. The few people who visited him during the gloomy summer of 2004 remember his diatribes against the relentlessness of the judges and the pettiness of the investors who had lost their savings when Sunset Partners went bankrupt. According to Bobby, the misdeeds attributed to his brother amounted to no more than peccadilloes, and, in any case, were hardly significant in comparison with the hundreds of lives saved and young patients returned to their families.

On house arrest since 2007, persecuted by the FBI, and pained to see his South-American friends distancing themselves from him, he drew his only consolation from his philanthropic activities, which, with the help of his loyal assistant Pamela, he had progressively refocused on Okaloosa County.

Bobby's health had severely deteriorated of late. He had complained to his doctor that his exercise sessions, which in the olden days were tantamount to bedroom marathons, now seldom exceeded twenty minutes. Shaniqua Richardson told the ambulance personnel that she had immediately recognized the symptoms of a disease that had already claimed one of her friends: moaning, shortness of breath, extreme weariness. Notwithstanding the intervention of emergency medical technicians, attempts to resuscitate Babbitt were unsuccessful.

A man of heart as much as a man of numbers, Bobby Babbitt leaves behind a disconsolate mother, Rita; two brothers, Tony and Mickey; as well as twelve nieces and nephews. He will be buried next Wednesday in the family vault at Harleigh Cemetery in Camden.

Instead of flowers or wreaths, the family requests that donations be directed to one of the dozens of charities that Bobby supported.

*****

From: Vlad Eisinger <vlad.eisinger@wst.com>
Date: Sunday, August 12, 2012 11:05 A.M.
To: Dan Siver <danielgsiver@gmail.com>
Subject: QED

Who said that writing literature and reporting news were mutually exclusive?

"In 1992, Consuela divorced by mutual consent." It doesn't make sense grammatically, yet it's the only sentence that even begins to tell the truth!

Other than that, I'm terribly vexed: how could have I missed the Miss South Beach Beauty Pageant Foundation during my investigation? I had heard that Babbitt had been briefly married to a beauty queen, but I never would have imagined that he had crowned her himself...

*****

Dan's journal

Sunday, August 12
An article, opposite Babbitt's obituary, is announcing the arrival of a swarm of several hundred thousand killer bees in the Golf of Mexico. The NFDN's meteorological experts predict heavy human and financial damages.

*****

From: Dan Siver <danielgsiver@gmail.com>
Date: Sunday, August 12, 2012 09:06 P.M.
To: Vlad Eisinger <vlad.eisinger@wst.com>
Subject: Indecent proposal

What if we wrote that book together? You, the press articles; Me, the description of their impact on Destin Terrace's residents. A radioscopy of the American soul, firmly rooted in its epoch.

*****

From: Vlad Eisinger <vlad.eisinger@wst.com>
Date: Sunday, August 12, 2012 09:07 P.M.
To: Dan Siver <danielgsiver@gmail.com>
Subject: Indecent proposal

I was afraid to ask. Do you think the *Wall Street Tribune* will grant us permission?

*****

From: Dan Siver <danielgsiver@gmail.com>
Date: Sunday, August 12, 2012 09:07 P.M.
To: Vlad Eisinger <vlad.eisinger@wst.com>
Subject: Indecent proposal

Of course they will: we'll tell them we made it all up.

PS: Any news from Vlad Eisinger?

From the same author

The Falsifiers (novel)

Fresh out of college, Sliv, a young Icelander, joins an environmental consulting firm. Soon his superior reveals that the firm houses the activities of a secret organization, the Consortium for the Falsification of Reality, which rewrites history and falsifies the world as we know it.

Who runs the CFR and for what purpose? That's what Sliv sets out to discover. His only chance: rise all the way to the top in record time.

The *Falsifiers*, a European best-seller, is the first installment of a trilogy. It is followed by *The Pathfinders* and *The Showrunners*.

The Pathfinders (novel)

In this second installment of the *Falsifiers* trilogy, the stakes have gotten higher. Sliv is tasked with daunting missions: help a small Asian country gain its independence, chase a rogue CFR agent, and convince the Bush Administration that Saddam Hussein no longer possesses weapons of mass destruction. Yet, in a post 9/11 world, Sliv and his colleagues are not the only ones tampering with reality.

The Pathfinders was awarded the prestigious Prix France Culture Telerama in 2009. It is preceded by *The Falsifiers* and followed by *The Showrunners* but can be read independently.

The Missing Piece (novel)

Between March and September of the year 1995, five murders shook the professional Speed Puzzle Tour. The modus operandi was always the same: the murderer would amputate the victim of a limb, then leave on the body a piece of a Polaroid photograph depicting the corresponding limb of another man. Evidently, speed puzzle, a sport by then as popular as football and basketball, had become the hunting ground of a serious killer.

Suspects are in no short supply: from the tyrannical president of the erudite Society of Puzzlology to the reigning champion who has mysteriously vanished to the billionaire who started the Tour.

Can you solve the puzzle?

The Missing Piece has been translated into a dozen languages.

The Disappearance of Emilie Brunet (novel)

Detective Achille Dunot suffers from a strange form of amnesia. Since a recent accident, his brain has lost the ability to form new memories. Every morning he wakes up with no recollection of the previous day. When the chief of police asks him to investigate the disappearance of wealthy heiress Emily Brunet, Achille decides to keep a journal in which he logs his findings of the day before going to bed. This diehard fan of Agatha Christie thus becomes the hero and the reader of a strange detective novel, of which he also happens to be the author.

Before long, all clues point to Claude Brunet, Emily's husband. Brunet had many reasons to kill his wife, has no alibi, and not-so-subtly boasts of having committed the perfect crime. As a world-class neuroscientist, he's also one of the very few people who can grasp Achille's ailment.

Legends (short story)

A civil servant of the British intelligence agency is tasked with animating a stock of legends - those disposable identities donned by spies during their missions.

Mr. Luigi's Binoculars (short story)

A young card player from Missouri is hired to help the world champion retain his title against the Russian rising star of the game.

7645009R00124

Printed in Germany
by Amazon Distribution
GmbH, Leipzig